MARTIAN DAWN

& OTHER NOVELS

MICHAEL FRIEDMAN

INTRODUCTION BY MOLLY YOUNG

Little a

D1153565

Martian Dawn was originally published by Turtle Point Press, New York, 2006.

This is a work of fiction. Names, characters, organizations, places, events and incidents are either products of the author's imagination or are used fictitiously.

Published by Little A, New York

www.apub.com

Amazon, the Amazon logo, and Little A are trademarks of Amazon.com, Inc., or its affiliates.

ISBN-13: 9781477828359
ISBN-10: 1477828354

Cover design by Ben Gibson

Library of Congress Control Number: 2014956584

Printed in the United States of America

PRAISE FOR MARTIAN DAWN & OTHER NOVELS

"Michael Friedman's metrosexuals are direct descendants of characters in Ronald Firbank and Ivy Compton-Burnett. Their wisecracking rises consistently to the level of poetry."

—John Ashbery

"Michael Friedman has one of the best sensibilities in contemporary lit. *Martian Dawn* possesses the impeccable construction, low gravity and shimmering surface of something written with a magic wand."

—Dennis Cooper

"Reading *Martian Dawn* is like watching an ultra-cool comedy of the future where familiar movie types develop into idyllic interplanetary characters in order to make yet more movies. It's as though *Star Trek*, *Pretty Woman* and *There's Something About Mary* had been sublimated in an unlikely fusion that is both comforting and hilarious."

—Harry Mathews

"Like soft-porn 'Pop' holographs crossed with Simenon, Socrates and reality TV produced by a punk Ivy Compton-Burnett, Michael Friedman's novels are analytical, fun to read and profoundly nourishing. He takes fiction seriously by *not* taking it seriously. Post-fiction, post-poetry, Friedman's buff concoctions offer bliss for hyper-aesthetic grown-ups: low-stress foreplay, high-brow tickling and Zen giggles."

—Wayne Koestenbaum

"In pitch perfect vernacular that's gauzy and precise, shallow and ambitious, and smugly hilarious Michael Friedman slaps our attention around like nobody's business while delivering the impossible: totally intelligent writer's fiction that's also a porny distraction for anyone who might want to graze like a silver drone or a celebrity whale (there truly is one in here named "Monstro") in the smarmy circles of entertainment culture, glam spirituality, eco culture and everyday dharma of the streets, restaurants, bedrooms and biospheres and of the hip haute global media bourgeoisie. It's almost hard to read alone it's so gorgeously nasty."

—Eileen Myles

For Dianne, Henry and Joe

CONTENTS

INTRODUCTION
By Molly Young

Sometimes you discover a good book, and sometimes it is prescribed to you. Nearly a decade ago I was visiting my uncle, Geoffrey Young, in Great Barrington, Massachusetts, where he runs a gallery and a small press called The Figures. It was winter, and Geoff's house is one of those rambling wooden structures with a thousand tangential corners and hallways—the kind of house that never fully warms once the temperatures dip into single digits. We walked around in layers and tight, condomlike wool caps, playing aerobic Ping-Pong matches and drinking tea to stay warm. One night during the visit I realized that a blazing-hot bath might be an effective thawing agent, and I asked if I could borrow the upstairs tub for a while. "Yes, one sec," was the reply. Geoff vanished. I went in search of towels. When he reappeared, he had a copy of Michael Friedman's *Martian Dawn* in his hand. "Here you go," he said, passing it over, as though it were obvious (and it is, I guess) that a person wouldn't want to marinate without at least 150 pages of experimental fiction for companionship. Some nieces have all the luck. Bath drawn and windows fogged and clammy exoskeleton submerged, I picked up my prescription and looked it over. If the title had William Gibson vibes, the cover painting by Duncan Hannah repelled any specific genre affiliations: In macaroon colors, an elemental man and woman face off in what could be Taos or the moon, each wearing sensible footwear and flowing garments with statement necklines. A pale sun or some other astronomical object glowed in the corner. It was around five by seven inches, my favorite size for a book: not quite pocket-size but scaled ideally to a woman's purse, like a derringer pistol. I started reading.

In all pieces of genuinely original fiction there's a moment when a reader halts with an internal *What the fuck?* and decides either to continue or to burn the book for fuel. In *Martian Dawn*, that moment starts at the tenth sentence:

> She watched Richard move silently through the house, stopping to rearrange the flowers and pictures. Sometimes, she reflected, he was like a wild animal—a black panther padding through the brush of Equatorial Guinea at dusk.
>
> She knew that Richard was a sucker for her "come hither" look. Lately he had been like putty in her hands.

It continues more or less throughout the book's twenty chapters, in a hailstorm of *What the fucks?* interspersed with the ticklish delight of uncovering a truly alien artifact. The passage just above brims with features that I would go on to perceive, in my cooling bathwater, as typical of Friedman: the obscene bursts of cliché, the mind-boggling specificity (Equatorial Guinea, dusk), the surgical transfer of surreal humans into quotidian situations and—just as often—the inverse.

As with any sufficiently enrapturing book, I started to wonder about the author: How old was this Michael Friedman person? Where was he raised? Who were his influences? The Wikipedia-grade questions were supplanted, as pages passed, by gauzier ones. What kind of cuss words did Michael Friedman use in conversation? Did he have recurring nightmares? What were his favorite chores? Had he ever bribed an official?

The Wikipedia questions were answerable after the bath. Updated for today, they are as follows: Friedman grew up in Manhattan and has published six collections of poetry. He cofounded the well-respected poetry journal *Shiny* in 1986, the same year he graduated from Duke Law School (an article published a decade ago in the Denver Bar Association's magazine describes him, delectably, as a "lawyer by trade, poet by habit"). *Martian Dawn* was his first work of fiction, originally published in 2006 by the excellent Turtle Point Press. He completed his second novel, *Are We Done Here?*, in 2009, and his third, *On My Way to See You*, in 2013. They are published here for the first time. Friedman lives in Denver, Colorado.

Martian Dawn's central figures are Julia and Richard, a Los Angeles show-biz couple enjoying a life of Rodeo Drive shopping sprees, dinners with costars, and casual Buddhism. Depending on readers' engagement with late-twentieth-century pop culture, they may realize immediately or never that Richard and Julia bear a resemblance to Richard Gere and Julia Roberts, as well as sharing certain qualities with the characters played by those actors in the 1990s Pygmalion tale *Pretty Woman*. (Which had, incidentally, a tag line that Friedman might as well have written: "She walked off the street, into his life and stole his heart.")

Each subsequent chapter of the book takes a hard left turn. First we transition to a group of researchers exploring the viability of interplanetary colonization. Next, a dip into the therapy session of a mildly racist movie producer and his psychotherapist. In chapter four, we're at the Yale Club bar discussing the erotic possibilities of blue whales. Then we get a whale's-eye view of the world, with brief reflections on the challenges of marine mammalhood. Naturally, it all comes together in the end.

Which brings us to clichés. Friedman's pages are filled with them. Two per page, at least, in each book. Characters hatch plans, enjoy whirlwind courtships, grab a bite, sleep fitfully, race against the clock, wax poetic, look like a million bucks, stand their ground, shoot themselves in the foot, remain calm under pressure, shake their heads ruefully, wait for the other shoe to drop, keep their emotions firmly in check, become wracked with jealousy or remain preternaturally calm. The clichés do different things: conjure a mood, signal wryness, give their speakers a dim-witted veracity. Some are punch lines. One thing they are not is lazy; on the contrary, a reader gets the sense of prose that has been harnessed in rigorous but invisible constraints—like a fresh-faced Gap model wearing a spiked leather codpiece beneath his chinos.

Indeed, these books have a perverse streak, but they are not disobliging. There's lots of dialogue, little figurative language, many short sentences that appear like blips across a radar screen. There are lists and geographical coordinates and a feather-light quality to the verbiage. You could read Friedman's sentences out loud to a fourth grader and the kid wouldn't have to look up any words. (He'd probably develop some interesting pathologies down the road too—an added bonus.) As for an adult reader, I felt the whole time as though I were being pleasurably hoodwinked, which is the exact response I prize above all else in literature.

Friedman's next two novels, *Are We Done Here?* and *On My Way to See You,* draw from the same tool kit but yield new inventions: They scoot among exotic settings (Paris, South America, the Betty Ford Center in Rancho Mirage), pop in and out of scenes with dronelike omniscience, and generally decline to recognize common sense. The end of *Are We Done Here?* finds two friends chatting at a bar in Minneapolis:

> "You know, there's a rumor going around New York that I've moved to Latvia."
> "I wonder how that got started?"
> "The grapevine," Thomas said dolefully.
> "Those grapes will soon be raisins."

This isn't the kind of exchange that two men have in a bar in a midsize Midwestern city; it's the kind of exchange that a singularly odd person invents in his head and, if we are lucky, commits to paper. If you had to guess at Friedman's influences, you might think, Joe Brainard? René Goscinny? Ronald Firbank? The Henry James novel *The Spoils of Poynton*, which revolves entirely around a family's minor furniture dispute? But with more dopamine squirts? It's hard to say. Friedman doesn't write like any particular predecessor. You could say he writes the way an eccentric billionaire spends money: unpredictably, in unusual denominations, with zero scruples. You could also say he writes like some other, smarter species imitating a human being.

The singularity of the books might be one reason it's so pleasurable to read them illicitly. For a real thrill, photocopy a chapter of *On My Way to See You* and read it during work hours at the office. Knit your brow and grasp a highlighter in one hand, hovering it above the pages to create a strong visual impression of industry. Teenagers, slip this volume between the "Stoichiometry" and "Covalent Bonding" chapters of your chemistry textbook and experience a whole new kind of catalysis. Jurors, whip out your copy midway through deliberation. The private joy of absorbing these works is accentuated when you do it in public, under circumstances that explicitly forbid recreational reading.

I love Friedman's books for the reasons I love the paintings of Jan Steen and the poems of Emily Dickinson and the symphony that Beethoven wrote, Symphony No. 2, about farting: He is weird and virtuosic, and this union of traits is agonizingly rare. He makes me laugh, he makes me sad, he leaves me feeling invested in my own freakishness. His books are wonderful to read in the nude. What more could you ask of an artist?

MARTIAN DAWN

CHAPTER ONE

Richard and Julia strolled along Rodeo Drive, monogrammed tote bags in each hand. The sidewalk was crowded, but they hardly seemed to notice. It was a bright, sunny day. Julia was momentarily struck by how beautiful the red awnings of the Beverly Wilshire Hotel looked against the pale, sandblasted façades of the hotel and boutiques.

They returned, exhausted from shopping, to their modernist glass compound nestled in the Hollywood Hills. Sunlight streamed through the glass-walled living room from the Japanese garden. There, Julia felt, they were away from it all—Morty, Mars, everything. It was just Richard and her. Her old life with Angel and the gang seemed like a distant Jacqueline Susann nightmare.

She watched Richard move silently through the house, stopping to rearrange the flowers and pictures. Sometimes, she reflected, he was like a wild animal—a black panther padding through the brush of Equatorial Guinea at dusk.

She knew that Richard was a sucker for her "come-hither" look. Lately he had been like putty in her hands. Because he would do whatever she wanted, she often had to pause to think about what it was she *did* want. And, too often, she didn't know. Did she even want Richard, now that she had him? Why not? He was a handsome movie star with millions of dollars. His intellect was passable.

"Richard," she said.

"Yes, Julia?"

"Come hither," she purred, and motioned with an index finger. She realized there was some truth to the observation Angel had made: Until recently she had been nothing more than a hooker in a plastic dress, taking on all comers at $500 a pop. Old habits die hard, she thought. "You know, Richard, before I met you I was only a cheap hooker in a plastic dress."

Richard smiled. "Not *cheap,*" he said.

Julia was aware that Richard was pulling a Pygmalion routine on her, though awkwardly at best. She sort of liked it. He was attempting to teach her about the finer things in life—how to dress, how to eat in fancy restaurants, how to converse with people "in the business"—not realizing that she was already quite advanced in these departments. Though only a high school graduate, she was a voracious reader and had bootstrapped herself quite an education.

Richard had also introduced her to Tibetan Buddhism. Through his fame, he had become friendly with the Dalai Lama. He had his own meditation instructor, with whom he met every afternoon, usually at home but occasionally at a local Buddhist center. He talked of taking Julia to visit a community of Buddhist practitioners in the mountains outside of Boulder, Colorado.

They traveled frequently: Santa Fe for the opera, Aspen to ski, Casa de Campo for golf, St. Bart's to relax and unwind, et cetera. Julia remembered once driving with Richard through New England in the fall to see the leaves. They had stayed overnight at the Red Lion Inn in Stockbridge, a rambling Revolutionary War–era hotel. They drove along Route 7 through West Cornwall, Sheffield, Great Barrington, Stockbridge and Williamstown. She remembered the stunning yellow, red and orange leaves.

She also remembered Hawaii, walking with Richard on the Big Island through a park known as Observatory Park, perched on a promontory overlooking the ocean. The observatory itself had seemed impossibly small, a white dome on top of a red-brick doll-house. It sat in disuse at the edge of the park.

Richard had pointed to a stand of bamboo nearby. "Do you know why the bamboo is there?"

"No."

He had grabbed her hands and looked into her eyes. "Waiting for the wind to touch it."

When not vacationing or on location filming, they enjoyed staying in for champagne bubble baths or candle-lit dinners. Richard was a fine cook. His specialty was baked Alaska.

Their social lives and business lives were intertwined. When they did go out, it was usually for a dinner or party given by or for a costar or partner, producer, agent or publicist.

Richard was constantly developing new interests in addition to Buddhism. Currently, he was taking weekly flower-arranging lessons at the botanic garden. He was becoming quite good at it.

On a typical morning, Richard, Julia and Jemima, Richard's assistant, worked out with Yoshi, their personal trainer, in the garden. Twice a week, Nigel, the gardener, came by to tend to the lawn, flower beds, trees and shrubbery.

Their lives seemed complete, but if Julia had learned anything from her studies in Tibetan Buddhism, she knew they were also completely empty.

CHAPTER TWO

Night was falling in the high desert all around the Biosphere. On a nearby rise, giant cacti were silhouetted against the sparkling blue-black sky. The Biosphere's transparent dome gave off a pale green light.

Dirk was alone in the rain-forest biome. Angelfish, parrotfish, triggerfish and others he couldn't identify swam in an oversize aquarium along one wall. He sat in a blue butterfly chair sipping coconut milk through a straw, watching a TV that was perched on a fluted pedestal. Several discarded coconuts were strewn about. The supply of tofu squares had run out. There was a golf match on, but Dirk was hardly paying attention. He was concerned that he and Monica were becoming careless, even brazen. But Monica would not take no for an answer. It was a dicey situation.

At the weekly teleconference with Trout that morning, Dr. Gold had recited a growing list of problems, including insufficient oxygen production and poor crop yields. Also, the water purification system was on the blink.

"Our self-contained, self-sufficient ecosystems appear to be slowing down and approaching stasis," Gold had reported. "It may be that our model for enhancing the possibilities for interplanetary colonization is flawed. The photosynthesis projections, for example, just aren't panning out."

"Yeah, I see what you mean," Trout said. "I'll have a team of scientists on the blower to you ASAP to see what the deal is."

"Also, morale has been suffering," Gold continued, "which has had an adverse effect on productivity."

"I'll get my people from Booz Allen involved too. We've gotta change the prevailing culture that's developed in there. That's how I see it. What else?" Trout said.

"Does anyone else have anything to add?" Gold asked.

No one did. Simon, Samantha, Judy, Dirk and Monica rounded out the team of biospherans sitting sullenly around the conference room table in the Biosphere's teleconference center.

"Well, listen, y'all," Trout said. "I have total confidence we'll get these little kinks worked out. This project is of major-league importance to the future of mankind. The Biosphere is the linchpin of my plan for turning this four-hundred-acre ranch of mine into a high-tech office park. We'll have our own golf course—and a Westin. This is big. Very big. The press has been talkin' all kinds of crap about the Biosphere, but you shouldn't even be reading that stuff. I know it's been rough in there. But we've got to stick it out. We'll have a company retreat to La Quinta when this is over. Keep your chins up. All right."

Trout's image on the video monitor suddenly went dark.

The meeting had ended, leaving Dirk feeling dispirited. He wondered what had happened to the "city of the future" that Trout had once spoken of in connection with the office park project.

Dirk pictured something along the lines of the futuristic office park on the outskirts of Paris, where he and Monica had once wandered on a gray fall afternoon. Outsize geodesic domes and scaled-down Bauhaus midrises: a toy city set in the shadow of the Grande Arche de La Défense. They had taken an elevator to the top of the arch for a Tintin exhibit: darkened galleries with wall-size, backlit comic-strip panels of Tintin in Tibet.

To his dismay, during the conference call Dirk had noticed Dr. Gold staring at Monica's breasts. What was worse was that Monica was actually flirting with Gold. Right under Dirk's nose! He had pretended not to notice.

∾

Late that night, Dirk and Monica pulled inflatable dummies out of the bedroom closet and tucked them into their queen-size futon. It was time for a pizza run. Once they were sure the others were asleep in their rooms, they tiptoed to the rear exit and slipped out. There was a full moon. It was a half-hour walk down the blacktop to the Domino's Pizza in a shoppette.

CHAPTER THREE

"Morty," Alice said.

Morty had just drifted off into a reverie.

"Oh," he said, suddenly snapping out of it.

"Have you had any dreams?"

"Yeah. I had one last night. A beautiful, charismatic artist had founded an art institute—on Mars. Someplace off the beaten track, anyway. I'm in her painting class. She'd studied with Hans Hofmann and was looking for a change. She's encouraging us to experiment with surrealist automatism. I want to impress her, but it's not working out. I'm feeling all bollixed up. My painting is crap. I look over at another student's—another guy's—canvas, and *his* painting is remarkable. Gray squiggles on a white background. Surprisingly simple. While looking at it, the teacher comments, 'There is perfect clarity and harmony at work,' or something like that. I'm worried she might stop and examine my painting as she walks around the studio. That's it."

"That's quite a bit," Alice said. "What do you make of it?"

"I'm not sure."

"What about the other student with the remarkable canvas?" Alice asked.

"It all comes so easily for him. You know, that part of the dream reminds me of what a rat race this business is. They're all ganefs. I'm trying to raise enough to get *Martian Dawn* going and make a little something in the process, and these Arab investors—what do they think, I'm a total schmuck? I've gotta put the sheik back in his cage before he walks all over me. This ain't my first dance."

"Of course not," Alice said. "You've produced several successful films."

"That's right."

Morty had been in therapy with Alice for the past two years. Mysterious Alice. He was strangely drawn to her. He couldn't quite explain it.

Alice had agreed to act as a consultant on *Martian Dawn* to help add verisimilitude to scenes involving Richard's character's psychotherapy sessions. Morty was hoping it might bring Alice and him closer together. He pictured long evenings with just the two of them working out scenes, reviewing storyboards, etc. Then maybe he'd wow her with his collection of Indonesian artifacts, including the pieces he'd picked up on his recent buying trip to Sumatra.

Alice had been excited about the movie's premise, as Morty remembered it. She was sensitive, intelligent, wise and—on occasion—quite funny. Did she remind him of someone? His Aunt Bella?

Outside, it was seasonably mild. The curtains were drawn in Alice's dimly lit arts and crafts–style office off Beverly Drive. A built-in walnut bookshelf lined one wall, and a colorful Léger print hung on another. The room had a calming effect on Morty.

"What about this charismatic art teacher?" Alice asked.

"I'm not sure."

"You didn't want her to see your painting," she said.

"No."

"What was your painting like? You didn't say."

"It was—all mixed up. A dense mass of tightly coiled black doodles—almost like something a child might do—against a blue background."

"What would the teacher have thought if she had seen those black doodles?" Alice asked.

"That I was in serious trouble."

"And that made you uncomfortable," Alice said.

"No question," Morty said.

"There's a lot going on in this dream that might help us. Let's think about it some more. But we're out of time for today."

"Are you coming to the party?" Morty asked.

"I don't know if that's such a good idea."

"Yeah, maybe you're right," Morty said disappointedly.

"See you next time," Alice said.

After Morty left, Alice thought about what had just transpired. She did, it was true, find Morty to be an appealing, outsize character—in a little Jewish body! *What is this,* she asked herself, *countertransference?*

CHAPTER FOUR

A blue whale appeared on the screen.

"There's Monstro," said the bartender, pointing to the small portable TV on the bar in front of Cap.

"Are you kidding?" said Cap. "Monstro could use that whale for a toothpick. Bill, you're a good, even great, bartender, but you know shit about whales."

"Nobody's perfect," Bill said.

Cap had been at the bar for about an hour.

"You know, it's only two o'clock. I'd like to go to the beach to do some whale watching," Cap said.

"The only whale watching you're doing is right here on television, my friend," Bill said.

There was a long pause.

"Yeah, I guess you're right. Let me have another spritzer."

Cap watched part of a show about whales as he finished his drink.

"What is it with you and Monstro?" Bill asked. "I'm no expert, but . . ." He didn't complete his thought. "It's like Ahab and the white whale."

"Ahab was an asshole," Cap said. He shot Bill a withering glance. "Wiseass."

"If I didn't know better, I'd say you were half in love with that whale."

Yet it *was* true, Cap reflected, that he had developed more than a passing interest in Monstro.

"Bill, can I confide in you?"

"Must you?"

"You *are* a bartender, aren't you?"

"I'm a *weird* bartender, not some garden-variety set-'em-up Joe."

"*Please?*"

"Oh, all right."

"You know," Cap deadpanned, "Monstro *is* a very attractive whale. I guess you could say the relationship is—bigger than the both of us."

Bill and Cap broke up laughing.

"Yes," Cap continued, "I can honestly say that I've never felt this way about another whale before . . . Though there *was* this sea lion in Nova Scotia . . ."

"Really?"

"No. Don't be an idiot."

Cap got up and went into the reading room. He sat in a red-leather club chair opposite the magnificent picture windows facing Grand Central Station, and let his body go limp.

Two men in gray business suits sat across the room reading newspapers. Cap had been coming to the Yale Club every afternoon for several months now to relax and have a few drinks. He wondered if Monstro was out there, off Montauk, basking in the sun close to shore. Or perhaps to points north, near Nantucket, making for the depths.

Cap had first learned about Monstro in an article in the *New York Observer*. A Park Avenue matron had been keeping a baby whale as a pet on her estate in Quogue. In a digression, the article had mentioned Monstro, who had been found as a baby by a conservationist couple after Japanese whalers had killed his mother. The couple had raised Monstro as a pet, but they knew that one day they'd have to let him go back to the ocean.

Someone had made a quasi-documentary film about it, featuring the couple and the full-grown Monstro, but with a stand-in for Monstro as a baby. Cap got choked up just thinking about it: a lone whale, a solitary romantic spirit, its life turned upside down by an unseen industrial complex intent only on profit and laying waste to the planet. Monstro was destined to roam the sea alone. *Unless . . . unless what?* Cap thought. *Unless, somewhere out there, he hooked up with someone . . . someone . . . at least simpatico.*

Just then Bill came in with a phone message for Cap.

"Monte just called. The new issue of *Whale Quarterly* is scheduled to go to press next week, and you were supposed to finish proofreading the galleys yesterday. He wants you to call him."

"Oh, boy," Cap said.

"You need to learn how to multitask," Bill said.

"Who asked you?" Cap said.

∾

Monstro had built up a good head of steam and was fast approaching Monhegan Island. It was a crisp, clear day. A few sculptural white clouds were fixed high above the horizon. Monstro had been developing a case of cabin fever in the familiar coastal waters in and around the Hamptons, even with the occasional trip to Block Island. He felt he needed to get away and explore, perhaps even venture out to open sea.

He was happy on his own, but he wondered about the couple that had raised him. Though he was getting used to it, it was tough, after a sheltered upbringing, to have to fend for himself.

CHAPTER FIVE

D ealer takes two."
Monica discarded two worthless cards and dealt herself two worthless others.

Simon looked at the two cards he'd drawn, which were the two clubs he needed. "The game is five-card draw," he announced excitedly.

"Yeah, yeah," Samantha murmured with evident boredom. "Whatever. Nice poker face."

"Where was I?" Monica asked.

"Dirk was having a crisis," Samantha reminded her.

"Oh yeah, Dirk was having a crisis. About taking a new job. So he went to see a psychic a couple of times."

"No way," Samantha said, while eying her pair of aces.

"Yup. I said, 'Dirk, have you completely lost your mind?'"

"Well, that is kind of kooky," Gold offered. "But changing jobs can be stressful. Were you there for him? Did you provide moral support?"

"No, not really," Monica said matter-of-factly. "How could I help?"

"Have you had any psychic training?" Simon asked.

"Not recently," Monica said.

"All right, the Dr. Ruth Show is over," Gold said. "Back to the main event."

Now everyone had their cards. Gold bet a dollar, and Samantha saw it. Simon saw Gold's dollar and raised another dollar. Gold tossed a blue chip into the pot, and Samantha, Judy Gold and Monica folded.

Gold eyed Simon, trying to get a read on him. Simon's stone face told him nothing. "All right, Steve McQueen. *Mano a mano.* Just the way I like it. Whaddya got?"

"Victory is mine," Simon declared, throwing a flush down on the table.

Gold had kings and eights. He sighed.

"Sweet victory," Simon chuckled, sweeping the chips into a pile in front of him.

"Don't gloat," Samantha said. "Win one hand, and all of a sudden you're a big swinging dick."

Simon shot Samantha a sarcastic half smile.

Monica passed the deck to Gold, who shuffled, then asked her to cut it.

"What'll it be? Texas hold 'em? Anaconda? Cincinnati?" Gold asked. Everyone seemed a little bored, he thought.

The Biosphere teleconference center looked out on the Sonoran Desert. The first lights of evening from a couple of ranches and a residential subdivision flickered in the distance.

"How did you and Dirk meet?" Judy asked Monica, picking up the thread from the earlier conversation.

"Do you really care?" Monica asked, looking Judy directly in the eye.

"Passionately," Judy said.

"Well, sir, he was eyeballing me in a gourmet food store. Practically stole the nuts and berries right out of my shopping cart."

"Land sakes," said Samantha in a faux Southern drawl.

"*Something* like that," Simon said. "I think I read about it in the Boulder *Daily Camera*. Wasn't it *you* who shamelessly undressed *him* with your eyes in the aisle? Does hunting him down like a dog in the street sound familiar?"

"Please, sir," Monica said, "you go too far."

"It seems like so long ago," Simon said. "Now you treat him like dirt."

∼

Birds twittered and crickets chirped in the evening shadows. Dirk floated on a pink rubber raft in the saltwater-ocean biome at the far end of the Biosphere. Johnny Cash moaned "Long Black Veil" on his Walkman. The lines about the mystery woman visiting her lover's grave always got to him. He also liked the part about how the fleeing killer and ill-fated lover looked a lot alike. He pictured a cemetery at dusk and a young man walking through it.

A voice crackled over his walkie-talkie. He picked it up off his stomach.

"Hello?" he said.

"Dirk, it's me. Come in. Over," Monica said.

"I'm sorry, there's no one here by that name."

"Ha, ha."

"What's happening?"

"We're still playing poker. I just wanted to see how you were."

"How do you think I am?"

"Just fine."

"Yes, you're right," Dirk agreed. "Things are perfect."

"I wouldn't say that."

"That's because you have no imagination. Not a scintilla."

"Not even a scintilla?"

"Not a microdot."

"I want a divorce."

"You got it."

"You'll be hearing from my lawyers."

"Always a pleasure."

∽

"Did I ever tell you about when I lived in Equatorial Guinea, conducting a study on the rain forest?" Gold asked the group.

"I don't think so," Samantha said.

"The prime minister and I became best friends. It's funny, he was only one generation removed from cannibals."

"Oh my God!" Monica exclaimed. "Weren't you worried?"

"Gold's got ice water in his veins," Judy commented sarcastically. "He's a stone killer. Didn't you know?"

Gold ignored his wife and continued. "The prime minister was a spectacular billiards player. He had a pilot's license. He could speak five languages fluently—four of them Indo-European—was a crack shot and could recite Byron's "So We'll Go No More A-Roving" by heart.

As if on cue, Simon suddenly stood up and held forth:

So we'll go no more a-roving
      So late into the night,
Though the heart be still as loving,
      And the moon be still as bright.

For the sword outwears its sheath,
      And the soul wears out the breast,
And the heart must pause to breathe,
      And Love itself have rest.

24

Though the night was made for loving,
> And the day returns too soon,
Yet we'll go no more a-roving
> By the light of the moon.

"*You* were the prime minister of Equatorial Guinea?" Monica asked Simon.

"Simon, you continually amaze me," Gold said.

CHAPTER SIX

Hal poked his head inside the trailer. "I've just seen the rushes from this morning and want you to look at the Mars shuttle scene."

"Okay," Richard said, in between swigs of beer. "Can I get you something?"

"Campari and soda," Hal said.

"Coming right up."

Richard's vintage Airstream trailer had been completely refurbished inside. He and Hal sat opposite each other in matching white-leather Knoll chairs.

Hal was Richard's kind of director. He wasn't looking for anything fancy. He was content to let Richard do what he did best: be Richard. A writer from the *Hollywood Reporter* had asked Hal about Richard for a story on *Martian Dawn.* "Richard is very . . . Richard," Hal had said. Richard loved that. He *was* very Richard. All he had to do on the big screen was exist: a larger-than-life Richard to the max—china-blue eyes, chiseled chin, etc. Good lighting and the camera would take care of the rest. Richard liked to think of each of his roles as a different "product" in his own personal line. The quintessential Richard character was slippery and unpredictable, but also a master of crocodile tears. When Richard and Julia were cast opposite each other, the audience expected a contemporary, comic spin on *The Naked Kiss*. Richard had to be strong—but also vulnerable.

"Richard, you're like liquid gold," Hal said. "You could be in the worst piece of crap, and just by virtue of your existence, you elevate the entire film to the next level."

"Why *liquid* gold?"

"The camera loves you. But that's what's great about this role—why it was written with you in mind. It's such a *Richard* role."

Richard listed the character's finer points. "Let's see . . . devastating good looks, check; razor-sharp intellect, check."

"See? What'd I tell you?"

"Yeah, but why *liquid* gold? Isn't that oil?"

"No, that's *black* gold."

As a rule, Richard didn't get caught up in the nuances of a screenplay. If a line didn't seem enough like "one of his own," he'd simply demand a rewrite. "I love it. I've come back to Mars for my twenty-fifth college reunion to reclaim Julia, my college sweetheart. I see her from across a crowded ballroom. The room has a three-hundred-sixty-degree view, glass floor to glass ceiling. The stars, as well as Earth and Saturn, are visible in the distance. The soundtrack is 'Aquarius' by the Fifth Dimension. I remember the first time I nailed her."

"Very touching."

"So that's how we'll shoot the reunion?" Richard asked hopefully.

"No, it'll be nothing like that, I'm afraid," Hal replied.

"Oh." Richard shrugged. He didn't really care. He was a hired hand. All he could do was sign on with the most experienced director he could, and hope for the best. There was a knock at the door.

"Yo!" Richard yelled.

"Yo, Richard, it's Morty."

"Morty, my man, come in," Richard said.

"I hate to break up this little lovefest," Morty said, "but I need to talk to you, Richard." He sat down on the couch.

Morty's instincts told him what was up: Hal had been feeding Richard that "liquid gold" shit he fed to all his leads, and generally stroking Richard's ego. "All right, Richard, you've had your quota of ass kissing for the day. Good thing I showed up when I did—before Hal blew you."

Richard smiled.

"Very funny," Hal said.

"What's up?" Richard asked.

"Well, for one thing, this trip you have planned to India to see the Dalai Lama—the insurance underwriter is very uncomfortable with the whole thing. And without insurance, our backers are gone. I'm behind you a hundred percent. I love the Dalai Lama, terrific guy. By the way, did you see the great piece on him in the new issue of *Tricycle?* Anyway, bottom line, it's a nonstarter. It's gotta wait till the movie's in the can."

"Hmmm," Richard said. "What else?"

"I wangled you and Julia a tour of that Biosphere in Arizona. It's supposed to simulate life on Mars. It's a good marketing opportunity for the movie."

"Cool," Richard said. "Can Julia and I hang out in the Biosphere? To soak up the vibes?"

"I don't know about that. Lemme find out. I'm not sure you wanna do that. I think those geniuses in there are a bunch of nut jobs—kooks."

Richard was only half listening. The trailer sat in the parking lot of the Griffith Observatory. He was looking south out the window at the Hollywood Hills. He pictured the transparent dome of the Biosphere and, inside, Julia in a white lab coat and tortoise-shell glasses, with her hair in a bun.

"I can talk to Carole Berman about the Biosphere to see what she thinks," Hal interjected.

Morty shot him a nasty look. "Who gives a fuck what Carole Berman thinks," he snapped. "Carole Berman . . ." Morty's expression became thoughtful. "When I hear the name *Carole Berman* I have to send out a search party to find my pecker . . . It would be a contest as to which would be more gratifying: being blown by her or by Ernest Borgnine."

They all laughed.

"Why is it that whenever you walk through the door, suddenly everyone's getting their cock sucked?" Hal asked Morty. "It's embarrassing."

"That's a very good question," Morty replied.

∾

After they'd left, Richard sat musing in his white chair. Where was Julia? he wondered. Then he remembered she was on location wrapping *Cat Fight at the OK Corral,* the story of supermodels on the loose in Manhattan. What did Julia want from him? She was . . . complicated. She had a gorgeous athlete's body, but she could take sex or leave it. She liked to spend lavishly, but her tastes were actually quite simple. He knew that before they'd met, she'd led a completely different life, which he could only dimly imagine. Who was this "Angel" to whom she sometimes referred? Latin lover? Hairdresser? Lay analyst? All of these? What did Hal expect of him? How was the plot going to fit around him? And why *liquid* gold?

CHAPTER SEVEN

Walter, he is good lover?" Svetlana asked Sylvia.

"I beg your pardon?" Sylvia said. She was annoyed with the turn the conversation had taken, but for Svetlana it was just getting interesting.

"Boris bores me. He is so dull."

"I'm sorry to hear it," Sylvia said.

"How did you and Walter meet? I would like Walter—I mean, I would like to *meet* man *like* Walter."

"Walter and I have known each other forever. We met in Houston. How about you and Boris?" Sylvia didn't trust Svetlana and was reluctant to provide her with anything but the most general information.

Svetlana followed suit and pared her story down to the bone. "I lived in Moscow when I meet Boris. I see what I want—I grab it."

Sylvia nodded.

Kremlin II floated four hundred miles above Earth. The titanium skin of the space station stretched over an aluminum frame in the shape of a large glazed doughnut. Sylvia and Svetlana sat across from each other in the galley. Walter was working about forty yards away, monitoring the core systems. Boris was even further removed, in the tech module, analyzing the day's data from several tests that were being run to determine the ability of various organisms to adjust to life in space. They were all in the middle of a three-month stint aboard Kremlin II.

Svetlana reached over to the intercom on the wall by the table and called the tech module. "Boris?"

"Yes, this is Boris."

"When you are done with highly important task you are doing, do my laundry, please, and then make dinner. I am hungry."

"Yes, Svetlana."

Svetlana turned to Sylvia and smiled. "Boris is good boy."

"Nice," Sylvia observed.

～

Svetlana tiptoed up behind Walter and covered his eyes with her hands. "Guess who," she said.

"Boris, are you up to your old tricks again?" Walter smiled.

"Walter, you make joke."

Walter swiveled around in his chair to face Svetlana. They were alone at the main control panel of the operations room.

"Walter, tell me about your house in Houston." Svetlana pronounced it *Hoo-ston*.

"Well, I've got a condo in a high-rise overlooking a park. Tons of space, open floor plan, great views of the city."

"Sounds very nice. You know, maybe I must be in *Hooston* on business. I could stay in hotel, but is so impersonal. And you have such big place, no? I can stay with you?"

"Uh . . . I'm not sure that's such a good idea. It's just that my place is not really all *that* big . . ."

"I can cook for you. I have written cookbook, *From Borscht to Crêpes Suzette.* You like spaghetti carbonara? Penne with vodka cream sauce? Gnocchi Bolognese?"

Walter listened while he looked out the porthole of the operations center into deep space. He felt it pulling him in. "Well, that does sound tempting, Svetlana, but I'm not sure Sylvia would go for it."

"Who?"

"That's funny," Walter said.

Svetlana put her hand on Walter's thigh. He left it there for a few moments, smiling back at her. Then he removed it.

"Walter, what is wrong?" she asked.

"This is the operations center, Svetlana. I need to keep my head in the game."

"That is what you think. This is sex module. Do not try to fight it, Walter. Do not make me beg."

"Phew! Is it hot in here, or is it just me?" Walter asked, pulling at his collar with his index finger.

"You are helpless to resist. You are in my power. You will do as I say," she cooed.

"Point taken," he murmured.

"I want to be sure. All right, Walter, I just leave you with something—something to think about."

"I've got a bad feeling about this," Walter said.

She shrugged, then turned and sauntered out, leaving him alone in front of the control panel. What had just happened? Was he developing more than just a passing interest in Svetlana? Were they going to *do* something—sometime soon? And how was her carbonara sauce?

CHAPTER EIGHT

Monica climbed into bed next to the inflatable dummies, closed her eyes and thought back.

Ten years earlier Dirk and Monica were known as the Archie and Veronica of the MFA program of the Jack Kerouac School of Disembodied Poetics at the Naropa Institute in Boulder. They had met at Alfalfa's Market during the first week of school. Dirk had felt her giving him the once-over in the fruits and vegetables section. Soon they were inseparable.

They communicated constantly through prototype cell phones.

"Monica, what's your position?"

"I'm leaving the Shambhala Hall and making my way to the parking lot."

"Check. Let's rendezvous at The James at thirteen hundred hours."

"Roger that. Order me an Irish coffee. Over and out."

They both had apartments on the Hill. Dirk spent most of the week attending literature classes and writing workshops. Monica was studying pre-Columbian art and Balinese dancing. Occasionally, they would drop by the Varsity Townhouses to swim in the pool or would take long walks in the meadow beneath the Flatirons. They spent several evenings a week with their Naropa clique in the Catacombs bar under the Boulderado Hotel. There were plenty of poetry readings at Naropa, Boulder Bookstore and Penny Lane coffee shop.

Monica was fickle, flirtatious, impetuous, unreliable, self-possessed and postadolescent, though a fully developed twenty-one-year-old woman. Dirk was popular with the ladies. His success was due, in no small part, to his dogged determination: He rarely took no for an answer. He was also prone to jealous fits. From the beginning, he sensed that his relationship with Monica was on a precarious footing and that, if someone more exciting came along, she might suddenly break away.

They tried to keep it casual. They might not see each other for a day or two, but as a rule one would usually drop by the other's place and spend the night. Monica was wary about approaching anything even vaguely suggestive of marriage. Dirk, too, was not eager to take the plunge, despite his possessiveness.

~

Monica used to hang out with Simon and Luke. At first, they had seemed a little odd to her. Simon, who'd graduated from Naropa's writing program several years earlier, used a portion of his trust fund to finance the installation of site-specific, abstract sculptures made of brushed steel on his estate-size lot, which abutted the open space along the west edge of town. He would call in the specs by phone from his studio to a metal shop in Denver, where the pieces were fabricated. He had his own publicist and had developed a profile as a local artist, something which in itself was not unimpressive, considering that he had had no formal training and hadn't been to an art museum since he was a young child.

Luke and Simon had gone to prep school together on the East Coast. Luke's wife had bought him a "hippie" candle shop on the Pearl Street Mall. He had two employees and dropped in a couple of times a week to check up on them. He hired someone to redecorate the store, and he paid a candle consultant and a retail consultant to prepare a business plan for a boutique candle business. The store had one or two regular customers, and a few walk-ins would come in every week. Luke and his wife lived in a custom home on Flagstaff Mountain just outside of town.

It became apparent to Monica fairly quickly that Simon knew as much about art and Luke as much about the candle business as her great-aunt Bessie. Simon's art studio and Luke's store were, essentially, not much more than elaborate stage sets in which very little happened. But she admired their ingenuity: There was a certain Dada genius in the intense focus each of them brought to simply creating and maintaining these façades. They were pretty dopey, it was true, but Monica couldn't help wondering what might happen if each devoted a fraction of those efforts to some kind of serious pursuit. She was certain the thought had never occurred to them. And, far from being oddballs in Boulder, they were fairly typical.

∽

Rinpoche was a great Tibetan Buddhist teacher. He lived in a four-thousand-square-foot ranch-style house with an indoor basketball half-court in East Boulder, along the thirteenth fairway of the Flatirons Golf Course.

To go with his profound state of enlightenment, Rinpoche had a childlike sense of humor and loved practical jokes, the sillier the better. His favorite ploy was to send Blackie Friedlander, the Beat poet who was the director and cofounder of Naropa's Kerouac School, phony letters from young poetry student admirers ("my fellow classmates tell me that I am quite beautiful," "maybe we can meet at Rinpoche's next happy hour," etc.). The letters were full of extravagant praise, not only of Blackie but also of Rinpoche, whom the "student" would claim to have recently met. Rinpoche dictated the letters to his secretary in his office at the Shambhala Center.

He enjoyed entertaining and hosted a happy hour on Friday evenings. He was known for his "world famous" whiskey sours.

∼

Richard sat meditating alone in the temple on the top floor of the Shambhala Center, a three-story, nineteenth-century brick building a few blocks from the Boulderado Hotel. The windows provided a view of the rooftops of the city.

Richard had come to Boulder for a weeklong residency in Buddhist studies at the institute. He was scheduled to give a talk and participate in a panel discussion, and had made an appointment for a private interview with Rinpoche, which was to take place now. Despite his regimen of Buddhist meditation and instruction, he was feeling anxious and wondered whether he was ready.

Rinpoche appeared suddenly in the doorway in an orange sarong, startling Richard.

"Rinpoche, this is a great honor. Thank you for agreeing to this private interview."

"Please don't get up. The pleasure is mine." He looked into Richard's eyes and held his gaze. Then he sat down opposite Richard in front of the large shrine in the center of the room.

Rinpoche proceeded to draw Richard out about his meditation practice. Next he listened to Richard describe some of his concerns and questions. Using some concrete examples from Richard's life, Rinpoche artfully suggested to Richard how he might, in a variety of ways that hadn't previously occurred to him, more easily clear away the confusion of ego in order to glimpse the awakened state.

Richard was deeply moved. He bowed his head and closed his eyes. When he opened them, Rinpoche was gone.

≈

Later that afternoon, Monica was checking Richard out from across the pool at the Varsity Townhouses. She was in the shallow end in a lavender bikini. He sat on the edge at the deep end dangling his legs in the water.

She swam over to him. "I really enjoyed your talk yesterday. Tibet must have been incredible." She flashed her best bedroom eyes.

Richard smiled, enjoying the attention but slightly embarrassed by it as well.

≈

That night Richard and Monica dined at Laudisio, a hip Italian restaurant located in a strip mall at Twenty-Eighth and Iris. Afterward they returned to Richard's apartment at the Varsity.

"What am I going to do with you?" Richard asked no one in particular. He was thinking of a girlfriend back in Los Angeles.

"Oh, I can think of a few things," Monica grinned.

Richard excused himself for a minute, went into the bedroom, undressed and lay down on the bed.

After a few minutes, Monica wondered why he hadn't returned to the living room. "Hey, where'd you go?"

"I'm in the bedroom."

The bedroom was dimly lit. She peered in at the doorway. Her jaw dropped.

≈

The next afternoon Monica was just opening the front door to her apartment when the phone rang.

"Monica, it's me," Dirk said.

There was a long pause. "Yes, how may I help you?"

"I'm sorry about our fight—I don't know what I could have been thinking."

"Listen, pal, you're a day late and a dollar short."

"What do you mean?"

"Do you know Richard?"

"Yeah . . . What about him?" Dirk had seen a couple of Richard's movies and was aware he had come to Naropa for a residency.

"I'm with *him* now," Monica said matter-of-factly.

"That's ridiculous. When did you meet him? We only just had our fight the day before yesterday."

"A lot can happen in a day and a half."

"Fucker," Dirk sputtered. "I'll kill him if I see him."

"Always good talking to you, Dirk." Monica hung up.

Richard was the sweetest lover she ever had. She thought wistfully about the night before as she gazed at the Flatirons from her living-room window. A few papier-mâché clouds floated slowly by.

∾

Dirk's worst nightmare had come true: Monica had been stolen right out from under him. He rode his bike to campus to see if anyone knew where Richard was and learned that he was giving a talk outdoors at Boulder Creek, near the public library. He rode there as fast as he could pedal.

Richard had just wrapped up his talk when Dirk arrived.

"Hey, you!" Dirk shouted, jumping off his bike.

"Do I know you?" Richard asked.

Dirk walked up and poked his finger in Richard's chest, then shoved him. Richard shoved back.

"So, this is a fight?" Richard asked.

"You're damn right," Dirk said.

"Why is it a fight? What's your problem?"

"Does the name 'Monica' ring a bell?" Dirk asked.

"Monica? Hmmm . . . Brunette? About five-nine?" He made an hourglass shape in the air with his hands.

Dirk nodded.

"No, no bells," Richard said, shaking his head.

They stood glaring at each other in the clearing next to the creek. There was silence except for the birds and the gurgling of the creek. It was a Mexican standoff.

CHAPTER NINE

Svetlana sat beautifying herself in front of her mini-vanity. The full moon glowed in her cabin porthole.

Sylvia was on duty in the operations area. She had left Walter napping in his cabin. Boris continued to compile data in the tech module.

Walter sat wide awake in his bed reading the note that had been slipped under the door.

Meet me in Docking Module at 1500.
Dress: casual.

It had been nearly a week since he and Svetlana had had their first assignation in the docking module. She had told him to be patient and wait for her to contact him when their next opportunity arose. In the meantime, they would go about their duties.

Walter was apprehensive. Svetlana's charms were considerable. Just how smitten was he? He wondered what would happen once they were off the space station and the initial excitement of their liaison had faded. What might their life together be like? Would Svetlana take up golf and round out his weekend foursome at the country club? Would she take to Houston society? Shop at Neiman Marcus? It was hard to say.

When he arrived at the docking module, the lights were dim. It seemed to be empty. Then Svetlana appeared in a silver lamé jumpsuit.

"Walter, you are late! But Svetlana forgives you. Svetlana forgives—but she does not forget!" she said, spanking Walter's behind.

"It's been *too* long," Walter said, moving close and embracing her. "You don't write, you don't call . . . I've been thinking about you."

"I know, Walter. But I have been busy. So much to take care of . . ." She hadn't been busy, and there wasn't much to take care of. The mission was going more smoothly than any of them could have hoped. Her ploy of feigned indifference was designed to pique Walter's imagination, in case he had any thought of ignoring her or fending her off.

"No problem," he said. "Now we're together."

"Walter, what will happen to us when mission is finished? You will return to *Hooston* with Sylvia? Shall I return to Moscow with Boris?"

He smiled and shrugged.

"Well, Walter, I am thinking. We will run away together. Boris and Sylvia will have problems, and I am feeling sad, of course, but there is American expression: Shit happens." She tried to look innocent.

Walter laughed, then caught himself. "Hmmm," he said.

Svetlana studied his face. Could she really rely on him? Eventually, she might get bored with him too. After a brief "honeymoon" phase, Svetlana had lost interest in all her prior lovers. Would it be any different this time?

Walter was developing a cow-eyed look. He wanted to know all about her: her childhood; her past loves; her "lost" years, as she referred to them, on the catwalks of Milan, before she returned to Moscow to train as a cosmonaut. She and Boris had met as trainees in the Russian space program.

41

"Walter, I have surprise for you."

"I hate surprises," he said under his breath.

"Excuse me, Walter?"

"Yes, Svetlana."

"Oh, Walter, you are so funny. I think you will like this," she said. *Maybe he will, and maybe he won't,* she said to herself. But *she* would like it. "You wait here. I am coming right back."

She disappeared around a corner into an alcove and slipped out of her jumpsuit. Then she lay on her side, resting her head on one elbow, and relaxed. She thought she would build up the suspense by making Walter wait a few extra minutes before making her entrance.

Svetlana loved surprises. She liked to keep her men on their toes, lest they become complacent. It kept things interesting. She would never let a relationship become *too* comfortable. None of her boyfriends had ever known exactly where they stood. Was Walter her boyfriend? Technically, Boris was her boyfriend. The idea of two boyfriends at once pleased her. If only Sylvia were out of the picture. Then how would the arrangement work? She had heard of such situations among the bohemian set in Moscow. Would there be a sign-up sheet? Would each boyfriend be "off" on alternate weeks? No, that sounded so bureaucratic. The ad hoc approach would be preferable. She must think.

Walter had waited long enough, she decided, and she made her final preparation. Then she appeared from out of the shadows looking very pleased with herself, and faced Walter, hands on her hips, wearing only a strap-on dildo. "Walter, you know I only want best for you," she said.

CHAPTER TEN

Richard and Julia sat next to each other in their Gulfstream jet, which Richard had leased. They leveled off to a cruising altitude of forty-five thousand feet for the two-hour trip to Arizona. Richard was reviewing the week's clippings from the tabloids and other periodicals that mentioned him or Julia. He read that he and Julia were moving to Paris because Julia's dream was to live there. The move was a done deal, he was reported to have said, because his priority was to keep Julia happy. Paris was like no other city in the world, Julia had confided to a close friend. She just wanted to be there, sit in a café, walk down the Champs Elysées, buy perfume.

The tabloids had it backward, he mused. Julia's carefully cultivated public image was that of a bright-eyed and bushy-tailed floozy with a heart of gold. He was supposedly the more analytical, worldly wise of the two. Another article had Julia considering a role as a comfort woman in a Japanese POW camp. According to a source, Julia had become fascinated with nineteenth-century captivity narratives and was also considering a script about a white woman taken prisoner by Indians. The truth was, Julia was a quick study whose generous physical endowments belied her intelligence. She had a clear-eyed view of human nature, cynical at times, beyond her years.

Her occasional temper tantrums were calculated for their dramatic effect. Richard tended to be the sentimental one, always ready to attribute the most altruistic motives to others. In some ways he was quite naïve. Julia, on the other hand, had grown up in the streets and viewed the world with the wariness of an Arab trader in a Middle Eastern marketplace.

He watched her sleeping peacefully in the seat next to him. He found her skin and lashes remarkable and felt compelled to touch her cheek, but he didn't want to wake her. She was breathing lightly and looked uncharacteristically vulnerable. Her perfection suggested an air of unreality. Julia's identity, Richard reflected, had in some sense become so fused with her public persona as to be indistinguishable from it. The "real" Julia hardly existed at all.

~

Further back in the plane sat Morty and Alice. Morty had been having a number of vivid dreams. He kept a notepad on his night table so he could write them down when he woke up. Later, he would discuss them with Alice in their sessions.

In a recent dream, he had fornicated with an old love interest, Bridget Byrne. It was exhilarating. Soon afterward, his college classics professor appeared as a Monday-morning quarterback and told him to, one, stick to the text and, two, not get too excited about Bridget because she'd dump him at the earliest opportunity.

It was a sad litany of dreams with a similar trajectory: utter joy followed by a punishing, humiliating blow. Through his work with Alice, Morty was starting to realize the metaphorical qualities of dreams such as these—that, in a certain way, they reflected his own view of himself. He sensed that part of his work with Alice was the painstakingly slow, almost imperceptible process of internalizing

Alice's good opinion of him so that it became part of his own view of himself.

Did he deserve happiness and success? Possibly. But his feelings of inadequacy had been an ongoing problem. Whenever he had his wits about him, he liked to say that he had simply been caught in the act of being himself. At those times, he would try his best to keep out of his own way.

~

A cloudless blue sky was visible through the dome of the Biosphere.

Richard and Julia had just finished autographing eight-by-ten glossies of themselves to be given out to the biospherans.

"In response to the readings, we can control many variables by artificially adjusting rainfall, temperature, relative humidity and oxygen output," Gold said.

"Yeah, that's interesting," Morty responded, suppressing a yawn.

Richard and Julia were lagging a few paces behind. Julia wished she could simply explore on her own. Richard was content for the time being to blend into the scenery.

"The Biosphere complex measures twenty acres. Essentially, it's a huge, airtight greenhouse. Each of the seven biomes represents a different wilderness ecosystem," Gold continued. "Right now, we're in the coastal-fog desert. The vegetation you see around you is typical. We'll also see the rain-forest biome and the saltwater-ocean biome, which contains well over a million gallons."

"What's in the water?" Richard asked.

"We have porpoises, sea turtles—even a whale," Gold said. "The whale's a recent addition. We'll see how he does."

"Cool," Richard said.

"Such a glorious view." Alice looked outside across the desert.

"Yes," Gold continued, "we get some beautiful sunsets over the Santa Catalina Mountains, and the turtles come up onto the beach."

"Isn't that something? Right up on the beach?" Morty asked with a great show of enthusiasm.

"Uh-huh," Gold responded proudly.

"Wonderful!" Morty bellowed. "But tell me something . . ." he continued, his brow furrowing. "These turtles—will they blow you?"

Gold suddenly looked confused. "Excuse me?"

"Oh, Morty," Alice said. "You never stop." She hit him affectionately with her handbag. "Don't pay any attention to him," she said to Gold.

Richard and Julia were laughing.

"Don't encourage him," Alice said to them.

"I'm sorry," Morty said, with as much contrition as he could muster. "It's the burlesque in my blood. I really am enjoying the tour."

"There are sensors," Gold said, picking up where he had left off, "that monitor light and carbon dioxide."

"So," Richard asked, "the point of all this is to create a self-sufficient environment to facilitate interplanetary colonization?"

"Exactly," Gold said. "Food cultivation and oxygen production are critical to survival—in the Biosphere or on other planets."

"At least one of us is paying attention," Richard said to Morty with a smirk.

"It must be tough," Alice said. "How long has your team been in the Biosphere?"

"The current team has been here for just under a year," Gold responded.

"Wow," Julia said. "How's it going?"

"Well, there are, of course, petty jealousies and squabbles that crop up. It's inevitable: who's not pulling their weight, who's making time with whom, et cetera. The usual stuff."

"Interesting," Morty said. "Tell us more. It sounds like a big soap opera in here."

"That would be one way of putting it. I have to watch Mrs. Gold like a hawk, for example—can't trust her as far as I can throw her," he deadpanned.

"Alice, you could have a field day in here with these geniuses," Morty said to Alice under his breath.

"Morty, he was kidding," Alice said, laughing.

"Oh really? Too bad. I was looking forward to meeting Mrs. Gold. Thought maybe I'd see if I can still throw the fastball," Morty said.

"Does anyone ever sneak out?" Richard asked.

"Oh no," Gold said, horrified. "Everyone's signed contracts."

They were walking in a circle on a path around the three-acre biome. The ground was hard and dry. There were several stands of small ponderosa and piñon pines.

"What kind of contracts?" Morty asked, his ears pricking up. "Agreements promising not to work for a competing biosphere?" he laughed.

"No, not exactly," Gold said.

"Excuse us for a minute, Dr. Gold," Morty said. "Richard, I've got an idea for a movie."

"Okay," Richard said. "Let's hear it."

"Two competing biospheres: a 'good' biosphere and a 'bad' biosphere," Morty said.

"I like it," Julia said.

"It's the old nature-civilization tension. Works like a charm," Alice said.

"Yeah . . ." Morty said thoughtfully.

They had arrived back at the biome entrance and now stood in front of a bank of video monitors displaying all seven biomes. The biospherans were at work on several screens. A blue whale was swimming alone in the ocean biome. The rain-forest biome appeared to be empty.

"We have these displays throughout the Biosphere," Gold said. He took a few minutes to explain the various tasks being carried out by the biospherans and what their typical day consisted of.

Morty noticed that Richard wasn't paying attention to Gold and had instead become fixated on an attractive brunette now appearing on the rain-forest monitor. She was brushing her hair while emerging from some very thick undergrowth. "Oh shit," Morty said under his breath. He nudged Alice and whispered, "Code red," nodding in Richard's direction. Alice nodded back.

Morty had enlisted Alice, in her capacity as a consultant on *Martian Dawn,* to help keep an eye on Richard. She and Morty had discussed Richard at length and agreed that it would be wise to make sure he didn't get into any trouble that might sidetrack production.

He took her by the arm, and they retreated about twenty yards so they could have some privacy while Gold droned on. "I think we've got a situation," Morty said gravely.

"Morty, let's not jump to conclusions," Alice said.

"I smell trouble," Morty said. "Who is that rain-forest bimbo? We need to find out. I've seen that look in Richard's eyes before. That was not a look of mild interest—more like an insatiable lion staking out a gazelle."

"'Insatiable lion'?" Alice said, trying to keep from laughing. "Interesting choice of words. Could be you're projecting a little, no?"

"Very funny. Look, Richard needs to be saved from *Richard,*" Morty said.

"I agree," Alice said.

"At least until *Martian Dawn's* in the can. Then he can do whatever the fuck he wants."

They both laughed, then silently rejoined the group. Morty had calmed down and began to focus on Richard more intently. Was he a sex addict in need of professional help? Or was it simply, as Richard had often claimed, that he was catnip to the ladies? The truth was probably somewhere in between. The situation might require some finesse, and Morty would need plausible deniability in case Richard figured out what he was up to.

"I thought we'd go to the teleconference center next," Gold said, "so you can meet Trout. After that we'll head to the rain-forest biome. There should be some good photo ops. Sound okay?"

Everyone nodded. Morty was watching Richard carefully.

"Morty," Richard said.

"Yes," Julia said, laughing.

"Is your name 'Morty'?" Richard asked her.

"No," she said, laughing some more.

"Yes, Richard darling," Morty said impatiently. "What is it?"

"Stop looking at me," Richard said. "I can feel you watching me. You're drilling holes in the back of my head. Would you just calm down?"

"No problem." Morty and Alice exchanged knowing glances.

They all stood on a gentle rise. Before long, a thick fog had descended on the group.

~

Morty had arranged Richard and Julia's tour of the Biosphere to generate some advance publicity for the movie. A publicist had flown in a photographer and set up some press interviews for later in the day to discuss how the two leads were researching their roles in a simulated Mars environment to bring added authenticity to their portrayals. The combination of Richard and Julia's Hollywood glamour and Trout's Texas oil money had been irresistible, and the press had eagerly signed on.

No sooner were Gold, Richard, Julia, Morty and Alice seated around the conference room table than Trout's image appeared on the screen. He was wearing a ten-gallon hat and a bolo tie, and there was a view of the Houston skyline behind him. "Hi, how y'all doin'?" he asked.

"This is some place you've got here," Richard said. "Thanks for allowing us to visit."

"My pleasure," Trout said. "Morty's an old friend. It's good publicity for us too. Morty, what's happening? How's business?" He didn't wait for a response. "You know what's all the rage in corporate America these days? Started on Wall Street and caught on like wild fire."

"No . . ." Morty said, his interest piqued.

"Janitors insurance." Trout paused dramatically and let his words hang out there for a moment for the group to absorb. Everyone around the table had a puzzled expression. "They also call it peasants insurance. The company gets life insurance on its employees—with the company named as beneficiary. It's a very hot product right now. You ought to think about it, Morty. I can put you in touch with one of the top guys at Prudential who came up with this. Guy's a genius."

"I will," Morty promised.

"How do you like my little theme park, Julia?" he asked.

"It's pretty great," she said.

"It's not perfect—not yet, anyway. But we're working out the kinks. And eventually we'll have our own high-tech office park and golf course. So, tell me about the movie."

"Well," Richard said, "it's the usual boy-girl story. Julia and I do a mating dance, opposites attract, one or possibly both of us turns out to have a heart of gold, et cetera. Think of it as *Bringing Up Baby* meets *Last Tango in Paris*—on Mars."

"I love it! Something for everyone! It's the American way," Trout boomed.

"That reminds me," Richard said to Morty, "I need to talk to Hal. I'm not sure just what he has in store for me."

"Richard, you worry too much. You're in the hands of an old pro."

"Julia's not old," Richard said.

"Very funny. Relax," Morty said.

∿

Alice lingered in the conference room for a few moments after everyone else had left. Outside, the light was fading. She stood by the windows looking out at the desert and distant mountains. She tried to imagine a life of total isolation in the Biosphere and pictured herself and Morty holding daily analytic sessions in an igloo. Had she been watching too many movies? Maybe. Was she losing her professional remove? Quite possibly. Would she, one day, help Morty cut through to his psychic makeup? The odds seemed pretty good. And who was that rain-forest bimbo? An owl hooted.

CHAPTER ELEVEN

R ichard, I've been sitting by the phone these past few years, waiting for you to call," Monica laughed.

"I thought you didn't have a phone in here," Richard smiled.

As Monica led Richard to a secluded clearing in the rain-forest biome, they began to reminisce.

"I was just a kid then," Monica said.

"You're still a kid, Monica. How'd you end up in here?" he asked.

"It's a long story."

He had a feeling it might be. "Are you still with that creep? The one that tried to clock me at Boulder Creek?"

"'*With*' is such a relative term, particularly here in the Biosphere," she responded in a world-weary tone. She draped her arms around his neck.

"It's just like old times at the Varsity Townhouses," Richard said, gently removing her arms from around him.

"Who's the chick I saw you come in with?" Monica asked. "She looked familiar."

"That's Julia."

"Is she your girlfriend?"

"No, she's my . . . psychoanalyst. Can't go anywhere without her. Nerves."

"Oh. Well, do you think your *shrink* would mind if she saw us together?"

"She trained in Vienna. Strict Freudian. She's been a tremendous help to me."

"Lucky you," Monica smirked.

"Don't you know who that is?" Richard asked.

"Yeah. Some second-rate actress."

"*First*-rate, my dear."

"So you're here because you're in a movie together? What's the picture?"

"Takes place on Mars. We're soaking up the vibes."

"Anyway, you're really involved with her?"

"'*Involved*' is such a relative term—particularly in the movie business."

"You're fucking her, right?"

"Be nice."

"I am nice. I'm just remembering old times—back in the Townhouses. How's your memory?"

"Amnesia."

"So, how'd you meet her?"

"She was turning tricks by the side of the road when I drove by in my Ferrari."

"Sounds romantic. No, really. How'd you two meet?"

"*Really.* You don't believe me?"

"No, of course not."

"So you just stay in the Biosphere all the time?" he asked.

"Yeah, except for my nightly pizza runs," she said.

"Ha, ha."

"Hey, kiddo. You ran away." Morty suddenly appeared and put a hand on Richard's shoulder.

Richard introduced Morty to Monica.

"So, how'd you wind up in here?" Morty asked her.

Just then Dirk appeared with a pitcher of iced tea and some glasses.

"This is my fiancé, Dirk," Monica said, introducing everyone.

"Would you all like some iced tea?" Dirk asked.

"Iced tea sounds good," Morty said.

"I'll stick with my Evian," Richard said.

Morty took Richard aside. "It's none of my business, but is everything okay here?" Morty asked gingerly.

"Morty, give me a *little* credit for a modicum of self-control," Richard said. He explained to Morty that he and Monica had met in Boulder and that anything between them was ancient history.

"I'm sorry," Morty said contritely. "I just let my imagination run away with me."

"No problem," Richard said. Then he turned to Monica and Dirk. "You two kids run along."

"But we don't feel like 'running along,' Richard," Dirk said. "Have some iced tea."

"Fuck your iced tea," Richard said.

Monica jumped between them, imploring them sarcastically. "Oh please, boys. Let's not revert to our old roles. Jeez, you guys are so corny. And now we will run along. Take my hand, Dirk. Ta-ta, everybody."

"Ta-ta," Morty called out, waving. "This iced tea is delicious."

CHAPTER TWELVE

Monstro swam lazily in the saltwater-ocean biome. A couple of terns standing motionless on a white-sand beach watched him gliding silently through the water. Judy Gold stood on the beach with her hands on her hips in lime-green Lilly Pulitzer clam diggers. The vast scale of the biome dwarfed her.

The scene appeared to Cap to resemble a *tableau vivant*. Was it true? he wondered. Had he found Monstro at last? He peered in from the breezeway outside the biome and noticed that Mrs. Gold was gazing lovingly at Monstro like a doting parent. Monstro was basking in the attention. Cap felt a twinge of jealousy. He was still early for his appointment, so he took out his cell phone and dialed Monte.

"*Whale Quarterly*," Monte said.

"Monte, it's Cap. I'm at the Biosphere."

"Good man. See what you can find out. I love that going-back-to-the-wild angle you pitched to me. Maybe Monstro has some dark secret in his past? Skeletons in his closet . . . I dunno—maybe he ate somebody and it was hushed up," Monte said.

"He's a blue whale. They eat plankton," Cap said.

"Oh, for chrissakes, I was only joking. But you get the general idea. Have you seen him yet?"

"Just through the glass. My meeting's not for a little while. But I'm sure it's him. He was with Judy Gold. They seem to have some kind of special relationship," Cap said.

"Hmmm . . . Maybe we can work on some kind of love triangle angle—'Monstro: The Whale I Left Behind,'" Monte offered.

"What is this, 'Page Six'?" Cap asked.

"Easy, now. Remember, we need a scoop, the inside story."

"Got it."

"Okay. Good luck," Monte said.

As soon as Monte hung up, Cap placed another call on his speed dial.

"Yale Club," said the receptionist.

"Yes, can you put me through to the bar?" Cap asked.

"Yes, sir. Hold for the bar," the receptionist said, before patching the call through.

"This is the bar," Bill said.

"Yes . . . This is the pro shop calling from Montauk Downs. Did you lose a white golf ball around the eighteenth green?" Cap asked.

"Why, yes. Have you found it?" Bill asked.

"Titleist number two?"

"That's it. Hey, Cap, where are you?"

"Listen, I've tracked down Monstro. He's in the Biosphere."

There was a long pause on the other end as Bill took this in.

"Bill, are you there?"

"I'm here. Hmmm . . . So, you're in Arizona? What are you gonna do? Try an intervention? It'd be more like a jailbreak."

"Whale break."

"Do you need help? I've got people I can call."

"I haven't decided yet what I'm gonna do. I'm on assignment for *WQ*. Monte sent me."

"Does Monte know about you and Monstro?"

"What's there to know? I've just developed a healthy interest in Monstro. It's perfectly normal."

"Okay, forget that . . . How're you gonna get him out of there?"

"I'm not sure he *wants* to leave. He seems pretty happy. There's a Mrs. Gold here, a scientist, who's all over him like a cheap suit."

"Brazen hussy," Bill said. "What's going on in that Biosphere, anyway? According to *Newsweek,* it sounds like midnight on Monkey Island."

"There's something about this place . . . I can't quite put my finger on it . . ." Cap said.

"Interesting . . . I oughta blow this Popsicle stand and come out there to get a firsthand look. If I like what I see, maybe I'll move in!"

"Hmmm . . ."

"Cap?" Bill said.

"I'm here. Something you said got me thinking. Anyway, I've got to run."

"Okay, bye," Bill said.

≈

Cap took in the sprawling Biosphere complex. Then he walked around to the main entrance. Judy Gold was waiting.

"Are you from *WQ*?" she asked.

"Yes. Cap Martin."

"Nice to meet you. I'm Judy Gold. I thought I'd take you inside the saltwater-ocean biome and let you look around for yourself. I'll come get you in half an hour, and I can answer any questions you might have for your article."

"Sounds good." Nice outfit, Cap thought to himself.

They went inside and passed a bank of video monitors. Cap noticed a handsome man who looked familiar—an actor, maybe— and an attractive woman with her hair in a ponytail walking in the rain-forest biome. He wondered who they were.

"I'm looking forward to seeing the whale," Cap said.

"Yes, dear Monstro. He's practically family," Judy responded.

So I noticed, Cap thought. He smiled at her, and she smiled back.

She led him down a corridor and directly into the saltwater-ocean biome. They stood on the beach watching Monstro, who looked even bigger up close. Monstro stopped swimming and eyed Cap with curiosity.

"Oh, Monstro," Cap said, as soon as Judy had left. "It really *is* you, isn't it?"

Monstro continued to swim, ignoring Cap. He seems to be enjoying himself, Cap thought. Monstro *was,* in fact, quite happy. How he had gotten there was a complicated story. The effort to reacclimate him to the wild in Iceland had been unsuccessful. He had turned up in Norway after years of being retrained for reentry into his natural habitat. He surprised the Norwegians, who petted and swam with him in the Skaalvik Fjord, about 250 miles northwest of Oslo. Volunteers continued to monitor him. Eventually, it was determined that he was not equipped to fend for himself. He showed little interest in feeding or mating. So the decision was made to find a suitable venue to house him in captivity, since he seemed to prefer humans to other whales.

A few giant sea turtles rested on the beach while some porpoises swam along with Monstro. The sun was setting. The clouds were pink, with shadows underneath. Cap and Monstro were finally together. The planet had stopped spinning beneath them, and they were frozen in time at the center of the universe. The intensity of the moment was palpable.

They would have no need for society: They would be a world unto themselves. Cap pictured the two of them leading a sublimely solipsistic existence together in the Biosphere, he playing Friday to Monstro's Crusoe. Then the two of them in a shiny, stainless-steel rocket hurtling through space to explore nearby planets. Cap wanted nothing more than to become lost in something greater than himself.

Monstro continued to swim around, oblivious to Cap, wondering when Mrs. Gold would return. But he half suspected, from the penetrating looks Cap was giving him, that Cap might be involved in some kind of foolishness.

CHAPTER THIRTEEN

Julia strode to the stage in a gingham Talbots dress, cardigan sweater, saddle shoes, horn-rimmed glasses and a pearl necklace with her hair in a bun. She climbed the steps, then turned to face the audience and struck a pose: head tossed carelessly to one side, eyes looking knowingly over glasses on end of nose, and hand on hip. Her attitude suggested there might be more to this shy librarian than met the eye. She held her pose until the music began: Marvin Gaye's "Sexual Healing."

She moved with the music, first tentatively, then with feeling. Before long she had let her hair down, stripped to just a G-string and begun to swing her bra over her head with abandon. She grabbed the chrome fireman's pole at one edge of the stage and curled a leg around it, arching her back and throwing back her head dramatically. The Friday-night crowd at the Baby Doll Lounge in downtown Phoenix whooped in appreciation.

Angel stood by the bar in a black-leather jacket taking it all in. It gave him a charge to see "Esmeralda"—Julia's stage name at the club—turning on the crowd. She had been an exotic dancer at the Baby Doll for the past two years and had spent the better part of the first year as a member of Angel's informal "stable," hooking on the side, out of the club, to support her heroin habit. Their courtship had begun in typical "office" romance fashion with flirtatious banter around the watercooler.

"Hey, Esmeralda, what're you doing this weekend?"

"The name is *Julia,* dick-for-brains. And it's none of your bees-wax. I ought to report you for creating a hostile work environment."

"There's probably no such thing as sexual harassment in a topless bar, so I won't lose any sleep over it—*Esmeralda.*"

One night he ran into her at a nearby nightspot after the club had closed.

"Excuse me, miss, I'm checking hall passes. Do you have yours?"

"Gosh, I seem to have misplaced it—somewhere or other. Am I in a lot of trouble?"

"You've been very bad. And I probably will have to punish you—at some point. But I think I can let you off with a slap on the wrist tonight. I just got blown in the bathroom," he announced with a wry smile.

"Let me buy you a drink!" Julia responded, without missing a beat.

"Yes. I'm parched."

They made their way to the bar. Julia wondered, *had* he just been blown in the bathroom? In fact, he'd been making out with a girl at the bar when the bartender told them to take it to the men's room. They did, and half the bar followed them in, cheering them on. Angel couldn't remember feeling so excited. He thought he now knew what Lee Trevino or Chi-Chi Rodriguez must have felt taking the victory walk up the eighteenth fairway.

"I don't mean to toot my own horn, but—"

"Please," Julia interrupted, "by all means, toot away!"

"It really took a lot out of me," he confided, sipping his bourbon.

"I can imagine. You must be exhausted," she said with mock sympathy.

"I think I'm getting a second wind, though."

"Phew. I was worried we might have to carry you out on a stretcher."

"Well, I think I'll be okay. But the crowd, the cheering—it was really all . . . too much . . ."

"Yes . . . too, too much."

They went outside to look at his newly restored black-on-red 1965 Ford Fairlane convertible. It was a clear, starry night. There had been an unpredictable three-ring circus atmosphere to the whole evening so far, and he didn't see any reason why it shouldn't continue. She leaned back against the car. He put his hands around her narrow waist and kissed her.

"Lightning can strike twice," he said.

They both laughed.

"Don't get your hopes up," she said. "Besides, a quiet, romantic night under the stars does nothing for me. I'll take a harshly lit, run-down men's room with a cheering crowd every time."

"Well, to each her own."

He drove her home. She invited him in for a nightcap. Two months later, Julia and her cockatoo, Spanky, moved into Angel's duplex not far from the club.

$\approx$

Angel and Julia spent five nights a week at the Baby Doll, which closed at 4 a.m. Their day started when they rolled out of bed each afternoon and headed to the greasy spoon on the corner for breakfast. They spent most afternoons placing bets at the dog track, attending stock-car races at the speedway on the outskirts of town or hanging out at the bar down the block from the Baby Doll with their friends from work. Angel also had a regular Monday-night poker game in his old neighborhood in South Phoenix with an unlikely assortment of drug dealers, pimps, lowriders, thieves, bikers, performance artists and millionaires.

$\approx$

As part owner of the Baby Doll, Angel had an intuitive grasp of rudimentary business management principles and did his best to boost morale at the club in an effort to enhance profitability. He gave out an employee-of-the-month award and held periodic contests. The contest for the cutest pet photo had been a big success. He had waged a vigorous telephone campaign among the employees on behalf of his cat, Fluffy.

Angel also enjoyed occasionally taking a few liberties with the truth and creating a little drama at the club as a means of fostering an atmosphere of competition among the girls—and demonstrating his innate sense of right and wrong.

"Hey, Josie, Donna said you don't know how to *do* it. No sense of theater, no foreplay. Just wham-bam-thank-you-ma'am. I said that was *bullshit*. I said, 'Josie can teach you a thing or two, *bitch*. You can't talk about Josie that way. If you persist with these outrageous allegations, it might be best if you were to consider employment at another place of business.'" He noticed the spare wigs on the bar and tried one on. He parted the long red bangs with his fingers so he could see Josie. He looked ridiculous, but, to his surprise, Josie didn't register any reaction.

"Like she's some kind of expert or something. *Puta*," Josie spit.

"Anyway, I just want you to know I stuck up for you, Josie," Angel said, in case his chivalrous role in the scenario he had just invented had been lost on her.

"I know you did, Angel. I appreciate that."

He nodded in approval.

"By the way, you look ridiculous in that wig, Angel," she said. "I'm telling you that as a friend."

〜

Julia sat wistfully on a rock in the Japanese garden of Richard's house. She and Angel and Fluffy and Spanky *had* been happy together. *And yet . . . and yet what?* she wondered. *Did Angel really get that blow job in the men's room?*

CHAPTER FOURTEEN

The screen went dark, and the lights in the chic, wood-paneled screening room of the smallish production facility on La Cienega suddenly went on. Morty blinked a few times as his eyes adjusted to the light. He rose to his feet and silently stumbled out of the room and into the parking lot outside.

The screening of the rough cut of *Martian Dawn* that Morty had arranged for Alice and him had just ended. Shooting had wrapped two months earlier, and Hal and his postproduction team had recently finished the rough cut. Hal's contractual arrangement with Morty, however, allowed Morty the final cut.

Alice followed Morty outside a few moments later. He seemed to be beside himself. She had never seen him this upset.

"Morty, what's wrong?" she asked. "You look pale. You rushed out without a word. Let's go back inside."

They went back inside and sat down.

"Didn't you see?" he sputtered.

"See what?" she asked.

"The ending is total crap. It's going to have to be completely reshot," he barked.

"What *exactly* is the problem?" Alice asked.

"For one thing, there's no chemistry. And the tone is all off," he sniffed.

"What happened? I thought it was going so well," Alice said.

"So did I. I turn my back on Hal for five fucking minutes, and everything goes to hell in a handbasket. I watched the dailies every day for months, until I was comfortable Hal had everything under control. I hadn't seen any of this footage before," he said.

"Uh-oh," Alice said.

"'Uh-oh' is right." Morty imagined giving Hal a public dressing-down. In his mind, it was all over but the shouting. Hal was going to have a hard landing. "What was I supposed to do, hold Hal's hand throughout the entire production? It's not his first dance. I just don't know how this could have happened."

"I liked the college reunion scene on Mars," Alice said, trying to cheer Morty up.

"Yeah, that wasn't too bad," Morty admitted. "But the scene where Richard and Julia make love in the Mars Ritz-Carlton falls completely flat."

"Uh-huh," Alice said. "So now what?"

"Well, this could cost a small fortune. We'll have to reshoot the entire ending. The investors are not going to be happy at having to pony up more shekels. But that's life. We'll more than make up for any cost overruns on the foreign rights. It should still be a sweet deal for everyone," Morty said. "Except for one thing."

"What's that?"

"Everyone will have to wait a little longer to get their return. We'll have to change the pro formas. I don't know if we can still make the projected opening date. It's going to be touch and go."

"Doesn't sound so bad," Alice said.

"No, I guess not. I just thought this time it would be different. I need to meet with Hal—alone. I'll break it to Richard and Julia later. I'd like to tear Hal a new one. But this has to be handled in the right way. I need Hal."

"Morty, remember, stay calm," Alice cautioned him.

"Yeah, yeah. I'll say one thing for Hal—he can flush money down the toilet with the best of them. A real champ."

"Morty," Alice said, reprovingly.

"I know," Morty said, apologetically. Then he looked at his watch. "I'm starving—do you have plans for lunch? I thought we could go to the Ivy."

Alice had been making an effort to keep a professional distance, but Morty sensed that her resolve might be faltering. He was quickly developing a romantic fixation on her. He wondered if any of it was reciprocated.

"Hmmm . . . Well, I suppose I could," she said, after some thought.

"Great. I'll call ahead for a table," he said.

They stepped outside the production facility for a second time into the bright afternoon sunlight.

❦

Richard and Julia sat reviewing scripts in their sunken living room. Unread scripts were piled in two neat stacks on the coffee table. Discarded scripts had been carelessly tossed on the floor around them.

"You always get the best scripts," Julia complained.

"That's not true," Richard said. "You get good ones too."

"The parts I'm offered are so one-dimensional. I think I have a much broader range. I only need to be given a chance to prove it."

"I think so too. Be patient. Remember, I've been at this a long time. I didn't just start out in roles as a doctor or lawyer or businessman. I only graduated to those kinds of roles after earning my stripes as . . . a gigolo, for example."

"Okay."

"Hang in there."

Just then the phone rang. It was Jemima, Richard's assistant. Richard rattled off a list of midcentury designer chairs he wanted her to look at for the house: Kjærholm, Bertoia, Jacobsen, Risom, Eames.

"Is anything available in pony skin?" he asked.

"I'm not sure. I'll look into it," Jemima said.

"Okay. Keep me posted. Thanks," Richard said, then hung up. "Julia, I'm going to be in the shrine room meditating for a while," he said.

"All right. I think I'm going to do some vacuuming."

"Really? Why? Dolores can do it."

"I know. But it's therapeutic—it relaxes me."

He nodded.

"What should we have Dolores make for dinner? Pork tenderloin?" she asked.

"How about grouper with cream sauce?" he responded.

"Fabulous. You know, your tastes are evolving very nicely."

"In tandem with yours."

~

It was the middle of the night, and Cap was sound asleep. He was talking to Monstro at the mouth of an intracoastal waterway in a "prophetic" dream.

Monstro said, "There's no reason for me to be with you. I'm not that kind of animal—a dog or a cat. Your sentimentality is so hardwired." He was giving Cap a gentle brush-off.

"How can you be so indifferent to something so sincere?" Cap asked from the dock.

Monstro betrayed no emotion. "My indifference is sincere," he said.

~

Morty sat behind his desk in a Century City high-rise. The desk and a built-in credenza behind it were finished in blond wood in curvy faux deco. A chrome lamp sat on the desk, and Eggleston photos hung on the walls. Through his windows he had a hazy view of the Hollywood Hills.

"Hal is here to see you," Morty's secretary, Roberta, said over the speakerphone.

"Okay. Send him in."

Hal entered with what Morty, in a moment of irritation, would have called a shit-eating grin.

"Morty, how's tricks?"

"I can't complain," Morty said. He got up from behind his desk to shake hands and motioned Hal to a brown-leather club chair opposite his desk. "Let me show you these photos of the stuff I picked up on my last buying trip to Sumatra." He pulled a heavy green photo album off the bookshelves.

"Wonderful!" Hal said.

Morty sat down in the matching chair next to Hal and spent a few minutes walking him through the recent additions to his Indonesian collection.

"Just great!" Hal commented, when they'd finished.

"Thanks."

"So, what'd you think of the rough cut of *Martian Dawn*?" Hal asked nonchalantly.

"Let me see . . . Oh yeah, I did get a chance to see the rough cut a couple of days ago."

"And?"

"Hal, I'm a big fan of your work. The film is terrific. Maybe your best yet. But the ending . . . it has its moments. I think there's room for improvement."

"All right, Morty, let's cut to the chase. What'd you really think of the ending?" Hal asked.

"What did *I* really think?"

"Yeah, what did *you*, Morty, really think about the ending?" Hal asked.

"Is there an echo in here? What I *really* think is . . . I haven't seen chemistry like that since Wilbur and Mr. Ed."

"Hilarious," Hal said.

"We're talking big-time chemistry here," Morty continued. "I haven't seen chemistry like that since . . . Yogi Bear and Boo-Boo. Look, the tone is all off. It's too campy. The first two-thirds of the film have a mercurial feeling. You can't quite tell if it's serious or funny. It's perfect. The ending just falls flat. It needs to be completely reshot."

"Reshot completely?" Hal asked in disbelief.

"*Completely* reshot," Morty said with conviction, looking Hal directly in the eye. "But let me speak to Richard and Julia myself. I know just how to handle this."

Hal left Morty's office with a hangdog look in spite of Morty's reassurance, "We'll nail it this time."

Alice shot down Sunset at dusk in her red Mercedes SL convertible on her way to her home in Laurel Canyon. *Morty, what have you gotten me into?* she thought. She could see that the boundaries she had tried to maintain were blurring beyond recognition. The screening and lunch a couple of days earlier had felt a lot like a date. Morty seemed devoted to her. Maybe it would be best if she found him a new analyst to work with. Nothing had happened between them yet. But it might. Did she *want* something to happen? She didn't know. But, she decided, she could not continue as Morty's therapist.

And what about Morty's psychotherapy? He'd certainly made a lot of progress since he'd begun his work with her. He was slowly but surely wrestling his self-destructive impulses into submission. The prostitutes, drugs, alcohol and car wrecks seemed to be a thing of the past. There was something about his nature Alice found appealing, even romantic. She had her own demons, she knew, and perhaps Morty sparked some impulses of her own.

She reached Crescent Heights and turned left into the canyon. She was looking forward to a hot bath and listening to jazz. It would be good to give this Morty dilemma a rest.

CHAPTER FIFTEEN

The shuttle descended over the vast canyons of the Valles Marineris and then slowed as it approached the passenger terminal on the outskirts of the Mars colony. Inside the craft, Richard and Julia prepared for landing.

The colony was located on the planet's southern hemisphere, where the cratered highlands resembled the surface of the Moon. The complex, which spanned several square miles, consisted of a master-planned, mixed-use grid of geodesic modules. The size and scale of the structures were impressive.

Richard still found it hard to believe that it had already been five years since Mars had first been colonized.

∽

Am I my usual self? Richard wondered, after they'd disembarked. He wasn't sure. He couldn't resist gently booting Julia in the butt.

"Richard, you're acting weird," Julia said.

"We *are* on Mars," he shrugged.

They headed for the baggage claim.

When they arrived at the Ritz-Carlton, they checked in and went straight up to their suite. Julia drew a bubble bath, and a few minutes later she slid into the Jacuzzi-style tub, which was now covered in bubbles.

"Richard," she called.

"Yes?"

"What are you doing?"

"Waiting for a streetcar. And putting my things away."

"Come in here—I want to show you something," she cooed.

"Okay," he said, reluctantly.

"And bring a bottle of champagne from the minibar and a couple of champagne flutes."

Richard suddenly stopped unpacking, and his face brightened. "I think I'm starting to feel like my old self again."

A few moments later he entered the white marble bathroom to find Julia luxuriating in the tub.

"Get your ass in here," she commanded, lifting an impossibly long leg out of the water for him to admire, in case he was having any doubts. Some foam fell from her foot.

He slipped in and handed Julia a champagne flute.

"To Mars," he said, lifting his glass.

"To Mars. I don't know why we don't come here more often."

Richard settled in at the opposite end of the tub.

"Richard."

"Yes, Julia."

"Come over here," she said and motioned, giving him the look he knew only too well.

He smiled at her as he put his glass down, and she did the same.

That night, Richard, Julia, Morty, Alice, Hal and Carole Berman, the line producer for *Martian Dawn*, met for dinner at the Ritz-Carlton.

"Well, Morty, I hope you're proud of yourself," Julia said, once they were seated.

"Meaning?" Morty asked.

"You've brought us here to the ends of the Earth," she said.

"Ends of Mars," Richard corrected.

"It was a figure of speech," Julia snapped. "Where was I? Oh yeah. Well, I thought the *old* ending to the movie was perfectly fine. So we have to traipse all over the solar system, *Richard,* to reshoot the ending?"

"Yeah, it *is* a bit of a schlep to get to Mars, no question," Morty said. "But you'll be singing a different tune when you're taking champagne bubble baths with the Oscar." He gazed at her pointedly, waiting for his words to hit home.

Julia's face suddenly lit up as she broke into a big smile. Morty folded his arms with a self-satisfied grin.

"I know *I* will," Hal said.

Everybody laughed.

"You'll be printing your own money, Julia," Morty added.

"I hate it when that happens," Richard deadpanned.

"By the way, how come Morty knows so much about my bathing habits, Richard?" Julia asked, with mock annoyance. "I'll speak to you later in private," she scolded.

"Let's face it," Richard said. "Yes, the film's ending did need a little tweaking. But the real reason we're here is so Morty and Alice can do a little therapy on Mars."

Richard could see the wheels turning in Morty's head. Alice blushed and smiled wanly.

"Not a bad idea," Morty said. The thought of it gave him a little charge. Just then he noticed the look that Carole was giving Hal. What was going on *here?* Were they an item? He made a mental note to take this up with Hal later.

"All right, enough with the jokes, I'm all out of ammunition. Let's order," Morty commanded. "In fact, I'll order for everyone.

Let's see . . . Richard, you'll have the . . . swordfish. Julia, the chicken. Alice, the duck. Hal, the goat. And Carole, the—goat cheese salad."

"Morty, I think everyone should decide for themselves," Alice said.

"Oh all right," he said, with feigned exasperation. "I'm too tense. Richard may be on to something. Alice, I think a session on Mars might really do me some good."

"We'll discuss it," Alice said, uncomfortably. "You know, I've recused myself as Morty's analyst."

"Really?" Richard asked. "I didn't realize that. Interesting . . ." He smiled broadly, and nudged Morty with his elbow.

"Morty, I'd like to confide in you. Richard and I took a bubble bath when we got here today," Julia said.

"You're kidding! Well, *that's* a first. I understand it's very relaxing. As a matter of fact, Hal and Carole have been slipping into the bubbles too," Morty quipped.

"Hal and Carole?" Julia asked with interest.

Hal shot Morty a dirty look.

"Morty, you're such a troublemaker," Alice said.

"I know. I can't help it. I just like to stir the pot. Excuse me, everyone," Morty said. "Hal and Carole have an announcement they'd like to make."

"Really?" Julia asked excitedly.

Alice rolled her eyes. Richard braced himself for the worst.

"We do?" Carole asked. "No we don't," she said sharply. "Morty, what *are* you going on about?"

"I thought you and Hal had something you'd like to tell the group," Morty said disingenuously.

"Yes we do," Hal said. He tapped the water glass with his fork. "Friends, Carole and I would like to announce our joint opinion that our producer is a horse's ass."

"You're too kind," Morty said.

The lights in the restaurant dimmed, and it began to fill with people. Through the wraparound windows in the distance, Earth was faintly twinkling.

~

The following morning, everyone met for the first day of reshooting.

The sets were strange and exaggeratedly futuristic while primitive looking at the same time: odd, biomorphically shaped rooms resembling caves, with state-of-the-art lighting and electronics. The interiors in the actual Mars colony were, in fact, not much different from some of the more progressive interior designs on Earth.

Morty and Hal had dropped by Richard's Gucci mini-trailer for a preshoot conference. The trailer was decked out in earth tones and bridle leather.

"You know, Richard, I'm worried about Hal," Morty said.

"You are?" Hal asked, surprised.

"You are?" Richard asked, equally surprised. "I've never known you to give a fuck about anyone—other than yourself."

"Richard, that's unfair," Morty said.

"Unfair—but true," Richard said.

"Well, it's just that Hal's got a lot of balls in the air these days," Morty said.

Richard smiled. "You just want to make sure that Hal's love life doesn't become too big a distraction."

"Exactly," Morty said, giving Hal a pointed look.

Hal, who was nonplussed by this unwanted attention, said nothing.

"Do you want to discuss it?" Morty asked, in his most ingratiating tone.

"No, Morty, I don't want to *discuss* it."

"Now, Hal, Morty has everyone's best interests at heart," Richard said soothingly.

"*What* heart?" Hal said.

"Somebody needs a hug," Richard said.

"Try it, and I'll coldcock you," Hal said.

~

That afternoon Morty, Hal and Richard watched the morning's rushes on monitors. Hal had calmed down after Morty promised to "butt out" regarding Hal and Carole. Everyone enjoyed the rushes, but Morty had a little trouble concentrating. He imagined a therapy session on Mars with Alice in the loggia of the Mars Guggenheim on a chaise longue beneath a Dali or a Tanguy. Just one more session with Alice for old time's sake, he laughed to himself uncomfortably.

~

Alice and Julia sat unwinding in the steam bath of the spa at the Ritz-Carlton. Morty was the topic du jour. Alice tried her best to avoid a breach of professional ethics by keeping her end of the conversation general, but Julia was enjoying the opportunity to play armchair psychologist. Did they come to any conclusions? It was hard to say. Morty was a man of many parts. Steam began to fill the room, and before long everything was completely obscured.

~

Later, Julia browsed alone at Harry Winston. She thought about how each role she played somehow contained a retelling of her story: the woman of questionable virtue making good. There was a lot to be said for branding—and brand loyalty—she reflected. After all, she had something to sell with a proven track record: "Julia."

She stared at the barren landscape through the glass wall.

CHAPTER SIXTEEN

Svetlana strutted dramatically through the Mars shuttle terminal as though she were back on the runway in Milan. Walter did his best to keep up.

"Walter, you are lagging behind," she complained. "You cannot keep up with Svetlana?"

"Evidently not," Walter responded.

"That is what I like about you, Walter. Always with witty retort."

"I try."

"There is something about this place," she said. "It has very cool, space-age feeling—like Tokyo or Seoul. I feel very *alive* here."

"Yeah, it's pretty hip," Walter agreed.

After picking up their bags they hopped on the monorail into town.

"Boy, I can really use some R and R," Walter said, after they entered their room at the Ritz-Carlton. "Being cooped up on that space station was getting old. No more sneaking around. Free at last."

"Yes," Svetlana chimed in, "we can just be ourselves." She became thoughtful. "You know what Svetlana would like right now?"

Walter tried to read her expression before responding. "I think I have a pretty good idea."

"Oh, Walter, you know Svetlana too well."

"Cherry Seven-Up with lemon?"

"You make joke. No, that is not quite what Svetlana had in mind." She undid his belt, tossed it on the floor and pulled down his zipper. "You would like Svetlana to suck your cock?"

"Well, that sounds like a pleasant way to pass the time."

"Just as I thought," she laughed.

~

Walter was still asleep when Svetlana woke up. She got dressed and went to the lobby to take a look around. She noticed a man looking in the window of Harry Winston. With the notable exception of beady, piglike eyes, his face was almost handsome. Just then he turned around, smiling at her, aware that she had been watching him.

"Excuse me, miss," the man said. "I could really use some help picking something out. Would you mind terribly?"

Svetlana gave him a noncommittal, measured gaze before walking over to him.

"Hi, I'm Richard," he said. "And you are?"

"Svetlana. I am cosmonaut here for R and R."

"Well, Svetlana, it's very nice to meet you."

The man looked familiar, Svetlana thought, but she couldn't place him. A friend of Boris's? "Do I know you?"

"I don't know. Do you?"

"Hmmm."

"Maybe you've seen one of my movies."

"Yes, yes, I have seen. You are that *guy,*" Svetlana said excitedly, as she recognized Richard.

"The very same."

"Why are you here?"

"I'm on location, finishing a shoot. In fact, we're having our wrap party next Friday night at seven—in the Metzinger Pavilion at the Guggenheim. You should come."

"Really? I would love to come. Thank you so much."

He said he would put her name on the guest list. "Svetlana" would be enough.

Just then Julia appeared and called to Richard from across the lobby. She eyed Svetlana suspiciously.

"Excuse me, I have to go. See you next Friday," he said cheerfully. "Good-bye."

"Who's the bimbo?" Julia asked, as soon as Richard had joined her.

"Just a Russian cosmonaut here for R and R."

"Cosmonaut, my ass. I can see I'm going to have to keep an eye on you, lover boy," she laughed.

"You have nothing to worry about."

⁓

Walter sat up in bed. He simply could not get enough of Svetlana and found himself constantly thinking about her. She was so unlike anyone he had ever known—certainly unusual for an astronaut. All that was missing was the sequined bikini and feather boa. And she probably had those in her bag of tricks as well. Then he wondered how Sylvia was faring. O Sylvia! How could he have treated her so shabbily? Had he left her for dead on the breakers? As for Svetlana, he had an uncomfortable feeling. Perhaps his life was about to change dramatically.

⁓

Monica, Dirk, Simon, Samantha, Dr. Gold and Mrs. Gold sat around the table in the Biosphere's teleconference center.

"This is a toughie," Gold said. "Because not everyone can go.

As you know, we've received invitations to the wrap party—on Mars—for *Martian Dawn*. But two of us have to stay here to keep the Biosphere up and running and monitor the systems until the others get back. I thought we should reach the decision as a group."

"And if we can't reach a consensus?" Samantha asked.

"Then I'll have to make an executive decision," Gold said firmly.

"Uh-oh," Simon muttered under his breath.

The tension in the room was noticeable.

"Well, I think Monica should go so she can rekindle her romance with Richard," Dirk suggested.

Everyone smiled.

"Ha, ha," Monica said. "And yet, there is a certain logic to Dirk's suggestion."

"I would, of course, have to go too," Dirk said, "to serve as a chaperone for Monica and Richard."

Gold laughed.

"I can't leave Monstro all alone for that long. He needs me," Judy Gold said.

"What?" Gold snapped. "You've got to be kidding. We won't even be away *that* long. He'll be fine."

"My mind is made up. My baby needs me. My parents left me with a nanny to go skiing in Cortina for two weeks when I was an infant. It was traumatic—I've never quite recovered. Didn't even recognize them when they returned. I promised myself that if I had a child of my own, I would never make the same mistake," Judy said.

Gold started to say that Monstro was not her child but thought better of it. Monstro might as well have been her child, he thought, so deep did her feelings for the whale run. "I guess it would be a bad idea for me to even consider going without you," he said.

"*Very* bad," Mrs. Gold said, shooting Gold a withering look. "I'm going to do you a favor. I'm going to pretend that last remark never happened."

"Thank you, dear. Well, I guess that takes care of it. Mrs. Gold and I will be staying here to give Monstro the nurturing he needs. Dirk and Monica and Simon and Samantha, pack your bags," Gold said resignedly. "Mrs. Gold, Monstro and I will hold the fort."

Dirk, Monica, Simon and Samantha all beamed with excitement.

∼

Bill sat beneath a large tree on the grounds of the Huntington in Pasadena. He had just viewed the Gainsborough collection. Were the women depicted in those paintings—with bouffant-style hairdos and elegant finery—eighteenth-century drama queens? he wondered. Did the rococo backdrops reflect some inner emotional complexity at odds with the stately bearing of the painter's subjects? He found the women appealing. Then his thoughts turned to Cap, with whom he had recently come to LA. His relationship with Cap was, he reflected, hard to define: He was part confidant, part shrink, part Boswell.

During Cap's many hours at the Yale Club bar, Bill had patiently listened to his hopes, dreams and relationship problems, as well as his infatuation with Monstro. His behind-the-scenes guidance had helped Cap navigate the tricky waters of his love life: Precious Flanagan, Molly Schwartz, Erica Wong—the list of girlfriends went on. Bill enjoyed playing savant, and it was true his life was richer for having Cap in it. At the same time, though, he chafed somewhat at what he perceived to be the second-fiddle aspect of this role. There was something about the sense of living vicariously through Cap's experiences that he resented. Was it even slightly unseemly or voyeuristic? The jury was still out.

Now Bill had written a treatment for a screenplay of the story of Cap and Monstro, which is what had brought the two of them to LA. He found it curious that all his most vital experiences were somehow mediated, secondhand. Was he consigned forever to play special guest star to Cap's top banana? Or would he strike out on his own? It was funny, he thought, how Monstro's story—his "captivity narrative"—struck such a deep, resonant chord with him.

~

Svetlana lay on a pink chaise longue, sipping a coconut daiquiri while watching Walter swimming laps in the pool. She was reminded of a photo shoot in Sardinia during her modeling days. Stars and distant planets were visible through the skylight.

"Somebody throw me a towel," Walter called to Svetlana as he climbed out of the pool.

"Walter, I have idea," she announced.

"Should I be worried?"

"Just listen."

"I'm all ears."

"Maybe we don't go to *Hooston.*"

"Not go to *Hooston?*"

"Yes. Maybe we just stay here—on Mars."

"In the Ritz-Carlton?"

"No. Condominium."

"Hmmm. You really like it here that much?"

"Yes. There is something about it Svetlana likes very much."

"Well, let's think about it. But you know how you're always changing your mind. You're very fickle, Svetlana."

She laughed. Walter started to think about it himself. The phrase "Martian fuckfest" echoed through his head as he tried to picture life on the Red Planet with Svetlana.

Later, Svetlana strolled through the lobby and past the shops. Moving to *Hooston* was not a good idea. Walter was becoming so predictable. *Hooston* must be very boring, she speculated. Was their romance losing its magic? What about Boris? She reflected on their years together: training at the cosmonaut institute in Moscow, Moon missions, weekend tennis at his dacha on the Black Sea, etc. Poor Boris. Boris was a good boy. She hoped he would be okay. Did she feel any pangs of guilt? Not really. Then her thoughts turned to the party next week, and she felt a sudden rush of excitement. What about that *guy*? Or would she meet someone new?

∼

Rinpoche entered the lobby of the Ritz-Carlton and approached the front desk. His journey had been tiring, but he had experienced a great sense of peace since arriving on Mars. *This must be a very spiritual place*, he said to himself.

An hour later, he was sipping a whiskey sour while reading the new issue of *Wallpaper* in the bar of the Ritz-Carlton. The bar, like the Saarinen-style hotel lobby, was all swooping shapes and soaring spaces. The surfaces were covered in carbon fiber and titanium. Rinpoche felt strangely at home on Mars, despite the fact that the Mars colony had no real history or culture. He remembered Blackie Friedlander telling him about how scientists believed that life as we know it had begun eons ago when a large chunk of Mars broke off and became a meteor that struck Earth, introducing Martian microorganisms: the first life on Earth. In a sense, Blackie had explained, we are all Martians.

CHAPTER SEVENTEEN

As Julia hurried by the bar on her way to the shoot, she noticed Rinpoche sitting inside. What was he doing here? she wondered. He was a puzzle.

She slipped quietly onto the set and stood behind Hal, who sat in his director's chair watching Richard hit his marks as the camera rolled. Once each scene was completed to Hal's satisfaction, he calmly gave out precise instructions to the cinematographer and crew for the next scene. It was the last day of shooting, and he wanted to make sure he had some continuity shots in the can to work with before they were done.

During a break in the shooting, Julia spoke to Richard. "You'll never guess who I just saw in the bar at the hotel," she said.

"Who?"

"Rinpoche."

"Really? What's he doing here?"

"I saw a flyer for a talk he's giving at the meditation center this afternoon."

"Wow. We should go. I'm going to call him right now." He picked up a courtesy phone, dialed the hotel and asked to be put through to the bar. When the bartender picked up, Richard described Rinpoche and asked to speak with him.

"Hello," Rinpoche said.

"Sir, it's Richard."

"Richard! Have you come all the way to Mars for my talk?"

"No, not exactly. I'm here on location. We're going to try to make it, though. Listen, I'd like to schedule a follow-up interview with you, if possible, here on Mars."

"Of course."

They scheduled a meeting for the next day, and Richard invited Rinpoche to the party the following week. After hanging up, Richard suddenly remembered how much Rinpoche liked parties.

∼

"Well, well. Look what the cat dragged in," Alice cracked when Morty appeared around noon and joined everyone on the set, now in the process of being struck.

"Yeah, yeah, yeah. Out of sight, out of mind. I'm gone for one week, and no one even knows who I am anymore," Morty said.

"We missed you terribly," Carole said.

"Thank you, Carole, I appreciate that. I've always said you were terrific."

Morty had just returned from a quick trip to Hollywood to attend the Golden Globe Awards dinner and work the after-party crowd. During his absence, Alice had noticed that she missed him. Or was it just being millions of miles away from home? And what was this business of Morty's about needing a session with her, even though she was no longer his analyst? Perhaps she could find him a referral on Mars.

∼

"Svetlana, you are really quite beautiful," Svetlana said to herself, primping and admiring herself in the bathroom mirror, flush with sexual energy. She sized up her breasts as she held them in her hands. She wondered if she would have more sex appeal if they were just a little larger. No, she decided, they were fine just the way they were.

Just then Walter called out, "What's going on in there? Are you still alive?"

"I'm just getting into shower, Walter, to cool off. You got Svetlana very hot." The shower was filling with steam. She slipped out of her terry-cloth robe and stepped in.

Walter lay exhausted on the bed. Svetlana had an insatiable sexual appetite. Sex was almost becoming like work: During each "session," they stripped, and she put him through his paces. If this is what life on Mars with her would be like, he wasn't sure it was for him. He thought back on their affair on the space station. It seemed less like something that had actually happened and more like something that Svetlana had invented. In a sense, he reflected, she *had*.

~

The Buddhist meditation center was located in a medium-size geodesic dome. Julia and Richard arrived a few minutes before the talk was to begin. The Mars Buddhist community had turned out in full force to hear Rinpoche. A large crowd had gathered inside by the temple doors. Suddenly, the doors were opened and everyone poured in. The center looked like the interior of an actual Tibetan temple that had been painstakingly reassembled on Mars: wood-paneled walls, beamed ceiling painted orange, shrines, altars, and ceremonial tapestries and figures. After they'd sat down, it was all Julia could do to stifle a yawn.

The lights dimmed, and then Rinpoche appeared on stage in an orange ceremonial robe, dramatically lit by several spotlights. He made his way to the lectern. The audience was hushed in silence. A purple and white banner with embroidered symbols hung behind him. Then Rinpoche bowed his head.

≈

Morty, Alice, Hal and Carole strolled down the main concourse at the center of the Mars colony. Skylights and panels of windows afforded a view of the rest of the brightly lit colony and the dark planet surface beyond.

"What's the name of the place again?" Morty asked.

"Moon Bus Excursions," Alice said.

"Remind me again why we're doing this," Hal said to Carole.

"Because it'll be fun," Carole said. "We can't come all the way to Mars and not do any sightseeing. Don't you want to see the real Mars? Take in some local color?"

"We've shot an entire movie about Mars without taking in any local color, why start now? So, we put on space suits and get to walk through craters?" Morty asked.

"Exactly," Alice said.

"Hmmm," Morty said. "So, it's like a white-water rafting trip?"

"More like one of those double-decker bus tours of Manhattan—but we can get out and look around," Carole said. "There may be a whole busload of new tourists looking to see the real Mars. I think the latest shuttle just landed yesterday."

"Will we see any Martians?" Morty asked.

"Anyone who was born on the Mars colony is, technically, a Martian," Hal said.

≈

Julia's mind was wandering. Why was she suddenly thinking about Angel now, on Mars, in the rarefied atmosphere of the temple? Was there something in the air, something more than just the excitement of finishing the production and the anticipation of the wrap party? She watched Richard, who in turn was gazing intently at Rinpoche, hanging on his every word.

"Man has a sense of self which, in his confusion, seems to him to be continuous and solid. The self is, in actuality, transitory. Experience continually threatens to reveal our true, transitory condition to us. It is because we have become so absorbed in our confused view of the world that we consider it real. This struggle to maintain the sense of a solid, continuous self is the action of ego," Rinpoche said.

CHAPTER EIGHTEEN

The average temperature here on the Red Planet is about negative fifty-five degrees centigrade. During the day, in the summer, it's about twenty-seven degrees centigrade. The surface gravity is lower than that on Earth, and Mars has a very thin atmosphere. In its early history, Mars was more like Earth. The average pressure on Mars is less than one percent of Earth's. But it is thick enough to support strong winds and vast dust storms. There are permanent ice caps at both poles. Mars is the fourth planet from the Sun and the seventh largest. Earth is the third planet from the Sun. Life on Earth began when a Martian meteorite introduced Martian microorganisms. Primitive life may have existed on Mars more than thirty billion years ago."

"Can I get a bite of that?" Morty pleaded.

"A small one," Alice replied, handing him a half-peeled banana.

"Mars has two moons, Phobos and Deimos. They are closer to their primary planet than any other moons in the solar system. They are so close that they cannot be seen above the horizon from all points on the planet's surface. They rise and set twice each day. There are space stations on each of them, and the very first Mars colony was built on Phobos. These days Phobos has a reputation as a nice spot for weekend getaways and time-shares. Okay. Enjoy the drive. I'll let you know when we get to our destination. We'll be able to get out and walk around and take in the view. But you *must* keep your space suits on at all times." The driver of the moon bus put the microphone down.

"My, *that* was interesting," Alice observed.

"*I* want to go to Phobos for a weekend getaway. Why can't *we* go to Phobos? We never get to go anywhere," Carole joked.

"I hate to see a man henpecked like that," Morty said. "Just take her to Phobos, Hal."

"I may just do that," Hal replied. "By the way, Morty, I really like you in that space suit."

Morty got up out of his seat and, with feigned enthusiasm, modeled it for the group. "I think I may pick up a pair of these moon boots to bring back home."

Hal and Carole nodded approvingly.

Alice started to chuckle. Morty tried to keep a straight face but broke up laughing.

The bus gradually picked up speed as it snaked through the outskirts of the colony in the shadow of curious, spirelike rock formations. Then the grade of the rough dirt road became steeper, and the bus started up some switchbacks. There were several other passengers besides Morty, Alice, Hal and Carole seated together toward the front of the bus. They chatted animatedly. There was also a very good-looking, mysterious man who sat apart from the others at the back of the bus.

"Who's the short dark stranger?" Carole asked Alice.

"I noticed him when we were waiting to put our space suits on," Alice said.

"*I* think he looks suspicious. I'm going to keep an eye on him. What's a guy like that doing on Mars?" Carole asked. "Though he is kind of handsome."

"Yeah, in a seedy sort of way," Alice said. "Ever had a Latin lover? I did once. Joan Maria. He was a Catalan diplomat from Barcelona."

"Very nice," Carole said.

"It was," Alice said wistfully.

Alice looked across the aisle, where Hal and Morty were sitting, to make sure Morty hadn't heard her. Morty actually had picked up bits and pieces about a Latin lover that had caught his attention. There was still quite a lot about Alice he didn't know, he reflected.

~

When the bus reached the promontory, it came to a stop, and everyone piled out awkwardly in their space suits and moon boots. The lights of the far-off colony were visible in the valley below. The road they had just taken was a black ribbon in the distance. Everyone stood in silence, awed by the vista of the dark, cratered landscape. Alice looked over her shoulder at the short dark stranger, who was now heading back to the bus.

~

The Ritz-Carlton was hopping. The lobby and bar were overflowing with the pre–wrap-party crowd. Dirk and Monica sat at the bar, and in a few minutes were joined by Simon and Samantha.

"It's like a Club Med here," Samantha said. "The only money they take are these plastic coins." She tossed one on the bar.

"Looks like a poker chip," Simon said, holding one up to the light between his fingers. "How much is this worth?" he asked, pretending to hide it in his jacket pocket.

"Hey, give me that back," Samantha said.

"I could use a drink," Monica said. "What time does the party begin, anyway?"

"I can't *wait* to see Richard again," Dirk said sarcastically. "Maybe he'll ask me out if I play my cards right."

"He just *might,*" Simon offered.

"I'm not sure that I'm at my most beautiful today," Dirk said.

"You mean 'beautificent,' don't you?" Simon asked.

"Yes, yes I do," Dirk said, after having paused for a moment to think.

Samantha and Simon laughed.

"Ha, ha," Monica sniffed. Her thoughts turned to Richard. He had more or less given her the brush-off back in the Biosphere. But, she said to herself, hope does spring eternal!

"Simon, should I wear my black catsuit or my black strapless?" Dirk asked.

"Boy . . ." Simon said. "Richard is so finicky. It's hard to know which one he'd like better."

Samantha chuckled. Monica fumed. "I hope you two are amusing yourselves," she said finally.

"Maybe the catsuit," Simon said, pretending not to have heard Monica.

"Yeah, I think the catsuit," Dirk said.

"Meow!" Simon growled.

They all laughed. Even Monica, despite herself.

∼

At the other end of the Ritz-Carlton complex, Morty sat in a chair by a poolside table. Alice was reclining next to him in a chaise longue. They were both facing the pool.

"What was your childhood like?" Morty asked, idly.

"Excuse me?" Alice said, caught up short by the question. "What is this, a session? Are you trying to analyze me?"

"Uh, no, not at all," Morty said sheepishly. "I'm just curious."

"Uh-huh. Well, the truth of the matter is, it doesn't really matter what your childhood was like after about the age of five. Your story is pretty much etched in stone by then. And I can't remember back *that* far."

"Hmmm. Okay." Morty scribbled a few notes on his pad.

"What did you just write down? Let me see that pad?" Alice said sharply.

"It's just a to-do list. Nothing to do with you. You just reminded me of something."

"Oh really? Read me some entries from this 'to-do list.'"

"Okay." Morty picked up the pad and read: "'Secure rights to update of *Le Morte d'Arthur*. Call landscaper.' Satisfied?"

"Yes. Where was I? Having said all that, my perception is that my mother was a bit self-absorbed and emotionally distant. And my father was a bit unstable emotionally. So, it was probably not the ideal environment."

"Uh-huh." Morty's expression betrayed no emotion.

"You know, Morty, if you're going to play shrink, it's okay to show some emotion. That stone-faced approach is old hat. No one does that anymore."

"I don't know what you're talking about. No one's trying to play analyst."

"Whatever. I'm just trying to help you out. You want to know about my recent dreams, I suppose?"

"Well, now that you mention it."

"Not a chance."

"Okay, it was just a thought."

"I've already had years of analysis—as part of my training."

"Oh really? I didn't know that."

"Turnabout is fair play. I think it's very interesting that you would like to play analyst to my patient. It says something very positive, I think, about—your own feelings about yourself."

Morty smiled nervously, then reached out for his glass of ginger ale.

CHAPTER NINETEEN

Angel entered the Metzinger Pavilion of the Mars Guggenheim, where the wrap party was now in full swing, and scanned the crowd.

"Look, it's the Short Dark Stranger," Carole said to Alice, nodding in Angel's direction.

"So it is," Alice said, sipping her champagne. "I think he's looking for someone."

"I didn't realize I'd made that big of an impression on the moon bus," Carole joked, pretending to preen.

From across the room, Svetlana was eyeing Angel. Who was *this* cute man? she asked herself.

∼

From the balcony, Morty and Hal surveyed the scene in the loggia below. Everybody was there: Richard, Julia, Alice, Carole, Rinpoche, Monica and some of the other biospherans, Morty's Saudi investors, the rest of the cast and crew, and many local guests.

"Hal, my man, you did it!" Morty said.

"*We* did it," Hal corrected him.

"Yep."

One of Morty's principal investors climbed the stairs and embraced Morty.

"Morty, you are the man," he said enthusiastically.

"No, *you're* the man, Ali. We couldn't have done it without you," Morty said.

Morty allowed himself to savor a brief moment of exhilaration. Then his thoughts turned to his next deal: remaking *The Fountainhead* with Richard and Julia.

"Ali, I've got a new deal for you," Morty said.

"Oh really? TCB!" Ali said, impressed.

"That's right, Taking Care of Business," Morty said. "Are you an Elvis fan?"

"Oh yes. *TCB* with a lightning bolt was emblazoned on the King's signet ring and on the tail of his private plane," Ali said.

"The *Lisa Marie*," Morty confirmed. "Have you been to Graceland?"

"Oh yes. I have been twice. I like Graceland very much. There are many good old Teddy boys there, visiting with their families. I picked up a limited edition *Speedway* plate on my last visit. So, what is this new deal? How is it looking for *Martian Dawn*?"

"The advance buzz on *Martian Dawn* is terrific. You and your partners will come out smelling like roses. As for the new deal, I'll get you some pro formas to look at. It'll be a home run. Both Richard and Julia have committed. I'd like you and your people to provide not just equity but also mezzanine financing."

"I think I can interest them. They are always looking for someplace to park their funds where they can realize a good return."

"Sounds good," Morty said.

Morty watched Alice talking to Carole. Would the evening turn into a "night of magic" for him and Alice? He wondered.

∼

Rinpoche was holding court by the bar at the party in the Guggenheim. Simon, Samantha, Dirk and several *Martian Dawn* cast members were listening attentively as he discussed the ancient Buddhist story of Marpa. "It is only at the point when you have completely let go of all expectations that your expectations will be realized. It is really counterintuitive," he concluded, taking a sip of his whiskey sour.

∼

Waiters and waitresses cruised through the Guggenheim galleries with hors d'oeuvres and champagne. Monica was wandering around the party when she spotted Richard in one of the galleries and sneaked up behind him. Partygoers mingled nearby. Large photographs depicting scale models of suburban houses, cars and families hung on the walls.

"Nice party," she said.

He turned around. "Monica! Wow! Where's the rest of your crew?"

"They're probably around here somewhere."

"I love your catsuit!"

"Thanks. So, you must be happy your movie's done. Congratulations!"

"I am. It'll be nice to get home. What about you? Back to the Biosphere?"

"I'm not so sure about that. I'm having some mixed feelings about the Biosphere. It's really not working out."

Where was Julia? Richard wondered.

"Look, there's Rinpoche," Monica said, in disbelief. She hadn't seen the great teacher since she'd left Boulder.

"Rinpoche, welcome!" Richard said.

Rinpoche entered the gallery with his group from the bar. Dirk eyed Richard suspiciously, but Richard ignored him and started a conversation with his guru.

~

Svetlana and Angel had been talking for some time. They were drawn to each other. Would they stay together on Mars? Go into business together? All seemed possible. She grabbed his hand and led him into a deserted gallery at the edge of the party. Dream drawings in charcoal rendered in a comic-book style hung on the walls.

As Svetlana held his hand, Angel reflected on the scene that had unfolded between Julia and him at the party not twenty minutes previous. Julia was a star. The dramatic "confrontation" with her he'd imagined had been, in actuality, less than he'd hoped. As he'd listened to her, it occurred to him that her new life was completely alien to him. Suddenly his burning desire to get back together with her seemed puzzling. Had he ever really known her? It seemed to him it wasn't Julia as much as the *idea* of Julia he had been so taken with after all. It was an epiphany.

~

Alice watched the group that had formed on the balcony around Morty. Was the movie really done? she asked herself. It was hard to believe. Where would things lead with Morty now that her consulting work was at an end? She was beginning to feel tipsy. How many glasses of champagne had she had? She'd lost count. Would Morty try to have his way with her? Just then Julia appeared at her elbow looking upset.

"I think I need professional help," Julia frowned.

"My professional hat is down around my eyes," Alice said.

"More like your ankles."

Alice looked around. "The Mars Guggenheim . . . What's so 'Martian' about this place, anyway?"

"Nothing. We could be anywhere."

"The Javits Center," Alice offered.

"Or the Kansas City stockyards . . . Alice, what's gotten into you?"

"I don't know."

"*I'm* confused—I'm in a state."

"So am I," Alice said.

"We're in this together," Julia said. "Can I tell you all my problems?"

"Sure, why not? The *short* version. I need time to get ready. I think I may do a fan dance later for Morty in my room."

"Good idea. It's a great icebreaker."

"So, what's going on?" Alice asked.

"Someone from my past has unexpectedly appeared and stirred up old feelings."

~

Richard joined Morty on the balcony.

"Richard, we had a situation, but everything's under control. A gate-crasher—an old flame of Julia's, apparently," Morty said.

"Who?"

"Some guy named Angel."

"Angel? On Mars? What's he doing here?" Richard said with concern.

"I don't know. I think he came with some idea of 'reclaiming' Julia. But he seems to have lost heart. Julia's a little shaken up by the whole thing."

"How do you know all this?"

"Julia told Alice."

"Where is he now? I can see Julia right over there."

"Seems he's gone off with some cosmonaut chick he met at the party."

"You're kidding! Svetlana?"

"I dunno. Some Russian fox."

Richard made an hourglass shape in the air with his hands.

Morty nodded.

Richard felt an uncomfortable mix of relief, jealousy and confusion as he watched Julia below in the loggia and pictured a mysterious "Angel" and Svetlana off alone together in the shadows.

∼

"You like Mars?" Svetlana said coyly, flashing a smile.

"I like what I've seen of it," Angel said, giving her a once-over.

"Svetlana was talking about planet."

"Oh."

Walter had left that afternoon for *Hooston*. She was to follow him there next week. But something told Svetlana she would not be going to *Hooston* next week after all.

∼

Julia collapsed on a Barcelona chair in the museum lobby, emotionally drained. Angel's appearance, Mars, finishing production, the wrap party—it was more than she could handle. Above the transparent dome of the pavilion the stars were pinholes in carbon paper.

CHAPTER TWENTY

Morty had slept fitfully. He sat up in bed in his rambling Coldwater Canyon Tudor and stretched. Morning sunlight streamed in through the windows. Then he remembered he wasn't alone and looked at the other side of the bed, where Alice was sound asleep. He stood over her like Cocteau's Death standing over Orpheus.

A little while later they were sitting on the flagstone terrace, having coffee and reading the *Los Angeles Times*. Hummingbirds twittered around the rosebushes. Morty reflected that he was as happy as he'd ever been. Was it too good to be true? He watched Alice carefully reading the paper. Their relationship was still new, and they were just getting to know each other's little idiosyncrasies. They had been spending many evenings at home watching videos from Morty's large collection. Alice had not been overly enamored of Morty's selection from the night before.

"You know what the difference between us is?" Alice said thoughtfully, looking up from the paper.

"No."

"*I* like character-driven movies. *You* like movies about flying dragons."

They both laughed.

"I'm speechless," Morty said.

"The truth hurts. By the way, was I snoring last night?" Alice asked.

"Like a pig," Morty joked. "I was too polite to say anything."

Alice was happy too.

∾

Was Angel her beautiful sex slave? Svetlana wondered. Where did she come up with such ridiculous ideas? But why not? And whatever happened to that *guy?* The actor from Mars. Maybe their paths would cross again . . . She tried to picture Angel's club in Phoenix, the Baby Doll, that he had told her so much about. She imagined taking to the stage and doing a striptease. She had no illusions. It would take some practice. But she was certain she'd be a natural once she got the hang of it. It was too bad, she thought, that she was staying on Mars and would never get the chance to find out.

She watched Angel sleeping silently beside her in their new Mars condominium. Outside the bedroom window, she could see the Ritz-Carlton, the lights of the colony and the desolate landscape beyond. How strange, she thought, that she should end up on Mars. Was it impetuous? No more so than anything else she'd ever done. Angel seemed different from the other men in her life. She had never been truly happy on Earth. Would she find the happiness that had eluded her here on Mars—with Angel?

She had gathered that another woman had brought him to Mars. Apparently, this other woman's charms had been no match for her own. Angel had dropped the woman like a hot potato when he'd met Svetlana, though there had been some mention of a reconciliation.

~

Richard stared out at the Hollywood Hills from the conference room in Morty's Century City offices.

"So, tell me all about it," Richard smiled.

"It's a remake of *The Fountainhead*," Morty said, pausing for dramatic effect.

"*The Fountainhead!*" Richard said, his expression brightening.

"You're made for this role. It's got *you* written all over it. I'm not sure there's anyone else with the size to pull it off and fill Coop's shoes—and make the role their own."

Richard luxuriated in the glow of Morty's praise.

"Who are you thinking of for the female lead?" Richard asked.

"Who else? Julia, of course."

"Julia?" Richard asked, after a long pause.

"You and Julia together are like money in the bank. We can get all the financing we need to green-light any project."

"I've got the juice to open a film without Julia."

"No question. But the two of you together are a huge draw. Remember, we need Saudi money, not just studio money. The Saudis are conservative. I promised them you *and* Julia."

"I hear you. But I think it would be a mistake for me to keep playing opposite Julia in every picture. I'm a serious actor. I've got my image to worry about. It's an unnecessary distraction."

"How so?"

"Well, the movie becomes the Richard and Julia show—a kind of sequel to the last mating dance we performed on-screen."

"You know, Boo-Boo was devastated when Yogi Bear broke up their act."

"Very funny. I think *Boo-Boo* will understand." Richard laughed uneasily. Privately, he had his doubts.

"Hmmm." Morty decided to back off for the time being. "Well, just out of curiosity, who'd you rather see in the role?"

Richard didn't know. But an involuntary smile came to his face as he considered the possibilities.

∽

Dr. Gold sat in the Phoenix Sheraton with his head in his hands.

"Good Lord, Harold, pull yourself together. It's not the end of the world," Judy said sharply.

Bacteria had been discovered in the Biosphere fertilizer, something that turned out to be the cause of the deficient oxygen production that had plagued the Biosphere almost from the beginning. Noxious gases had continued to build up, the water in the ocean biome had turned acidic, and the site had been overrun by "crazy ants" and morning glories. A complete overhaul of oversight and operations was in the works. To the outside world, it was being cast as a restructuring. In truth, it was much more: The Biosphere was to be shut down indefinitely. Gold had been pink-slipped.

"Not the end of the world?" he said dejectedly. "I suppose not."

"Stop sulking," she snapped.

"Your sympathy is touching."

"Thank you. Don't forget, I'm out of a job too."

"Yeah, but I'm looking at the bigger picture. This could be a huge career black eye. It may not be as easy to line up the next gig as it was in the past. And we're not getting any younger. I thought we could make a go of it with the Biosphere."

Mrs. Gold's eyes narrowed, and she said nothing.

Just then the phone rang in their hotel room.

"Hello?" Gold said.

"Dr. Gold? It's me, Monica. Dirk and I just wanted to call to see how you were. We feel terrible about the Biosphere being shut down."

"Monica, you're a sweet girl," Gold said. "Your call means a lot to me. By the way, I know you kids were sneaking out for pizza."

"Dirk wants to speak with you too," Monica said. "Don't worry, it's going to be all right."

"Thank you for the kind words," Gold said.

She handed Dirk the phone, and Dirk extended his best wishes before they both hung up.

Judy Gold took a break from pacing the room to look out the window. Gold joined his wife and looked out at the palm trees that ringed the hotel swimming pool.

Judy thought wistfully of Monstro.

~

Angel had kissed his old life good-bye. What had possessed him to stay on Mars with Svetlana? Life on Mars *was* very relaxing, he had to admit. Did he miss everyone from the Baby Doll? Fluffy? His Monday-night poker game? Yes. But there was more to life. And what of Svetlana? She was a dynamo. Was she crazy? They seemed perfectly suited to each other.

He watched her puttering about their apartment. How funny, he thought, that his quest to reclaim Julia had somehow led him here to Mars with a former model and cosmonaut sex maniac! It could be a lot worse. He had joined a Friday-night poker game with some of his new Buddhist friends on Mars and had entered a billiards league with some of the same people. Then his thoughts turned to Julia, and everything seemed bittersweet.

~

"It was an epiphany you had with Monstro in the Biosphere that first day," Bill observed.

"Yeah, I guess you could say that, now that I think about it," Cap said.

They sat on the patio of the Chateau Marmont. A few other luncheon guests sat nearby. The sky was relentlessly blue.

A short time later Morty joined them, and they introduced themselves. They made small talk for a few minutes, then Morty got down to business.

"I thought the treatment was interesting," Morty said. "But why is there a different name on it?"

"That's my pen name," Bill said.

"Oh. Okay. Tell me a little more about the story, the characters."

"It's the story of a guy and a whale that he chances to meet. Kind of an update of *Moby Dick*. Let's say *Moby Dick* meets *The Apartment*. A number of societal forces conspire to keep the two of them apart. The whale takes on a totemic quality," Bill said.

"Okay, it's the story of a quest. Does this guy have any love interests?" Morty asked.

"No, it's not that kind of story," Cap said with annoyance.

"Well, it's an interesting premise. I've visited the Biosphere, so the treatment caught my interest. I'm not sure we could sell our backers on this particular project. There's no real hook, no haymaker—nothing I think I can pitch with any success. But if you have other ideas in the future, I'd be interested in hearing about them."

"We've got lots of ideas," Bill said.

Morty smiled. The three of them sat talking enthusiastically for a few more minutes, then Morty took his leave.

∾

Richard and Julia were having a quiet dinner alone at the Ivy. The conversation turned to Richard's script meeting the other day with Morty.

"So, what's the picture?" she asked.

"*The Fountainhead.*"

"I love *The Fountainhead.*"

"Morty wants me to play Howard Roark."

"Great. How about the female lead?"

"I think he's going to ask Patricia Neal to reprise the role she created."

"It just might work," Julia said sarcastically.

"Your name came up. But Morty thinks it would be a bad career move for us to keep playing opposite each other."

"Morty does, does he? So who do you see in the role? Some bimbo whose pants you can get into, no doubt," she snarled. She could feel herself starting to fly into an uncontrollable, jealous rage. She turned red with anger, and her eyes began to tear up.

"Julia, calm down." He could see a temper tsunami about to engulf the premises.

"I'm very calm," Julia said softly. She rose and yanked the tablecloth away, sending glassware, silverware and dishes flying. "Very calm," she muttered, and stormed out.

Richard smiled and tried to make the best of the situation, as everyone in the restaurant was now staring at him with a mixture of shock and sympathy. He shrugged, as if to say, "She does this all the time. I'm her long-suffering friend."

~

Monstro had had enough of captivity. It was time to return to the ocean. He eyed Cap, who was standing on the end of the jetty. Was Monstro prepared?

Cap knew this was good-bye, but he understood it was for the best. He also felt he and Monstro had developed a mutual respect and understanding. How had they ended up in the shallow waters off San Diego? Because of the Biosphere's closing, Monstro, like the Golds, was out of a job. Tearfully, Judy Gold had determined Monstro was now, finally, ready to be released.

Cap turned to Monstro.

"You watch yourself, big fella. I'm not going to be there to cover your back. There are a lot of mean fuckers out there."

Monstro nodded.

Cap continued. "Everything is so vast. Man's desires are petty by comparison. You are so big—bigger than life. Identity is complicated. Who are we? Do we have anything unique to offer that separates us from the crowd? Are we walking on a high wire with no one to catch us if we fall? Monstro, you're at the center of the universe with all the planets spinning around you on their axes. Only apart from society will your life find meaning. You exist on a solitary, sublime plane—in a world both ancient and futuristic. There, I've said my piece."

It was an emotional disquisition, and Monstro rather enjoyed it. He sensed that Cap was trying to articulate something grand beyond his ability to express. Then the great beast turned and with a swoosh of his giant tail plunged into the deep.

ARE WE DONE HERE?

~

CHAPTER ONE

Amanda paced the room. "Can you tell me *why* you only love me for my money?" she fretted.

"Not *only* for your money," Todd laughed. "You have many good qualities. *Especially* your money."

They sat in the breakfast nook of her beautifully appointed prewar apartment on the Upper East Side, wearing matching his-and-hers striped silk pajamas.

"Excuse me while I storm out of the room and sulk," Amanda sniffed.

"Turnabout is fair play. Sometimes I think you just love *me* for my body. I don't think you respect my intelligence," he complained.

"What gives you that impression?" she asked coyly. She lazily stroked his chest with her finger.

The doorbell rang.

In the foyer, which was furnished with antiques, eighteenth-century prints and an Oriental rug, Amanda strained to look through the peephole. She gasped, hopped back a step, then slowly, tentatively, opened the door.

"Jason?" she asked, in disbelief.

"Yep."

"But . . . you're dead. You've been dead for five years, since you fell overboard in a storm en route to Tahiti on a scientific expedition. Are you a ghost? Is this—"

"A dream?"

She nodded.

"Nope," he said, shaking his head. "I washed up on a deserted island, where I lived on conch and coconuts for five years. Then I was rescued."

"Oh my goodness."

"Aren't you glad to see me?"

"Well, of course. But this is all so sudden. I need to get used to the idea that you're alive. It's all so . . . confusing . . . I gave a beautiful eulogy at your funeral, by the way."

"Thanks."

"You're welcome."

"So . . . Is there anything I should know?" he asked, edging toward the kitchen.

"I, um, thought you were dead."

"So I gathered." Jason peered down the hallway.

Amanda jumped in front of him to block his view. "It was very lonely once you were gone," she added, pouting. "I brooded and brooded. I asked the gods why they had taken you from me. You were so young."

"Yes, I was."

"Had your whole life ahead of you."

"I'm sure. Anything else?"

"No, that's it," Amanda said.

"Well, I'm glad we cleared that up."

"So am I. I feel a lot better. Now, do you think you could go back to being dead for just one more night, or at least come back alive tomorrow?"

"Not a chance," he said.

"I didn't think so."

Thomas shifted uneasily in his seat.

"Stop fidgeting. Sit still," Lisa whispered. "It's almost over."

The curtain fell, and the house lights came up.

In the front row, David turned to Thomas. "What did you think of Harper as Amanda?"

"Hideous." He rolled his eyes.

"Yes, but we love her and want to support her," Lisa said.

"I didn't think she was so bad," David said cheerfully.

Lisa and Thomas each shot him a sideways look.

A short time later, the three of them sat with Harper in her dressing room.

"Do you know what stinking out the joint really means? Because I just did it," Harper announced.

"C'mon, Harper, you were fine," Lisa reassured her.

"I don't know why I thought I could act. It seemed like fun at the time," Harper continued. "I should have gone into medicine like my dad wanted me to."

"Don't be so hard on yourself," Thomas said. "You looked like a million bucks up there."

"Really?" Harper looked at him shyly.

"Absolutely," David chimed in. "You're cutting your teeth on this role. It's a learning experience."

"Gosh," Harper giggled, her spirits suddenly lifted by the words of encouragement.

"So," Lisa said, "we thought we'd all go out to Pastis for dinner."

On the street outside the theater, it was an unseasonably mild late-winter evening. They piled into a cab and headed downtown to the

Meatpacking District, speeding along the West Side Highway past the piers and ship terminals. Lights flickered in New Jersey across the Hudson.

"Do you know who I miss?" Harper lamented. "The squeegee men. How can we lure them back to Manhattan?"

"Yeah, they were great," Lisa said.

"I'm not sure they ever actually left town," David reflected. "I think they simply transitioned to other careers when the bottom fell out."

"That's exactly right," Thomas said. "My stockbroker, for instance, used to be a squeegee man."

"Wait a minute. How could there be a bottom?" Lisa asked.

"Well, you've heard of subbasements," David said.

Harper sat glumly at the table in the restaurant wearing a feather boa and a sequined drop-waist dress. Thomas, Lisa and David shared a quizzical glance. Finally Thomas broke the uncomfortable silence.

"You're not still wringing your hands over the play?" he chided her.

"When Jerome and Elaine roped me into this, I thought I could do it. I let them sweet-talk me. After all those rehearsals . . . Boy . . ." Harper shook her head ruefully.

"I thought you were terrific," Lisa said. "We all did."

"You're too kind," Harper said. "I appreciate your loyalty."

"How did you hook up with Jerome and Elaine, anyway?" Lisa asked.

"Elaine used to work at the gallery with David. She and Jerome started the theater company together," Harper said. "They used to have a small theater company in Chicago before they moved to New York."

"They asked me if Harper had ever done any acting. They said she had 'star quality,'" David said dramatically.

Harper struck a pose, and they all chuckled.

After dinner, once they'd said their good-byes, David and Harper walked to their town house in the West Village while Thomas and Lisa took a cab to their Tribeca loft.

Later that night Lisa and Thomas gazed admiringly at their living room, which had recently been redecorated.

"You're so brilliant," she said.

"I am, aren't I?" he laughed.

"Which is why I married you."

"I know. It seems like the day before yesterday we wrote our own vows and walked down the aisle," he declared with a wry expression.

"I seem to recall that *you* wrote the vows, including the part about 'I acknowledge that you, Thomas, are the best thing that ever happened to me, et cetera.'"

"Yes, it was ridiculous, now that I think about it . . . By the way, are you all set for the big adventure?"

"I think so," Lisa replied.

Thomas began to read Lisa's travel checklist, pen in hand. "Mosquito netting?" he said.

"Check," she said.

Thomas made a note. They went over the list in this fashion. Occasionally he interjected questions about the climate, terrain and onset of the rainy season to satisfy himself that nothing had been omitted. The list included a global positioning system, water purification tablets and malaria pills. As they neared the end, Thomas quipped, "Compact, lipstick, handbag."

Lisa paused for a moment. "Roger that," she smiled.

"The banks of the Orinoco await you, milady." Thomas bowed.

∾

Harper lay on the couch in the study, staring at the ceiling.

"C'mon, Harper, snap out of it," David said sharply.

"What good is all my father's money if I don't have artistic fulfillment?" she protested. "I'm going to snort a line. Where's my bag?" She looked around. "How about a line? Care for a line?"

"You don't need that," David shot back, grabbing her handbag from the ottoman and marching out of the room.

"But I must, I must."

"You know what's going to happen?"

"What?"

"You'll end up in the Betty Ford Center."

"I *adore* the Betty Ford Center."

CHAPTER TWO

"You were a foolish woman when you first came to live in the village," Manolo said with a twinkle in his eye.

"What do you mean?" Lisa objected. They conversed in the Yanomamö language.

"You were easily intimidated when you bartered with us and made many bad deals." He sighed. "Those days are gone."

Lisa nodded and smiled.

"By the way, I think you should know there is talk in the village about you and Padre Higgins," Manolo said.

"What kind of talk?"

"The women say you are two lovebirds. They say you kayak to the mission in the evenings with romance in your heart, and that the two of you take long walks and speak of intimate matters. Sometimes you have a dinner lit by candles where he woos you by complimenting your womanly charms or by waxing poetic about the land of his ancestors in Chile and its great physical beauty."

"Hmmm." She knit her brow. "What else do they say?"

"You want to hear more?"

"Sure."

"They say Padre Higgins has exceptional personal magnetism, that he is popular with the ladies and that you behave like a young girl in his presence."

"Fascinating," she chuckled.

Manolo burst out laughing.

"You were laying it on a little thick there," she said.

"Yes."

"So, you don't really believe all that, do you?"

"No, of course not. But the women in the village are incorrigible gossips. In fact, everyone in the village is. They are convinced you two are involved in a courtship ritual of some kind. They speculate that that is really what brings you back to the village—and that the study of our customs is just a smoke screen. But they find the ways of the whites very puzzling in general."

"Indeed."

"I think what gives rise to the gossip is that you are not chaperoned on your visits to the mission. The women say one of them should accompany you to make sure Padre Higgins doesn't get up to any monkey business."

"I'll take that under advisement." She used the English words for "under advisement."

"What does that mean?"

"It means 'I'll sleep on it.'"

He nodded.

They lay in adjoining hammocks on the porch of Manolo's hut overlooking the Orinoco River and the distant peaks of the Sierra Parima. The remote village, located in the tropical highlands of the Amazon Basin in southern Venezuela, was surrounded by huge, vine-covered Brazil nut, kapok and balsa trees. Monkeys and birds called, and insects hummed in the fading jungle light.

"Daughter," Manolo said solemnly.

"Yes, father."

Manolo had "adopted" Lisa in an elaborate ceremony on her last field trip to the village, making her an honorary member of the tribe.

"I think I may be having problems with one of my wives, Sonia. I abducted her on a raid on a rival village last year. At first we were very happy together. Then an issue of that magazine *Cosmopolitan* found its way to the village. I had Padre Higgins translate some articles for me. One was about the 'ten trouble signs your spouse is cheating.'"

"What were they?"

"A sudden and unexplained interest in beautifying yourself and adorning yourself in finery, unaccounted-for absences, low interest in marital relations, presenting lavish gifts to your spouse to assuage your guilt, among others."

"I see."

"As soon as I heard this, I thought it sounded just like Sonia."

"So, what did you do?"

"I'm keeping an eye on her, but I haven't discovered anything."

"Maybe you're just jumping to conclusions."

"Yes, that could be," he said thoughtfully and looked away.

Lisa, too, became reflective. The list of trouble signs had given her pause, and she was feeling uneasy. Was she suspicious of Thomas? She'd never had any reason to be. But she considered the fact that some of Thomas's behavior fit the pattern of the *Cosmo* telltale signs.

Manolo noticed the change that had come over her. "What's wrong?" he asked.

"I don't know—it's Thomas . . . It's probably nothing."

"Your husband is not treating you well?"

She wasn't sure how to answer but thought it might be fun to play along with Manolo. "No, no he's not, now that I think about it. He's been beastly," she said. "He's just no good."

Manolo nodded, then rested his chin on his clasped hands, sizing up the situation. "Where is the village of Thomas's ancestors located?" he asked.

"Scotland."

"Yes, I have heard of it from Padre Higgins. It is a distant land, and they have strange customs there. Tell me, what is your mother-in-law like? Does she live with you?"

"A hateful woman," Lisa said. "Fortunately, she only travels from her village to visit us once a year."

"Well, this is very serious," Manolo said. "I recommend that you have some of the old women from your neighborhood meet with you and a local shaman when you return home to hold a ceremony, so your husband will once again be under your spell. They should make you a special charm bracelet and also a love potion for you to put in his lemonade."

"Really? You think it will work?" Lisa asked.

"Without a doubt."

He sensed that Lisa was anxious and wanted to reassure her. She was charmed by his homespun advice, drawn from his life in the village. Its applicability was dubious. If she had been having some nascent doubts about her relationship with Thomas, they had now evaporated. But she was enjoying the consideration and sympathy she had elicited from Manolo too much to let it end. Lisa continued to feign distress, frowning and casting her eyes downward.

"I just don't know." She shook her head. "I don't know what to do. But maybe following your advice *would* be best, father."

He smiled. "Yes, your village father knows best."

They stared wordlessly at the river. Manolo thought it would be a good idea to try to relieve the tension and get Lisa's mind off of Thomas for a while.

"You know," he said, "I've been meaning to warn you—we are not immune to attack by a rival village."

"What do you mean?" She was genuinely, if mildly, concerned.

"If another village sends a raiding party, they will try to abduct our most desirable women. The attacking warriors will be looking to take wives."

"Surely they wouldn't be interested in little old me."

Manolo ignored her and continued.

"I will, of course, do my best to protect you both in my capacity as village headman and as your father. But should I fall in battle, it is possible you would be taken captive and become the woman of a man from the raiding party. You would be taken to live as his wife in his *shabono*."

"Goodness gracious," she said with mock alarm.

"After my death, I would, of course, undergo a change and travel to a different realm, where I could sometimes be seen as clouds," he intoned with a faraway look in his eyes.

"I see. Manolo, why are your people always engaged in warfare?"

"It is in the nature of men to be *waiteri* because the blood of the moon spilled on this layer of the cosmos," he declaimed somberly.

"What would become of me?"

"Well, you would live in your new *shabono*, weaving baskets and growing *hukomo* in a *hikari täkä*. You would gossip with the other women about goings-on: who is making time with whom, who has been insulted, who has lost his blowgun, who lives in the nicest *yanos*. Of course, it would be necessary for you to please your new husband sexually. In all likelihood there would be a wedding ceremony shortly after your arrival."

This picture Manolo had painted of her life as a captive bride amused her. Manolo was a great kidder, and she'd assumed he was once again pulling her leg. But his demeanor had remained quite sober, without a trace of humor, and it suddenly dawned on her that he might, in fact, be serious.

"Are you playing with me?"

"A little," he smiled.

"How little?"

~

"Wife," Manolo said.

"Yes, husband," Sonia replied.

"Do you miss your mother?"

"Sometimes. Why do you ask?"

"Because you're going to be seeing a lot more of her if I have to take you back to your village."

"Have I displeased you, husband? Come here so I can apologize by hitting you over the head with this bowl." She grabbed a large wooden bowl, let out a war cry and began chasing Manolo around their hut.

He darted out the doorway with Sonia in close pursuit, to the amusement of the old ladies of the village. "She is a crazy woman!" he shouted, making sure to stay at least one step ahead of her.

CHAPTER THREE

Harper's phone call to Hector had been brief.

"Doberman pinscher," Hector had answered.

"German shepherd," she'd responded, providing the password. Then she placed an order.

Hector had pretended not to recognize her voice and maintained a curt, businesslike tone. Harper loved it when he did that and had trouble suppressing a laugh.

After hanging up, Harper left her town house and took the subway to Washington Heights. When she arrived at Hector's building, a dilapidated midrise, he buzzed her in. She slid an envelope of bills under his apartment door. Then she heard footsteps.

Suddenly Hector broke character. "Harper, is that you?"

"No, it's Eleanor Roosevelt."

He opened the door and sheepishly invited her in for a cup of coffee, handing her a packet of cocaine.

"What's your story?" he asked, once they were seated in his cramped kitchen.

"Oh, I've been up to no good. You know me."

He nodded. "Weren't you having an affair with that guy from the workshop?"

"Oh God, that was so long ago. He's married now."

"What kind of parts have you been getting?"

"If you get me started on my acting, all that's going to lead to is a monologue on my low self-esteem."

"Yeah, you were always down on yourself."

"That's what my shrink says. So what about you?"

"I've just had an audition."

"Good for you! You were great when we did those scenes from *The Cherry Orchard* and *Long Day's Journey* in workshop."

"You thought so? Thanks."

"So, what's the part?"

"It's off-off-Broadway. A Puerto Rican mugger. Big surprise. My character realizes he went to elementary school with his victim. We have a charged confrontation in which we discuss the divergent paths our lives have taken and reflect on how we've ended up where we are."

"Marvelous," Harper offered.

"Oh, yeah," he yawned. He cut several lines of coke on a mirror with a razor blade. They snorted a couple of lines each with a rolled-up dollar bill.

"Are you still with Bob?" Harper asked.

"As much as anyone can be."

"He's very difficult, isn't he?"

"That's one way of putting it."

"Why do you stay with him?"

Hector shrugged.

"Have you tried couples counseling?"

"Yeah, but it backfired. Bob got interested in the counselor."

"I hate it when that happens."

Harper had a buzz on as she left the building. She had planned to return home but stopped on the sidewalk and thought for a minute. *No, I don't have to go home,* she told herself. She hailed a cab on Broadway and took it to the Cloisters.

～

It was midafternoon, a brisk spring day, and Harper was the only visitor in the Cuxa Cloister. She savored the solitude. From the tower she gazed across the Hudson to the Palisades, then went inside to see the unicorn.

"Hi, cutie. I see they still have you on a leash. I'm just like you, except my leash is really, really long."

She looked over her shoulder to make sure no one but the unicorn was listening.

"They say you're elusive and magical, but we both know that, at heart, you're a homebody who enjoys life's simple pleasures: lying about the castle, swimming in the moat, puttering around the herb garden. I gotta go now, but listen, my darling, I'll be back soon."

On the A train, Harper mused about her life—her addictions, her fragile relationships, her defective personality. She was . . . who she was. She was dimly aware that self-destructing in one way or another and watching a proscenium, backdrop and stage set fall to pieces around her were, if not exactly enjoyable, somehow satisfying. Why, she couldn't say.

CHAPTER FOUR

The area to the north of the village was rugged and hilly, covered by dense jungle. The village itself was situated on a hill that rose one thousand feet above sea level. To the west was a relatively large natural savanna. The vista to the south offered a spectacular view of a lush valley and the Mavaca River.

A narrow trail led east from the village down to the Orinoco. Because of the thick rain-forest canopy, the trail was typically gray and gloomy. The ground was sparsely covered by undergrowth. Along the riverbanks, where the sunlight could penetrate, heavy vegetation grew, including Amazon lilies.

Lisa handled her kayak ably on the one-mile trip upriver from the village landing to the Catholic mission late one afternoon.

~

"You know, the villagers have been talking about us," Lisa remarked to Padre Higgins soon after arriving at the mission.

"Oh, really?" He was amused. "Well, let them enjoy themselves," he laughed.

"Yes, let them."

"They're harmless," Padre Higgins's pet macaw added. The precocious bird, named Billy, sat on a perch on the veranda of the clapboard mission house. The padre pronounced his name "Bee-ly."

"What would you know about it?" Lisa asked.

"I see, I observe," Billy said.

Esteban Higgins had been at the mission for five years. He and Lisa had met a couple of years earlier on her first field trip to Venezuela. Almost immediately they had established a bond of friendship based on a mutual appreciation of the majesty of the isolated region and the simple ways of the Yanomamö. He was kind and resourceful and had earned the respect of the villagers. Early in his tenure he had established himself as someone not to be trifled with. Since then, the villagers had been wary of crossing him, and he had largely been spared the abuse typically suffered by outsiders. The confidence and trust Padre Higgins placed in Lisa resulted in the villagers holding her in high regard as well.

The mission had a global positioning system, a satellite phone, an emergency generator and numerous other amenities, as well as generous stores and provisions, all of which Padre Higgins had obtained from the diocese in Caracas. A native of Chile, he had found that the missionary life suited his solitary, independent nature. His time was largely his own. He enjoyed taking walks along the river trail in the early morning or at dusk during the golden hour, as well as hikes along the jungle trails, listening to the cries of parrots and howler monkeys, alone with his thoughts. Sometimes he reflected on his home in Santiago or his time at seminary in Mexico City. He had enjoyed city life, for the most part. What had brought him to the middle of nowhere to live a simple life among the natives? He wasn't sure.

The Yanomamö were, he found, childlike in many ways, though he knew they were also capable of great brutality. His official duties involved introducing the village to Western ideas and ways, including

Catholicism. He was aware that Lisa, as a cultural anthropologist, did not approve of his efforts to "Westernize" the villagers, but when the subject came up, it was always in jest.

For dinner, he served Lisa a chicken fricassee accompanied by a bottle of a Chilean cabernet sauvignon.

"Billy loves Lisa," Billy suddenly called out.

"I'm flattered," Lisa chuckled. Then she added, "The feeling is mutual."

Billy squawked with glee.

"That's enough from you tonight, Billy," Padre Higgins scolded. "I want to have a word with you later." He turned back to Lisa. "He's very forward. He gets it from the villagers. My apologies."

"No need to apologize. I think he's charming. Say, how's the Westernization going?"

"The electric toothbrushes aren't working out. It was a mistake, I admit it."

She nodded, trying to conceal a smile.

"But you know what *is* popular? The microrecorders."

After dinner they adjourned to the veranda, and Lisa reported on the progress she'd made with her taxonomy of the village's oral traditions and her analysis of their kinship system. He listened intently and occasionally offered an observation based on his experiences with the villagers. Then they took a walk along the river.

"You know who's coming back? Caio," Padre Higgins said.

"Oh, you never told me about his audience with the pope."

"Caio treated the pope deferentially, giving him a *guacamaya* parrot and calling him *shorima*. I remember he was impressed by the Roman ruins. He told me he approved of the high regard the present-day Romans have for the ruins—assurance that present, past and future are unchanging and indistinguishable."

By the time they returned from their walk, it was dusk, and Lisa was eager to make it back to the village before nightfall. She and

Padre Higgins said good-bye. "So long!" Billy called as she walked down to the landing.

She switched on the kayak's deck-mounted mini-lantern and in moments was paddling downriver. Crickets chirped. *What will I say to the village women if they voice their suspicions?* she wondered. *I will simply declare, Padre Higgins is a fantabulous lover, and no matter what happens, it was worth it! In fact, I can't get him out of my head!*

≈

A few days later, several villagers carried one of the older men, Pablo, in on a litter. He was very weak, having fallen ill on a hunting expedition. A native taboo prevented Pablo from being given anything to drink, because the villagers believed he was being punished for having killed a jaguar. For several days and nights the shamans said prayers.

Manolo and Lisa called on Pablo in his hut. Pablo lay in his hammock, surrounded by his wife and family. Lisa could see he was suffering from dehydration. She felt his forehead: He was burning up with fever. Immediately, she went to her hut and made a pitcher of lemonade, then returned, waving off all protests, and explained that this was very powerful medicine.

"What kind?" Pablo whispered.

"American."

He nodded.

A knowing glance passed between them as he gulped down the first glass of lemonade.

≈

Lisa strolled along the riverbank. It was a beautiful evening. She was getting used to Padre Higgins's home cooking, she mused. The fare in the village was at best bland and at worst inedible: plantains, palm fruits, avocado, papaya, sweet potatoes, armadillo and grubs. Despite having her own hut, she hardly ever had a moment of privacy, as the villagers rarely left her alone. The bugs, heat and humidity were at times unbearable. And she slept fitfully in her hammock, which was far from comfortable.

Sometimes she felt lonely. She missed Thomas. Yet her trips to the Amazon fulfilled a profound need to get away from everything and everyone familiar to her. Thomas had never understood this. He was the quintessential urban dweller. What would it be like to "go native," she wondered, and kiss her old life good-bye? Would she and Esteban set up house together in the mission with Billy? The idea amused her. And what of his vows of chastity? She sensed there was more to him than met the eye: He came across as urbane, even suave. She thought about a friend in New York who had become a Franciscan monk. The chastity vow appalled her, but he'd confided that, as a practical matter, it was left up to the individual to determine the appropriate interpretation of the vow. And wasn't she always reading in the newspaper about small-town Catholic priests in Ireland with children and mistresses? The local parishioners simply looked the other way. She wondered if beneath Esteban's unflappable exterior there was a sensual Latin lover experienced in the ways of the world. The thought excited her . . . It was as though she had been reading too many Barbara Cartland novels.

∽

Lisa woke at dawn to a great commotion in the village and cries of *Whaaa! Whaaa!* Startled and still half asleep, she peeked out the window. The shamans were inhaling *ebene*, a hallucinogen, and were leading the warriors in chants and songs. The men had painted their faces with charcoal and were brandishing spears and bows overhead.

Then they stood in a row forming a *wayu itou*, the warrior lineup. The tension in the air was palpable. They began to shoot arrows into a *no owä*, a straw figure, at the far end of the gathering. The men boasted of what they would do to their enemies. The women wept or shouted encouragement. "You tell him!" "That's right!"

Lisa approached Manolo to ask the reason for the raid on a neighboring village.

"Why are you launching this *wayu huu*?" she asked in a whisper. "Is it women theft?"

He shook his head and explained that the recent death of Alfredo, his brother-in-law, had been attributed to witchcraft: a spell cast by a shaman from another village. Suspicion had been building for some time. The casting of the spell that killed Alfredo was an outrage that demanded revenge.

"Sonia and I will guard the village," Lisa smiled.

Eight weeks after her arrival, Lisa made her farewells and prepared to return home. A day's journey by a small launch brought her down-river from the mission through the jungle to a small airstrip at the edge of a frontier town. From there she took a puddle-jumper over the jungle and mountains to Caracas. As the plane touched down in Caracas, she sighed, both sorry to leave and excited to go home. The tires squealed and gave off puffs of blue smoke. When she stepped outside the tiny door, a blast of hot air swept over her, and the concrete runway disappeared in the heat waves on the horizon.

CHAPTER FIVE

Barbara and Harper sat in Harper's room in the Betty Ford Center in Rancho Mirage, California, comparing notes on the day's events.

"Should we kill her?" Barbara asked.

"Let's do," Harper said.

"Okay. Knock on my door later tonight—that'll be the signal. This'll mean one less orderly to fuck with us."

"Amen."

They broke up laughing.

~

Two weeks later, Harper paced near the entrance of the center. She watched David walk toward her from the parking lot on the palm tree–lined sidewalk.

"Well, well. If it isn't Dr. Jekyll and Miss Hyde," he said breezily. Harper blushed. David thought she seemed unusually fragile. "Should I treat you with kid gloves?" he asked.

"Yes, please. I'm feeling a little rickety just now."

He hugged her, and she smiled weakly. There was time to spare before their flight back to New York, so they stopped at an IHOP for lunch. Harper had just completed a sixty-day inpatient program at the center, and David was anxious to hear all about it. She launched into a catalog of her activities: group and individual therapy, drug addiction counseling, fitness training, lectures, movies, nature walks, birding, tennis, archery and skeet shooting. It had reminded Harper of summer camp in Maine as a young girl. She told David about how she was ignored at first but finally accepted by the other patients.

"Who were they?"

"Let's see. Trustafarians, executives, actors, lawyers, stockbrokers, ski bums, housewives, writers, pilots, professional athletes, newscasters, race-car drivers, professors, jockeys, country-and-western singers, stand-up comics, circus performers, ballet dancers, detectives, pop singers and Gypsies."

"Wow. Really?"

"No, silly boy."

They both smiled. David was glad to see some of her old spark returning.

Harper told him about the close friendship she'd developed with another patient, Barbara. They were so much alike, sometimes Harper thought Barbara was her. They did everything together. They stayed up all hours talking. In group therapy sessions, they wouldn't let anyone else get a word in edgewise. They pranced around together in Pucci, went to breakfast in terry-cloth robes with their hair in curlers and beauty "masks" on their faces. Everything Barbara did made Harper laugh: Barbara was outrageous and didn't care what anyone thought. They wore each other's clothes and liked the same movies, books and music. Their childhoods were nearly identical. They were twin daughters by different mothers.

"Your doppelgänger," David said.

"Exactly."

"I'm waiting for the other shoe to drop."

"Meaning?"

"Meaning I know you."

Harper smirked.

"Keep going," David prompted.

"Well, we OD'd on each other." She searched her lap and frowned.

"That's it?"

"We had a big blowup. It was ugly. We both said very cruel things to each other. We couldn't go back to the way things were before. She said I was a nutcase and needed round-the-clock psychiatric care."

"You know what I think?"

"No, what?"

"I think your intimacy with Barbara scared you. I think you felt you didn't deserve to be admired by her, so you torpedoed the relationship. You need to stop beating up on yourself."

"That's what the shrink there said too. He's very optimistic about my prospects for recovery, by the way."

"That's great news! You know I'm there for you."

Harper beamed.

On the plane, David made sure Harper had a blanket, pillow, magazines, juice and the window seat.

"I *need* to be coddled," she said.

"I know. You're in the hands of a seasoned, semiprofessional coddler."

She dozed off with her head on his shoulder.

~

"Have you ever worn women's clothes?" David asked Duncan.

"Why do you ask?"

"No reason."

"Are you considering it?"

"Not exactly," David said.

"Ever try on a pair of Harper's panties when she was out?"

Duncan closed his eyes and mimed holding a pair of panties to his nose and being transported. Then he cocked his head and opened one eye to gauge David's reaction to his performance.

David smiled uncomfortably.

Duncan wondered if he might have been hitting a little too close to home and said nothing.

They continued to walk around the Chelsea gallery where David was the director, looking at the work in a newly installed group show. Duncan occasionally asked about an artist, nodding approvingly when they came to something he liked and quickly passing the rest by.

"I'm not a big lover of conceptual art," Duncan said, by way of explanation.

"I know. You think artists should do it the old-fashioned way: Earn it."

"Precisely. I want to see some evidence of craft."

David nodded. He admired Duncan's art and hoped one day they could work together, perhaps with Duncan as a member of the gallery's stable. David wanted to know him better. He enjoyed gossiping with him, listening to stories about his ex-girlfriend the dominatrix and her dungeon. The time she'd become violent had been the final straw in an already-precarious relationship. It was hard to imagine that had been almost ten years ago . . .

"How's Harper managing?" Duncan asked hopefully.

"She's doing great. I think it may stick this time. Apparently, she got hooked on watching golf on TV when she was in rehab."

"Now I've heard everything."

"She's home watching a PGA tournament right now, practicing her putting on the living room rug. She's become something of a student of the game."

"Harper? How bizarre."

~

What do I think I'm doing? I must be crazy, Harper thought. *Do I want children? Plants. No children.* She walked over the Bow Bridge in Central Park, found a bench and tried to read but was too distracted. She put her book down and watched the rowboats on the Lake. Dogwoods and rhododendrons were in bloom in the Ramble.

She let her imagination run free. Biarritz? Buenos Aires? The Hebrides? No, Cap d'Antibes best suited her mood. Her lover stood with his back to her on the balcony of their hotel suite. The Mediterranean was spread before them beneath a cerulean blue sky. She tried to picture his features, but they remained fuzzy. "Shall we play 'Good Samaritan' or 'Rapist' this afternoon?" she asked him coyly, letting her negligee fall to the floor. The horizon became streaked with pink and red. He turned to her and smiled.

An oriole landed next to her on the bench. Harper looked at the little bird, which returned her look with interest.

She thought about her upcoming audition. It made her anxious. Would she be able to pull something riveting out of herself? That seemed unlikely: She was stuck with her nonacting acting style. She'd always gotten by on her striking good looks and attention-getting outfits. She sensed that, at best, she was a mediocre talent with only rudimentary technique. "I'm never going to make it," she said.

"You never know," the oriole said. It shivered for a moment, then flew away.

~

In his studio, Duncan relaxed in a club chair, listening to Chet Baker. A freshly stretched canvas sat on his easel, and a half-finished nude rested against a wall. Oona was scheduled to arrive later that morning to pose. Outside it was drizzling. Lazily, he pored over vintage girly magazines from his collection.

The doorbell rang, and Duncan greeted Oona, showing her to a study where she could undress and put on a robe. When she came back into the room, he was wearing an ascot and a beret.

"Nice outfit!"

"Thank you, my dear. Just thought I'd get into character." He picked up a brush and struck a thoughtful pose, sizing her up.

He couldn't hide a smirk, and she began to chuckle. He took off the ascot and beret and tossed them on a chair in the corner.

"You've probably done this a million times before," Oona said.

"Yes," Duncan responded in a mock world-weary tone. "Listen, I'd like you to sit on this chair right here." He motioned her over from where she'd been standing. "How about if I give you a novel to read? What do you like?"

"Oh, something light—Mickey Spillane, Henry James—stuff like that."

Duncan lit up at the mention of Mickey Spillane, disappeared and then came back with a first edition of *I, The Jury* with colorful pulp cover art, which he handed to her. Sitting naked on a wooden chair, Oona held the novel, pretending to read. "Perfect," he commented, after he'd returned to his easel to take in the tableau.

He began to work on an outline of Oona, keeping up a steady stream of patter to relax her. She seemed a little uneasy to him. "Where'd you grow up?"

"Bolinas."

"The 'psychedelic Peyton Place.' "

"Exactly!"

"Interesting . . ."

"You're a friend of Lisa and Thomas, right?" she asked.

"How'd you know?"

"Lisa talks about you all the time. 'Duncan this, Duncan that.'"

"Really?"

"Oh, yeah."

"How do you know them?"

"She's my aunt by marriage. Her older sister is married to my dad."

"How funny."

"I had dinner with Lisa last month," Oona said.

"I didn't realize she'd come back already. I thought she was still in the jungle. Say, would you mind leaning a little this way?" he asked, motioning her forward. "Hold it . . . right . . . *there*. So, how is Lisa?"

"She seemed concerned about her relationship with Thomas. She thought he was acting strangely: suddenly lots of late nights at the office and unexpected business trips. Lots of little things, but they weren't adding up."

"So you think he's on the loose behind her back?"

"Hmmm. I'm not really an expert in these matters. There's probably a perfectly plausible explanation."

Harper sat nervously in the lobby of an alternative performance space in the East Village. A number of other actors were also sitting or milling about in the dimly lit, run-down venue.

Harper's friend Bart, the author of the play for which she was auditioning, had wangled her an invitation to read for a part. A dozen actors in all, six men and six women, had been assembled. They were being called into the theater in pairs to read scenes.

Harper was thinking about golf, wondering what kind of clubs she should buy.

Suddenly the theater doors opened, and Bart gestured to Harper. "Let's go, honey, c'mon in," he said. "Stand up straight. Look more confident."

"I'm not feeling confident."

"Fake it."

Then Bart ushered Harper and another actor, Jeff, into the theater. The director and the company's artistic director sat in the front row.

Harper and Jeff stepped onto the stage.

That evening Harper took a nap and dreamed she and Barbara shared an apartment. They were corporate lawyers in the Paris office of a large, international firm, but they also moonlighted as exotic dancers. There was a constant risk they might be found out by a senior partner or important client who happened into the gentlemen's club where they worked at night and on weekends. Practicing law enabled them to support themselves so they could devote their free time to something they truly loved.

Lisa poked her head into the bedroom. "Hey, I didn't know you were in here," she said. "Don't we have plans tonight? I let myself in."

"I was just having a little nap and lost track of the time. Jeez, I was having this weird dream."

"Did you get the part?"

"No, it didn't work out. I gave it the old college try, but I just didn't have it."

CHAPTER SIX

Four years earlier, in the fall of 1995, Lisa and Harper were introduced at a Bikini Kill concert at Woolsey Hall on the Yale campus by a mutual friend, Jessica. Later, they joined Jessica's clique, a hip group of pixieish lesbians, at the Anchor Bar off College Street.

Lisa and Harper sat next to each other at the large table, smoking, talking and giggling.

"Jessica said you were great, but I had no idea *how* great!" Harper gushed.

"Gosh, I—"

"Will you be my best friend?"

"Okay."

"Hey, everybody," Harper announced. "Lisa is my new best friend."

"Cool," Jessica observed dryly, before diving back into her conversation. After a few minutes, Jessica tapped her glass with a spoon to get everyone's attention and began singing at the top of her lungs. Immediately, the girls at the table joined in:

Bull-dog! Bull-dog! Bow, wow, wow,
Eli Yale!
Bull-dog! Bull-dog! Bow, wow, wow,

Our team can never fail.

When the sons of Eli break through the line,

That is the sign we hail.

Bull-dog! Bull-dog! Bow, wow, wow.

Eli Yale!

"Encore!" Harper shouted.

Without hesitating, Jessica and the gang launched into another old campus favorite:

Bingo, Bingo,

Bingo, Bingo, Bingo,

That's the lingo,

Eli is bound to win.

There's to be a victory,

So watch the team begin!

B-B-B-Bingo, Bingo, Harvard's team cannot prevail,

Fight! Fight! Fight with all your might for Bingo, Bingo,

Eli Yale!

A month later Harper gave up her apartment on Whitney Avenue and moved into a spare room in the rambling Victorian that Lisa and a few other graduate students had rented on Science Hill. Lisa was pursuing a PhD in anthropology, and Harper was a costume design student at the Drama School. They quickly settled into a routine of meeting for a drink at the Anchor Bar, which had become an informal clubhouse for their circle on weeknights, before heading back to Science Hill.

One night Harper joined Lisa for vodka gimlets at the Anchor. They held hands and looked into each other's eyes.

"Are we having a moment?" Harper asked.

"I think so."

"You know why we get along together so well?" Harper said.

"No."

"Because we're opposites."

"Go on."

"You're bookish, reserved, together. I'm quirky, neurotic, an outrageous dresser and I say whatever comes into my head."

"That sounds like us!" Lisa laughed.

"Listen, you've got to come to the opening of the Athol Fugard play next Friday."

"That's right, I almost forgot. Who did you say did the costumes again?"

"Very funny."

"Seriously, I can't wait to see what you've done."

"Good! You need a break, anyway. You've been killing yourself preparing for your orals."

"Ain't that the truth. Tell me, is the play any good?"

"No, of course not! No one goes for the play. The actors just need an excuse to dress up and emote."

~

David rummaged through Harper's dresser drawers and closet. A few minutes later he appeared in the living room wearing a pair of her panties, a camisole top, her robe and bedroom slippers. It was the first time he'd acted on this impulse. He couldn't believe how exhilarating it was! The thought of her catching him in the act sent a shiver through his body. He pictured her walking in, pretending not to notice that anything was amiss, then observing that he looked different, asking if he'd gotten a haircut.

~

At the World of Golf in midtown, Harper buttonholed a clerk.

Holding up a club, she said, "What's this club, a mashie? I really need a mashie."

Lisa did her best to keep from laughing.

"Mashie?" the clerk said.

"Yeah, you know, peach cobbler," Harper said.

"Not familiar with it," the clerk said

"Ever heard of Ben Hogan?" Harper asked.

When Harper was done shopping for clubs, she and Lisa headed to the Dean & DeLuca in SoHo for coffee.

Lisa sighed and stared out the window.

"What's up?" Harper asked.

"Do you really want to know?"

"No, I just like saying, 'What's up?'"

"My marriage has gone to hell."

"In a handbasket?"

"Yes."

"Care to divulge any details?"

"Thomas has lost all interest in me."

"That's crazy. What makes you say that?"

"He's distant, cold."

"How cold?"

"Cold. And I caught him quickly hanging up the phone the other day when I walked into the room. There are a lot of late nights at the office—that kind of thing. Nothing I can really put my finger on."

"Could any of it be in your head?" Harper asked.

"I don't know . . ."

Lisa looked down and sipped her coffee. Harper couldn't read her expression and began eavesdropping on the conversation at a nearby table. A woman was holding forth.

"I've been so happy since Marco and I got married. I have Louis Vuitton luggage and a gold Rolex. We live on Park Avenue, have a summer house in the Hamptons and spend every Christmas in St. Bart's," she declared.

Harper and Lisa looked at each other and burst out laughing.

"Have you told your shrink? What does he say?" Harper asked.

"About Louis Vuitton?"

"Ha, ha! No, about Thomas."

"He's taking it very seriously and wants to hear more about my feelings about Thomas, the relationship, our sex life."

"*Ooh la la!* Is Thomas romantic with you at all? I mean, you two still do it, right?"

"He thinks he can have his way with me anytime."

"You know who I'd like to have my way with?" Harper said.

"Who?"

"*Duncan.* Duncan, Duncan, Duncan. 'Oh, Duncan, you're so naughty! Come out from behind that easel right now!'"

"You're kidding," Lisa said.

"He's been on my little mind."

"I can't believe it."

"Neither can I."

"You're really interested in him?" Lisa asked.

"Aren't we curious? I think *you* might have a crush on him too!"

"I do not!"

"Do so!"

"Well, I'm going home to kill myself. Are you coming?"

"No, call me later. I'll be at the library."

"Oh, the lie-berry," Lisa said.

"See ya."

"No you won't. I'll be dead."

"I'll view the remains," Harper said.

"You do that."

CHAPTER SEVEN

What kind of lingerie do you wear?" David asked.

"Why do you ask?" Hester was amused by the question.

"No reason."

"Yeah, right."

"Okay. I'm preparing to have a daydream about the two of us slipping away to a tropical isle."

"Oh!" Her expression brightened.

"Where do you think we should go?"

"What are my choices?"

"Let's see. Mykonos, Ibiza, Sardinia."

"Not very tropical. I vote for Mykonos."

"Have you been?"

"No, how about you?"

"I got laid under a windmill."

She arched an eyebrow. "Nice."

They sat at a conference table in the gallery office. The gallery walls were festooned with the work of Jim Shaw, Mike Kelley, Laurie Simmons and a number of rising stars.

"Yoo-hoo, David!" a voice called from the front desk.

"Wendy, is that you? Come back here," David said.

An attractive older woman joined them in the office. She wore a vintage Rudi Gernreich pantsuit and exuded an air of confidence that suggested she might once have been that designer's muse.

"Hester, this is Wendy, Harper's interesting mother," David said.

"Listen, honey," Wendy said, "you've got to watch this guy. Has he asked you about your lingerie? He's quite the connoisseur."

"Oh, stop," David protested.

"I'm here on a mission," Wendy announced.

David shot Wendy a wary glance. "What mission?"

"Let me tell you about my daughter. We've never gotten along. She's a real daddy's girl, but I love her and want the best for her. I'm a little worried about her. David, tell me, are you two shtupping regularly?"

"Morning, noon and night."

"Excellent," Wendy smiled.

"Bravo!" Hester exclaimed, following suit.

David rolled his eyes. "Satisfied? Because I've got work to do."

"Don't be rude," Wendy frowned. "I love that one," she said, pointing to a large black-and-white canvas on the far wall depicting vaguely sinister-looking versions of characters from *Archie* comics: Jughead, in his signature crown cap, but sporting stubble, was sitting in a hot tub flanked by Betty and Veronica in the midst of what appeared to be a swingers party. "I'd like to see how it would look at our place. Could you have it sent over after the show is down? Unless, of course, it sells."

"Sure. It's by Jim Shaw. You might also like to look at Richard Kern's photographs." David lowered his head and faintly smiled.

"You are bad," Hester said, laughing.

"What am I missing here?" Wendy asked.

"Oh, boy," Hester said. "Well, those photos may be a little transgressive for you and your husband."

"Nonsense. We're not old fogies yet," Wendy said sharply. "It seems like ten minutes ago, Harper was in diapers. If David recommends it, I'm sure it's fine. I have complete confidence in him. By the way, David, did I ever tell you about the time Harper ran off with the neighbor boy when she was five? We had to call the police. Finally found them sitting on a hill overlooking the interstate. They'd packed little bags and were ready to run off together. Harper was quite the tomboy as a child, always climbing trees, catching tadpoles down by the creek and building tree houses. Then, when she was twelve, she was bitten by the drama bug. Her first role was Wilma in *The Flintstones*. And she would write little plays, and she and her brother would put them on for us at home. And, oh my God! The puppet shows! She would do all the characters and voices. I still remember one in particular—her version of *Love Suicides at Sonezaki* by Chikamatsu. It was brilliant! I sometimes wonder if she ever got enough attention from her father and me. We were so self-absorbed, particularly Jack. And he was a drinker. We both were. Poor Harper, her self-image must have suffered because of our shortcomings as parents. Well, I've got to dash. I'm running late. So nice to have met you, Hester. David, I'll call you about the arrangement for the painting. And if you can send over the photographs too, that would be great. Good-bye." She turned and sauntered out.

"Wow," Hester said. "What was that all about?"

David had a puzzled expression. "I'm not sure."

David lay down on the Eames couch in the back room of the gallery and closed his eyes. He daydreamed about being with Hester on Capri, the two of them riding the funicular up to the town and strolling hand in hand through the Piazzetta.

≈

"Are you playing footsie with me?" Duncan asked Harper.

They were sitting opposite each other in wing chairs. She'd slipped out of her pumps and had placed her feet up each of his pants legs.

The cocktail party they were attending at an expansive loft at Broadway and Bleecker was bustling. There were several bartenders, and waiters were serving hors d'oeuvres. The space had been meticulously renovated to resemble a Park Avenue apartment. The living room windows offered a view of the West Village cityscape.

Across the room, Jeni and Lee Ann observed the goings-on between Duncan and Harper with interest.

"My, my. What do we have here? Could anything be developing?" Lee Ann asked.

"No, she's just had too much to drink. She's a booze hound!" Jeni said.

"I hear that Duncan is quite the roué!"

"You think he's after her?"

"I do."

Harper moved her chair closer to Duncan's. Her eyes were bright with excitement. "We're making a spectacle of ourselves," she exclaimed. "Everyone's talking about us!"

He feigned surprise. "They are? I wonder why. By the way, is Lisa going to be here?"

"I hope so," Harper said.

A few minutes later Thomas joined them.

"Where's your wife?" Harper asked. "We were just talking about her."

"Oh, she'll be here soon."

Duncan told them about Medieval Week, a reenactment that occurs every summer in a walled Swedish city that he had once visited.

"Buxom milkmaids in period costume—is that it?" Harper asked.

"Yep," Duncan laughed.

"Lisa could have a field day with that kind of thing—from an anthropological perspective," Harper said.

"No, she's too faithful to her Amazon tribe," Thomas replied.

The hostess of the party took Thomas by the arm and introduced him to Jeni and Lee Ann.

A short time later, Lisa arrived. She immediately noticed Duncan and Harper in a corner alcove making goo-goo eyes at each other and smooching. It caught her up short to see that Harper's relationship with David might be on shaky ground. *What's wrong with everybody?* she wondered. *What's wrong with* me?

CHAPTER EIGHT

"D o you like to travel?"

"I like to fuck," Harper said.

"Do you think there should be a separate state for Palestinians? If so, where?"

"In my pussy," Harper said. "These are great questions, by the way! Where did you get them?"

"Are you being sarcastic?" Jane asked.

"No, absolutely not," Harper protested.

"Okay." Jane was defensive. "These are our standard interview questions at the magazine. It's our house questionnaire."

"Terrific."

"Have you ever read *BOMB*?" Jane, an editor at the magazine, asked suspiciously.

"Oh, yeah . . . of course. I'm a regular reader. An avid reader— in good standing."

"Uh-huh. Let's talk about your movie."

"It's called *Are We Done Here?* It's an indie film that showed at a bunch of festivals, and it's just been released in honest-to-goodness theaters."

"You're great in it!"

"Do you really think so? Thank you!"

"Tell me about your role."

"Well, I play Mona. She's a scene maker, an outrageous dresser, a flirt, kinda quirky. I'm more or less playing myself, I must admit. I think I finally found my métier. I really can't 'act' in a conventional sense—you know, do a 'character' or something like that. I'm a terrible mimic, and I can't tell a joke to save my life. Anyway, Mona is a librarian by day. But then she becomes the queen of East Village nightlife."

"And she has a drug problem?"

"Yeah, exactly. I've been in and out of rehab because of a substance abuse problem. So that part was easy."

Harper and Jane sat on a couch in MercBar. It was a weekday afternoon, and they had the place more or less to themselves. Four months had passed since Harper and Duncan had made a spectacle of themselves at the cocktail party. *BOMB* had approached Harper for an interview because *Are We Done Here?* had opened to positive reviews. Her endearing performance as a female Holden Caulfield for the punk-rock set had suddenly made her an it girl among the city's downtown crowd. Harper, who had already downed three screwdrivers, was drunk and becoming increasingly unpredictable.

She ordered another drink as the photographer, Gretchen, arrived for the photo shoot. They went out to the sidewalk, where Harper vamped, pulling the straps of her cocktail dress off her shoulders and donning sunglasses.

"Fantastic," Gretchen said, snapping away with her Leica.

"I'm worn out," Harper announced when they returned to the bar. She collapsed on a couch in the corner and promptly passed out.

"Oh, boy. What do we do now?" Jane asked Gretchen.

"Call David," Gretchen responded without hesitation.

A half hour later, David walked into MercBar. The *BOMB* girls had revived Harper a few minutes earlier.

"My savior!" she exclaimed woozily, draping her arms around his neck before collapsing back onto the couch.

David shook his head in exasperation. Outside, they hailed a cab and headed to their town house in silence.

∾

"Look, Harper had this nice interview, and they killed it," Thomas said.

"Your point being?" Lisa asked. "I thought the photo they ran of her was very flattering. Didn't you like the caption, 'A bookish librarian we chanced to meet'?"

"Harper's a screw-up. She's become an expert at shooting herself in the foot."

"I don't think that's fair. She's really trying. It's not easy for her. Have a little compassion. In any event, she was in rare form when she got wind that the interview was killed. You should have seen her. She had some choice words for the *BOMB* staff."

"I can imagine," Thomas laughed.

Lisa and Thomas were having breakfast in a booth at Jerry's in SoHo on a Saturday morning.

Suddenly Lisa became weepy.

"What's wrong?" Thomas asked.

"I think we need to talk about our relationship," she sniffed. "And you never want to. Every time I bring it up, you act like a jerk and shut me down."

"That's ridiculous. Everything's fine," he snapped.

Lisa burst into tears.

∾

Thomas and Lisa took a cab to a Chelsea nightclub for a party honoring *Are We Done Here?*. She was still fuming over the incident from that morning and rebuffed his efforts at small talk.

As they entered the club, Harper and a redhead were in the midst of a wild, drunken fight by the coatroom. They were pulling each other's hair, scratching, kicking and screaming. Thomas and Lisa looked on in horror.

Suddenly, Harper ripped out a hank of the girl's hair and shoved her to the ground. Then she ran to the bar and stood up on a barstool, waving the hank of hair in the air above her head and whooping like an Indian. "I am a Chippewa brave!" she shouted, just before losing her balance, tumbling off the stool and cutting her head on the bar.

~

A week later, after making arrangements with the Betty Ford Center, David accompanied Harper to LaGuardia, where she boarded a plane for the trip back to Rancho Mirage.

"Welcome home, partner," Barbara smiled, as Harper approached the reception area inside the center.

"It's great to be back, Barbara. You're looking spiffy."

"You're pretty spiffed up yourself."

"What have I missed?"

"Not much."

"You mean the lunatics didn't take over the asylum in my absence and swing from the chandeliers?"

"Oh, *that* . . . So, what kind of trouble have *you* been getting into?"

"Don't ask! It was the usual litany of ugly scenes."

"Drunken excess, debauchery, blackouts, catfights, tantrums and severed limbs?"

"Absolutely."

That night, Barbara dropped by Harper's room for an impromptu sleepover. They would bury the hatchet and catch up. It had been six months since Harper's initial stay at the center. Barbara had returned a month earlier.

After smoking and gabbing, they fell asleep in each other's arms on Harper's bed.

The next morning, as the two of them entered the center's café for breakfast, they noticed a bunch of new girls.

CHAPTER NINE

"Nope, can't do Thursday . . . No, sorry, not Friday. Nah . . . How about never? Does never work for you?" Thomas asked. Then he said good-bye and hung up the phone.

Thomas sat with his feet up on the desk in his spacious, modern corner office, located in a newly constructed building west of Hudson Street, with views of the river. He was a senior editor at a major publishing company.

The phone rang. "Paul is here."

"Thanks, Mary," Thomas said. "Would you walk him into the conference room? I'll be right there."

A few minutes later Thomas arrived. "Great to see you, Paul. What's your pleasure? Coffee? Bromo?"

"Bromo," Paul said.

"Mary, please get Paul a bromo."

Thomas and Paul took seats at the conference room table.

"So . . . *The Death Machine*." Thomas said.

"How do you like it?"

"Well, I like the infidelity. And the bayoneting of the baby, of course. But I think the book could use a little more fantasy."

"Okay. We'd be glad to have your input on the editing front if you decide to publish. What else?"

"I wasn't completely sure about the narrative arc. What do you see as the central conflict?"

"Well, I'd say it's the dispute that's arisen among the girls of the coven as to who will be the warlock's primary girlfriend," Paul said. "Two of the girls are best friends but end up rivals for his attention."

"That works," Thomas agreed. "We might want to sharpen the conflict a bit. Also, I have a question about the marketing of the book, if we were to take it on. What do you think the author's brand consists of?"

Paul reflected for a moment. "Teen necrophilia."

"Perfect!" Thomas exclaimed. "I'm going to recommend that we offer your client a contract, and, as you know, my recommendations are generally accepted. But, of course, I have to run it up the flagpole with our business people and discuss numbers with them. You've indicated what kind of advance you're looking for, and I think we'll be in that ballpark."

"Thanks, Thomas. When can I expect to hear back?"

"Give me a week to ten."

"To *The Death Machine*!" Paul held up his glass of bromo.

"The Death Machine." Thomas raised his Coke.

~

Oona sat in a club chair in Duncan's studio. Duncan was working on a study of her in charcoal. When it was time for a break, she declined the robe he offered. She strutted about in her panties and bra.

"You're a bit manic today," Duncan observed.

Oona disregarded his comment. "Why don't I pose in a Roman toga with a fluted column?" she suggested.

"That's not really what I do," he frowned.

"C'mon, Duncan. You've got more than one arrow in your quiver. Don't be such a wet blanket!"

He laughed, shaking his head. "No sulking!" he admonished.

"You know, when this extra flesh on my legs, waist and thighs is pinched, it remains in a pinched position. Wanna see?"

"No, I don't, Oona," Duncan said impatiently.

After the break, she resumed her pose.

"Say, what do you think about this thing in Kosovo?" Duncan asked.

"You know, if a NATO peacekeeping force was actually sent in under a UN mandate and some kind of safe zone was put in place, I'd piss my pants with joy."

"Hmmm. Wouldn't that just be a Band-Aid? I think they're going to need a political solution. Until the nations with clout put economic pressure on Milošević, no lasting peace is gonna happen."

"Oh, shut up, Duncan. That'll take forever. Meanwhile, those Serbian monsters are raping and destroying entire villages."

"Can you turn your head this way a little?" he asked.

"Like this?"

"Yep. I don't disagree with that, by the way," Duncan said.

Oona nodded. "Say, what do you hear from Harper?"

"She's been in rehab."

"Oh, right. It's kind of a revolving door, isn't it?"

"I wouldn't say that," Duncan said guardedly.

Oona shot Duncan a skeptical look. "I wonder if she'll ever get it together."

"I have complete confidence in her," Duncan said.

"You do?"

"Not really," he confessed.

"Neither do I."

"What's the Betty Ford Center like?" Oona asked.

"I wouldn't know."

"What I imagine is a bunch of crazy-ass people basically just running amok—under some nominal psychiatric supervision, of course."

"That sounds about right."

~

Thomas and Lisa sat in the back room at Raoul's perusing the menu.

"Did you know that among our friends we're known as the Battling Bickersons?" Lisa asked.

"John and Blanche Bickerson. That was Don Ameche and Frances Langford, right? No, Rocky, I didn't know that," Thomas said.

"Well, why do you think that is, Bullwinkle?"

"Because you're always picking a fight with me?"

"With good reason. For example, where've you been lately? I can never reach you," Lisa complained.

"I've told you—work has been brutal. I've been holed up in a conference room at the office trying to pull together this dumb deal that's going to send us on a Uruguayan vacation."

"Okay, Bullwinkle, why don't you give me a blow by blow?"

"Don't be silly. We're working on *The Death Machine*," Thomas said with annoyance.

"Oh, that bore."

"No, it's going to be terrific and will lead to a huge television contract. Teen necrophilia."

"Can I take your order?" asked their waiter, who had just appeared.

"*May* I take your order," Thomas corrected him. "Rocky, can he take your order?"

"I'll have the dead moose," Lisa said.

"I'll have the dead squirrel," Thomas said.

"Very good, sir," the waiter replied.

"Just kidding, we'll have the Chateaubriand for two," Thomas grinned. "Idiot . . ." he added, under his breath. "Incidentally, waiter, that triphthong in 'Raoul's' is really obnoxious. And, waiter, did you know that Don Ameche invented the cell phone?"

"Sir?"

"Carry on," Thomas said, turning back to Lisa. "So, will the field-work keep going?"

"It's almost a wrap."

"Taxonomy of the oral traditions?"

"All done."

"What about the kinship system?"

"Done."

"You're amazing."

"I'm going to try to get these findings into *Current Anthropology*. But, to be honest, I'm of two minds about ending it . . ."

"Say, wasn't a definitive kinship study already published in the *Oxford Journal of Anthropology* back in fifty-seven?"

"Don't be a brat."

CHAPTER TEN

On the afternoon before her thirtieth birthday, Harper walked through the front door of her West Village town house. That morning, she'd been discharged from the Betty Ford Center and had taken a flight back to New York.

A couple of hours later, Lisa dropped by.

"My long lost friend!" Lisa shrieked, hugging Harper in the doorway.

"Oh, Leese, I feel like I haven't been a good friend—that I've let you down," Harper frowned. "I just upped and took off and abandoned you. I feel terrible."

"I'll get over it," Lisa said, "after my lawyers cream you in court for breach of friendship. The important thing is, you're getting well. Say, how are the preparations coming for the big birthday bash?"

"David and Hester have it planned down to the last dessert spoon. All I have to do is show up."

"Excellent."

"Oh, yeah . . . Besides, it keeps them out of trouble," Harper said. "How's the old tribe?"

"You mean the Cleveland Indians?"

"No, the Atlanta Braves."

"Oh, it's all good. Speaking of which, guess what? I may bring Manolo here for a visit."

"The headman? Here? No way."

"Yes, and I was wondering if you could put him up," Lisa said.

"You're kidding."

"I'm kidding."

∾

The next night, Harper, Lisa, Thomas, David, Duncan, Oona, Hester, Wendy and the *BOMB* girls, Jane and Gretchen, sat around a table babbling and drinking champagne. Two hundred or so other guests at Harper's party fluttered about the Campbell Apartment at Grand Central Station.

David leaned over and whispered in Harper's ear, "Are you feeling up to it, honey?"

"Why not? And no time like the present," Harper smirked and excused herself, stepping up to a mic at a podium that had been erected at the back of the bar.

"Speech, speech!" someone shouted.

She held out both arms in a gesture of supplication. "Fans," she said, "for the past two weeks you have been reading about a bad break I got. Yet today I consider myself the luckiest man on the face of the earth. I have been in ballparks for seventeen years and have never received anything but kindness and encouragement from you fans. Look at these grand men. Which of you wouldn't consider it the highlight of his career just to associate with them for even one day? Sure I'm lucky. Who wouldn't consider it an honor to have known Jacob Ruppert? Also, the builder of baseball's greatest empire, Ed Barrow? To have spent six years with that wonderful little fellow, Miller Huggins? Then to have spent the next nine years with that outstanding leader, that smart student of psychology, the best manager in baseball today, Joe McCarthy? Sure I'm lucky. When the New York Giants, a team you would give your right arm to beat, and vice versa, sends you a gift—that's something. When everybody down to the groundskeepers and those boys in white coats remember you with trophies—that's something. When you have a wonderful mother-in-law who takes sides with you in squabbles with her own daughter—that's something. When you have a father and a mother who work all their lives so you can have an education and build your body—it's a blessing. When you have a wife who has been a tower of strength and shown more courage than you dreamed existed—that's the finest I know. So, I close in saying that I might have been given a bad break, but I've got an awful lot to live for."

Wendy, who was standing nearby, moved to the microphone and nudged Harper gently to the side. "Let's hear it for my baby!" she shouted, clapping. "I couldn't be more proud of Harper tonight. She was a difficult teenager—we didn't know what was going to become of her! She was constantly sneaking out of her bedroom window and climbing down the trellis in the middle of the night, drag racing by the fairgrounds, drinking, smoking hashish, giving her boyfriends hand jobs in the family room, cutting classes. The nuns at her school were beside themselves! Except for Sister Beatrice, her Latin teacher, who always had a soft spot for Harper and thought she was brilliant . . ."

"That bitch," Harper whispered to Lisa, who had left the table and was standing next to her. "She's not upstaging me again."

Harper threw a hip at Wendy, pushing her out of the way, and regained the mic. "Please take a seat. Let's hear it for Mother!" she screamed, leading the crowd in a round of applause.

A small older man approached Harper. "Lou, I feel terrible about your condition," he said. "How long are they giving you?"

"Three months," Harper said.

"What'd you hit last year, Lou?"

"Three forty-eight. I can always go back to acting if my hitting falls off," Harper said.

"No, Lou, you're a shitty actor."

"Well, pal, you got that right. Say, who the hell are you?"

"Let's just say 'a friend.'"

"Jesus, you look like Meyer Lansky!" Harper stared at the little man in the chalk-striped suit, before excusing herself and rejoining the group at their table.

"Boy, I can't wait for the cruise," Harper said to Thomas.

"Me neither," he replied. "In fact, I'm going to wear my bathing suit under my clothes on the plane to save time."

"Good thinking! I may do the same."

CHAPTER ELEVEN

While everyone slept, their chartered yacht cruised through the night over a calm ocean. In the morning, when Thomas, Lisa, David, Harper, Duncan and Lisa's cousin, Stephen, meandered onto the aft deck, the captain had already dropped anchor off the coast of Anguilla.

The 150-foot yacht contained three bedrooms and a stateroom. It was manned by a crew of eight. Its equipment included a Zodiac with a sixty-horsepower outboard motor.

"Wow, I can't believe we're here!" Harper shouted. She was wearing a blue-and-white polka-dotted bikini, oversize white-framed sunglasses, platform sandals and a bucket-style hat.

"It was sheer genius of you to arrange this," Duncan said to Thomas.

"Thanks, my friend," Thomas said.

"I can use something in the way of a drink," Stephen sighed.

"At this hour?" Lisa, still in her pajamas, rolled her eyes and lay down on a chaise longue.

Stephen had been eyeing Harper since being introduced to her, but Lisa was there to look out for her friend. "Don't even think about it, Stephen," she admonished him in a stage whisper.

He looked down sheepishly. Harper, who was well aware of Stephen's interest, chuckled.

Stephen was a last-minute addition to the party. Lisa had thought the trip would do her cousin some good, but now she was beginning to wonder if she had underestimated the effects of his obnoxiousness and drinking.

$$\sim$$

The group traipsed around the island in their "finery," explored its secluded, palm tree–lined beaches, snorkeled in the clear water along the reef at Rendezvous Bay, shopped, went out to eat and toured the local nightlife. One evening, they took over a club, and Harper entertained them with an impromptu "interpretive dance" performance while they listened to CDs by Air and Ladytron from David's collection of French and English electronica.

Stephen's clumsy attempts to win the group over consisted of making piña coladas and daiquiris for everyone each afternoon, as well as his own concoction, the "coco loco," a frozen rum drink served in coconut shells.

"Fire in the hole!" Stephen shouted, as he handed Duncan a drink.

"I'm having so much fun!" Harper shrieked.

"Yes, but we're all going to die . . ." Duncan intoned with mock solemnity.

"No one's going to die. We're all immortal!" Stephen chided him.

"We are?" David smiled. "What'll they think of next?"

"A list of things to do for an eternity," Lisa answered gravely.

"In any event, I will live on in my work long after we're all gone," Stephen proclaimed. "Like Villon, Pound, Céline. The funny thing is, Pound and Céline were actually wonderful people. I think their views have been unfairly maligned."

"Oh, really?" Thomas said. "Fascinating."

"Pound was fond of telling Olga Rudge, 'Don't fall in love with the merchandise,'" Stephen added.

"Didn't Pound moonlight as a Jewish pawnshop owner?" Harper asked.

"More likely as a pimp," Lisa replied.

Stephen, unfazed by these quips, continued. "Céline liked to say that he found the Chinese unreliable. He told his wife to just do the shirts at home."

"Ste-phen," Lisa said reprovingly, wagging her finger at him, before abruptly changing the subject. "Hey, Harper, how was the snorkeling this morning? Did I miss anything?"

"Bor-ing. I'm done with snorkeling," Harper said wearily.

"Snorkeling is so yesterday," Lisa agreed.

They smiled at each other conspiratorially.

~

One afternoon, the yacht took them to Sombrero Island, a desolate moonscape with an abandoned lighthouse. They anchored and climbed into the Zodiac, which sped them to shore.

Once on the island, Harper went off on her own to explore. After two hours had gone by without any sign of her, the other members of the group became concerned and began to search for her along the rocky shoreline, shouting, "HARPER! HARPER!"

"What are we going to do?" David wondered.

"Let's go back to the yacht and call the police," Thomas said.

Once they were back on board, Harper suddenly appeared on deck. "Ha, ha! You thought this was *L'avventura*! But I'm not Anna. I'm Harper! I'm Harper!" She nearly fell down.

"You're drunk," David said angrily.

"Not cool," Duncan said. "We thought you were dead, washed out to sea. We looked under every stone for hours."

Lisa shot Duncan and David dirty looks. She put her arm around Harper protectively, walked her down to her room and put her to bed.

≈

The following evening, Stephen and Duncan were lounging on deck. David had volunteered to accompany Lisa on an excursion to a bird sanctuary on Anguilla, and they weren't back yet.

"Hey, let's get Harper to go skinny-dipping off the yacht," Duncan suggested, looking dreamily out to sea.

"Great idea," Stephen said.

They went below and knocked on Harper's door, but no one answered. They strolled down the hall to the stateroom, where Thomas and Lisa were staying, and, seeing the door ajar, pushed it open.

"Whoops," Duncan said.

"Oh my God!" Stephen exclaimed.

Thomas and Harper were lying on the bed with their clothes on but looking very cozy together. Quickly, they sat up.

"Nothing happened," Harper said contritely. "It's not what you think."

"What *do* we think?" Stephen asked.

"Yeah, what *do* you think?" Thomas chimed in.

"My mind is a blank," Stephen answered.

"What about you, Duncan?" Thomas asked.

"Mine's blank too," Duncan said.

"Mine too," Harper added.

"So we're agreed. Our minds are blank," Thomas said. "Harper, do you have anything sharp? This calls for a blood oath."

"I have a darning needle," she replied.

"Go get it," Thomas barked.

Harper fetched the needle and gave it to Thomas. He pricked Stephen's finger to draw a few drops of blood.

"Ouch!" Stephen complained. "What are you doing?"

"Swearing you to secrecy."

"But Lisa's my cousin," Stephen protested.

"We don't care if she's your mother!" Thomas snapped.

Then they all shook hands.

"Aren't you supposed to prick *your* finger too, to make it official?" Stephen asked.

"*No*," Duncan said emphatically, shaking his head.

Later that night, after everyone else had gone to bed, Thomas and Stephen had a nightcap together on deck, watching the lights in Blowing Point Harbor.

"We had a few drinks, and all of a sudden we were getting chummy. It was nothing really," Thomas remarked.

"Okay," Stephen said. "Whatever."

"Yeah, whatever," Thomas said.

~

"Let's blow this joint and swim to St. Bart's together," Stephen proposed to Harper. "I'll go to any lengths to prove my devotion. We can study the natives together poolside at the Eden Rock."

"I don't think so," Harper said forcefully.

"Oh, really? Do you truly care about David?"

"Are you referring to that silly little thing with Thomas?" She shook her head and quickly made her way on deck, leaving Stephen alone in the dining room.

"Is there a way we can get rid of Stephen?" Harper asked.

"I thought you were amused by him," Lisa said.

"He's impossible," Harper said.

"Let's toss him overboard, or set him adrift in the dinghy with a bottle of rum," Duncan offered.

"Can we?" David asked.

"Oh, c'mon, he's not *that* bad," Lisa implored. "Our mothers go way back."

Thomas looked at Lisa sideways and said nothing.

CHAPTER TWELVE

What are you cooking?" Lisa asked. "It smells wonderful."

"Mmm . . . armadillo," Padre Higgins replied. Wearing a white apron, he was tending to the grill on the porch of the mission.

"I love armadillo," Billy chirped from his perch.

When dinner was ready, they sat inside at the dining room table. Lisa eyed her plate suspiciously.

"I don't think I can eat this," she confessed.

"Try it. We have ice cream too. Carvel."

Tentatively, she tried a small bite. "It's great. It tastes just like anaconda."

Padre Higgins smiled and nodded approvingly.

She looked around. "By the way, the mission looks different than when I was last here. Have you redecorated? I don't remember this skylight in the dining room."

"It really opens the place up, doesn't it? I had Manolo put it in for me. I brought him a tear sheet from *Architectural Digest* to give him an idea of what I had in mind."

"I love it." Looking up, she admired the late afternoon sunlight.

There was a knock at the front door, and Padre Higgins went to see who it could be. "May I help you?" he asked.

A tapir was at the door with a shy, inquisitive expression on its face. "Am I interrupting?" it asked. "I just came to see if your water has gone off."

"Not now, Louis," Billy snapped. "We're having dinner."

"I'll come back later."

"Some people," Billy said with exasperation.

Padre Higgins rejoined Lisa, and the conversation turned to gossip about the tribe.

"How many wives has Manolo had, anyway?" Lisa asked.

"Oh my God, let me get my calculator! Let's see . . . By my count, well over nine hundred."

"I had no idea! Tell me about them."

"Which ones? I can give you a rundown of some of their idiosyncrasies."

"Great." Lisa was enjoying Esteban's company. She sensed herself being drawn into his sphere. At the same time, she couldn't help worrying about Thomas back in New York.

"Squawk! Squawk!"

"That's enough out of you, Billy," Padre Higgins chided.

"You and Billy are like an old married couple," Lisa observed.

"It's true," Padre Higgins lamented. "Billy has . . . issues."

"I see."

"I'm not sure that you do."

Padre Higgins and Billy both laughed, making Lisa uneasy.

"Say, where's Caio?" she asked, changing the subject.

"Caio has gone to the Great Beyond. I was afraid to tell you," Padre Higgins answered.

"Boo-hoo," Billy said.

"Billy, you're treading on thin ice," Padre Higgins warned.

"I'm so sorry," Lisa said. "Were you close?"

"Loathed and despised him. Shall we listen to the Victrola? I've got Tetrazzini doing 'Saper vorreste' from *Un ballo in maschera*, with 'Caro nome' on the flip side."

"I love Tetrazzini. What a dear old girl."

"Old? No, Lisa—here and now, past, present and future, forever unchanging."

"We could try contacting spirits from the other world," Billy suggested.

"How many times have I told you not to mention that?" Padre Higgins said sternly.

"I didn't know you had special powers like Manolo," Lisa said.

"None of us has any special powers," Padre Higgins replied coldly.

"Esteban, are you a dream?" Lisa asked.

"If it pleases you."

"It pleases me."

"Then wake up."

"No, stay, Lisa," Billy implored. "We want you here with us . . ."

Lisa opened her eyes. The sounds of the jungle became faint.

"And give my best to your distinguished husband," Padre Higgins added.

Lisa sat up and rubbed her eyes. "I'll do that."

"Do what?" Thomas asked, sitting up in bed next to her.

"Give Esteban's regards to you," Lisa said.

"How is the old boy?"

"Well, we were eating armadillo a second ago."

"What does it taste like, and don't say 'chicken'?"

"I'm not sure. Carvel?"

"You think?"

"He can contact spirits from the other side. No one's supposed to know."

"Is that right? So, I can't tell anyone?"

"Ha, ha."

"Lisa, did you know that men were created by drops of moon blood, and women come from a fruit? Moon blood spilled on this layer of the cosmos, causing men to become fierce."

"Okay, you've made your point . . ." Lisa said.

"You taught me everything I know."

"Yeah, I taught you everything about *The Death Machine* . . . Being facetious just makes everything worse. How do you love me? Tenderly, totally, tragically?"

"No, it's totally, tenderly, tragically," Thomas corrected.

"Why isn't this working?" Lisa blurted out.

"You mean us?"

"Yes, us."

"Come here," he said softly.

"Who, me?"

He hugged her and planted a kiss on her lips. "Rocky, we're going to get through this—together. Do you believe me?"

Lisa's expression brightened, and she nodded.

CHAPTER THIRTEEN

Lisa met Manolo at the gate at JFK Airport upon the arrival of his Varig flight from Caracas. He had come to New York for a one-month stay—his first visit outside the Amazon. He recounted for Lisa his trip downriver from the village by motorboat to Esmeralda, a desolate town on the banks of the Orinoco, followed by a flight on a twin-engine bush plane to Caracas. Lisa was excited to gauge Manolo's reactions to his new surroundings, but she knew him to be a cool customer who prided himself on his ability to remain calm under pressure. Consequently, she was careful not to patronize him or to become overly demonstrative. Though he was out of his element, his gait and expression while they strolled through the terminal suggested the equilibrium of a seasoned traveler. As they drove into the city, Lisa matter-of-factly pointed out the skyline and its particular buildings and monuments. Manolo expressed only polite interest.

"I want to see the Little Church around the Corner," he announced.

"Why?"

"It's part of your religion."

"I've never been there," she admitted.

Manolo proceeded to tell her about its picturesque English garden, visible from the Empire State Building, and its long-standing connection with Broadway show people.

"Manolo, you are incredible!" Lisa enthused. "And, by the way, I love your outfit."

Manolo smiled. He was dressed in a brown cowboy-style shirt with white piping, black jeans and sandals.

Shortly after they arrived at her apartment, Thomas called.

"How's it going?" he asked.

"Fine, but I think Mawobawä is a little wiped out from the trip. He's taking a nap in the guest room."

"Who's that?"

"That's Manolo's real name."

"Oh," Thomas said. "Well, should I be jealous?"

"I dunno—should you?"

The next morning, Lisa and Manolo took a cab to Central Park, where they explored Belvedere Castle and the Ramble. Standing on a rock in the Ramble, Manolo appeared to be in a reverie. He was, in fact, experiencing a moment of introspection. He had become enamored of the park's natural beauty, which provided a dramatic contrast with the nearby apartment buildings, and he sensed he would return at a later date to renew himself spiritually. Certainly the park must be the home of spirits from the other world. Away from the stresses of life in the village and the constant threat of warfare with neighboring tribes, Manolo now had the leisure to reflect. Was he, at the core of his being, of the forest or of the village? He didn't know . . .

They went to the Metropolitan Museum, where Manolo pored over the artifacts in the Egyptian collection. He called them "the belongings of the ancestors."

~

At the top of the Empire State Building, Manolo looked into Lisa's eyes. They spoke softly in the Yanomamö tongue.

"It's so high here, like a mountain," he said.

She noticed his hands trembling. "What is it, Manolo?"

"I don't know, but it's probably not good."

"Why don't you know what's wrong?"

"I don't know everything."

"You can turn people into birds."

"That's the only thing I can do."

From out of nowhere, a large purple and green cloud appeared in the sky, and a storm broke out.

"Hold onto me!" Manolo shouted.

People were running off the observation deck. Then, just as suddenly, the storm passed.

Lisa stared wide-eyed at Manolo. "Manolo, did you do that?"

"I forgot about these kinds of changes in the weather. I can't help it. It happens deep in my head. It's not something I can do whenever I like. Just the birds."

~

David and Duncan sat in David's office at the gallery. Hester was next door at the reception desk. The gallery was quiet.

"David, did you hear? Manolo, Lisa's headman, is in town," Duncan said.

"Yeah, I heard that. How's it working out?" David asked.

"She's been showing him the sights since he arrived a few days ago. He's a serious shopper. She couldn't get him out of J.Crew," Duncan said.

"Really?"

"No!" Duncan chuckled. "Hey, Hester," he called out, "when are you going to come over to my studio and model for me? I have a Roman toga with your name on it."

Hester appeared at the door. "I dunno, Duncan . . . I don't think it's gonna happen. It's not really my thing. Anyway, I thought Oona was your muse."

The phone rang, and Hester returned to the desk to pick up.

"Wendy just gave Harper and me a check for a thousand dollars each," David confided to Duncan.

"What for?" Duncan asked.

"She said Harper's was payment so she'd treat me better. And that mine was so I'd stop wearing women's clothes."

"She knows about it?"

"Doesn't everyone?"

❦

Late the next afternoon, David and Hester were relaxing over a beer in the back room of the gallery, after deciding to close early. From the window they saw the sky suddenly turn green before unleashing a brief but tremendous downpour.

"Wow, that was strange," David remarked.

"According to Lisa, Manolo might have something to do with this freakish weather," Hester offered.

"What—he's magic or something?" David looked at her skeptically.

"Well, yeah, supposedly."

"Jesus!"

"You know, Lisa doesn't kid around with that shamanic stuff. She's pretty serious," Hester observed.

"What has she told you?" David asked.

"Manolo is going to . . . cast a spell on you so I'll finally get to curate the solo show of Richard Kern photos I've been angling for."

"Ha, ha! What do you like so much about his work?"

"It speaks to me."

"What does it say?"

"I love you."

"Really? Pretty girls jumping up and down? Who would've guessed? Well, where are Lisa and Manolo now, anyway?"

"He's gone to the dog races in New Jersey."

CHAPTER FOURTEEN

David was in his study reading the current issue of *Artforum* when the phone rang.

"David, it's Lisa."

"Hi, honey. Are you looking for Harper?"

"No. Are you alone?"

"Yeah . . . You're not going to ask me what I'm wearing, are you?"

"Can you meet me at the King Cole Bar in the St. Regis in thirty minutes?"

"Are you kidding? What's this all about?"

"Listen, I've got a situation, and I need to see you right away—you're the only person I can speak to about this."

David hesitated before responding. "Okay, I'll be there," he said.

"You're a good friend, David," she said and hung up.

How weird! He'd never known Lisa to be a drama queen. It had to be something really important, he thought. He hailed a cab and in minutes was sitting across from her at a small table far from the bar.

After they exchanged pleasantries and ordered drinks, she launched into an explanation. Oona had called earlier in the evening. She had just seen Harper and Thomas leaving the Mark Hotel together. They were all over each other. Thomas had told Lisa he had to work late. It wasn't adding up. Or was it? The blood drained from David's face. He wanly recounted that Harper had told him she was having a girls' night out. Lisa nodded.

"David, we've got to kill them both," she announced.

"Lisa, that's something Harper would say," David said calmly.

"Shit, you're right. I'm going nuts here."

After another round of drinks, they discussed possible courses of action, until suddenly a plan came to Lisa, which she then laid out: She and David would simply go about their business and not let on for a couple of days. In the meantime, Lisa would extend an invitation to David and Harper to join Thomas and her at their place for drinks a couple of nights later. Then she and David would confront the unsuspecting culprits. They would play the rest by ear.

~

Over an egg cream at Veselka, Manolo reflected on his day. It had begun with a walk at dawn down Broadway, past Trinity Church and through the deserted Financial District to South Ferry. From the deck of the Staten Island Ferry, he had marveled at the scale of the Statue of Liberty. Later, he visited Fraunces Tavern, where the display of Revolutionary War–era antiques caught his attention. Lisa had given him a list of important sites and shared her impressions, and he was eager to return to her apartment to compare notes.

Venturing around town, Manolo was unusually alert, as if all his senses were heightened, the way he felt along the Upper Orinoco when he explored an unknown savanna or tributary for the first time. He chuckled to himself as he recalled how that morning he saw a tall, striking blonde woman on the ferry and imagined abducting her and taking her back to his *shabono*. He closed his eyes and pictured what their life together would be like.

~

Harper and David arrived at Lisa and Thomas's loft for after-work cocktails. Lisa hugged David tightly and ostentatiously gave Harper the cold shoulder. Thomas fixed everyone drinks, and they sat together in the living room.

"Sweetheart," Lisa turned to Thomas.

"Yes, dear."

"David and I want to know how long this has been going on between you and Harper." Lisa flashed her biggest and brightest smile.

Harper and Thomas each eyed the other, looking for a clue as to how to respond. Their faces were ashen.

"Don't be coy," Lisa insisted. "Let it all hang out. It'll do you worlds of good. Don't even think about denying it. *How long?*"

Thomas did his best to maintain some composure. "Uh . . . um . . . not long—"

"Two years," Harper blurted out.

"Oh my God!" Lisa gasped.

Thomas's jaw dropped, and he shot Harper a horrified look.

Lisa pulled a Luger out of her handbag.

"Is that a Luger? Amazing. Where did you find it?" Thomas asked.

"eBay. Now up against the wall, motherfuckers!" she shouted, waving the gun around.

"Give me the gun, Lisa," David instructed.

"Oh . . . sorry." Meekly, Lisa handed the pistol to David.

"You know, you're really very bad," Lisa chided Harper. "Why did you do this?"

"I don't know," Harper shook her head. "It seemed like . . ."

"Like something fun to do?" David cracked.

Thomas turned to Lisa. "You'll see, darling, it'll all work out," he offered cheerfully.

At that, Lisa shrieked and, leaping on Thomas, began to choke him. Harper stood by trembling. After letting her have at him for a minute, David peeled Lisa off and got scratched on the face for his trouble. Thomas staggered away, flushed and gasping.

"At least let me kill this one!" Lisa glared at Harper.

~

The following Sunday afternoon, Lisa and Manolo were having brunch at Savoy in SoHo. She found it remarkable how quickly he had adapted to city life and been able to make his way around on his own.

Thomas had moved out of their apartment. Lisa had told Manolo everything, and that had drawn them closer. Their relationship had become a valued one for her. Almost overnight, each had come to rely on the other for moral support—she because her foundation had recently been shaken, and he because his new environs had caused him to question who he was and what made him tick.

After checking to make sure their waiter was nowhere in sight, Manolo surreptitiously offered Lisa a potion in a small bottle. He assured her that it would ease her nerves.

"I'm already on Paxil," she replied.

"Throw that crap away. This is much better."

"Will this turn me into a pigeon?"

They both howled with laughter, until tears rolled down their cheeks.

"For a while I thought you were just treating me as a study subject," Manolo said. "I'm glad you can confide in me."

"You know, we have psychiatrists here, if you'd like professional help."

"Oh, please!"

~

Despite his disappointment, David was unwilling to give up on Harper. In the days that followed the ugly scene in the loft, he let Harper know that he could find it in himself to forgive her if she would make a clean break with Thomas. Then they would try again. It was difficult, but, surprisingly enough, they began to muddle through.

Lisa, however, was of a different mind about Thomas. She wanted nothing further to do with him, and after that week, they never saw each other again.

CHAPTER FIFTEEN

David was philosophical about Harper's affair. He was able to put it behind him and move on. Increasingly, Harper looked on David as her Rock of Gibraltar. Two weeks after the unfortunate confrontation, he had brokered an uneasy truce between Harper and Lisa. Now the two old friends were smoking the peace pipe. One night, the three of them were having dinner at David and Harper's town house.

"Thank God I didn't kill you. I'm not even mad at you," Lisa sighed.

"How can you not be?" Harper asked, in disbelief.

"Because I'm a saint."

"No, you're not," Harper laughed.

"Of course I'm not. In fact, I'm really sorry I didn't kill Thomas."

"Why don't you move in with us?" Harper suggested.

"Well, I'm thinking of returning with Manolo to the village," Lisa replied.

David and Harper looked at each other quizzically.

"Listen," Lisa continued, "will you come to a poetry reading with me tomorrow night? My cousin Stephen is reading at the Poetry Society of America. I know he's a pain in the ass, but come. For my sake. I don't want to be sitting there alone."

"Stephen is a major creep," David smiled.

"Indulge me," Lisa pleaded. "I guess I'll bring Manolo along."

"How will he understand the poems?" Harper asked.

"He'll get Stephen's vibe," Lisa said. "It's easy for him to read people by their body language and tone. He understands a little English—he just doesn't like to speak it."

"We'll go, darling," Harper reassured her.

~

In his studio, Duncan was gazing thoughtfully at Hester, who was posing on a chaise longue in a Roman toga. He was working on a study in pastels.

"Are you going to capture the *real* me? Or just me?" Hester asked.

"Oh, yeah . . . absolutely . . . that's what I do," Duncan said absently.

"Which one?"

He didn't answer.

"Say, what happened with Lisa and Thomas?" Hester asked. "It sounds like all hell broke loose."

"Yep. I hear it wasn't pretty."

"What's Thomas up to now?"

Duncan shrugged. "He moved out of the loft. We're not really in touch. He's become a bit radioactive." He shot her a pointed look.

"Where's his new place?"

"Latvia."

They both chuckled.

"Adultery is such an interesting life theme," Hester observed.

"It certainly is. By the way, don't forget we've promised Lisa we'll go to Stephen's reading tonight."

"Who's Stephen again?"

"Lisa's cousin."

"*Must* we?"

"For Lisa."

"Okay," Hester said. "For Lisa."

∾

At the Poetry Society of America, before his reading, Stephen was holding court with a few friends and admirers. The society was located in a historic town house on Gramercy Park South.

When Lisa and Manolo arrived, Harper caught sight of them and waved. "We're over here—I saved a couple of seats," she called.

David, Hester, Duncan, Oona and Wendy were seated in the row behind Harper. They all exchanged greetings with Lisa and gave Manolo a warm welcome. A capacity crowd, composed of a mix of Stephen's friends and poetry devotees, filled the intimate performance space.

"What's happening?" Lisa asked.

"We're going to kill Stephen," Harper whispered.

"We'll finish what we started on the yacht," David chimed in.

"Is it true Stephen is your cousin?" Wendy asked.

"Second cousin," Lisa said.

"Hmmm." Wendy smiled. "Will you introduce me to him afterward?"

"Mo-ther," Harper grimaced. "I know what you're thinking."

John Ashbery, who had curated the reading, approached the lectern to introduce the poet. There was a palpable excitement in the room when Ashbery appeared. He read a list of Stephen's publications and accomplishments, and stated how pleased he was to introduce Stephen's work, which he regarded as a well-kept secret. Then he continued, smiling wryly.

"Stephen sends his lyrics into outer space through liquid air. His poems offer seriocomic cartoon likenesses of fragments falling by parachute. He assists police investigators by taking precise measurements of nimbostratus cirrus. Meanwhile, ants get bigger and wear pants and skirts. We are all citizens of the nation of poetry, and Stephen is our president."

Ashbery turned to Stephen, seated in the front row, motioning him to the lectern.

"Mr. President . . ."

There was applause as Stephen thanked John and stood behind the lectern wearing a purple paisley shirt. He tested the mic to make sure everyone could hear him. After informing the audience that the first poem was called "Anatomy of Melancholy," Stephen explained the feelings he was trying to evoke in the piece and apologized for the mournful subject matter. Then he began.

> O my beloved,
> Why were you so sad on the porch?
> As before a languid summer afternoon's rain
> One hears the leaves whispering
> And notices each small dip in the barometric pressure,
> So it was then.
>
> Remember the night we got lost
> And how, when we turned around,
> Uncertain we were going in the right direction,
> Our headlights flashed on a red fox
> Alone in the moonlight—
> A beautiful, ghostly presence?
> The fox held us in its gaze for a single moment,
> As if wondering what the future might hold
> In store for the two of us
> In the years to come,
> Before darting off the highway
> Into a deep, dark thicket.

We remember brightly colored summer lanterns

Strung between Adirondack pines

And a nest of starlings murmuring overhead.

The lake glitters,

The lakefront disappears into memory.

A fading landscape,

And always the mournful high notes

Of a piano in the distance.

As the reading continued, the audience rolled their eyes, snickered or dozed—all except Wendy, who was attentive throughout. The reading ended to halfhearted applause. Stephen seemed inured to the mild response. A wine and cheese reception followed.

Lisa introduced Manolo to John Ashbery, who burst into fluent Yanomamö.

"One of my classmates from Deerfield Academy was from the Amazon Basin. He taught it to me," Ashbery revealed to an astonished Lisa and Manolo.

They were interrupted by Stephen. "What's everyone doing now?" he asked. "I have a key to Gramercy Park. Why don't we take the reception outside and have a stroll?" After a few minutes of successful cajoling by Stephen, who was now tipsy and swigging wine from a bottle, a contingent that included Lisa and her group, John Ashbery and a few of Stephen's friends poured out of the building and across the street. There were pink and white blossoms on the ground and flowering crabapple and cherry trees in bloom in the park, but there didn't seem to be much to do. Lisa was so amused by the unlikely spectacle of the nighttime walk that she momentarily felt her cares slipping away.

"This is the boringest park I ever saw," Harper complained in kindergarten-speak.

"I couldn't agree with her more," Manolo confided to Lisa.

Stephen had disappeared, seemingly in mid-stride. A pigeon strutted beneath the statue of Edwin Booth. Only Lisa understood what had happened.

"Where did Stephen go?" Ashbery asked.

"Oh, he's around here . . . somewhere," Lisa said. She pulled Manolo aside. "Why did you do turn him into a pigeon?"

"Well, he's a terrible poet, isn't he?" Manolo grinned.

~

"You'll never guess who David and I ran into last night at the Le Tigre show at Irving Plaza!" Harper gushed to Lisa.

She, David and Wendy were having coffee with Lisa at her loft.

"Hmmm . . . John Ashbery? I don't know," Lisa said.

Harper paused for dramatic effect. "Jessica."

"You're kidding!" Lisa exclaimed.

"I'm not. Physically, she hasn't changed a bit. Except the spiky hair is gone."

"What's she doing now?" Lisa asked.

"She's an investment banker," Harper said.

"I don't believe it," Lisa said.

"Plus, she's married," David added gleefully.

"Huh . . . wow . . . that's a lot of information to absorb," Lisa reflected.

"I know!" Harper said. "But don't forget, she went to Groton and is from a family of Wall Street types, after all."

"So, she's no longer a hard-core punker dyke?" Lisa asked. "Then what was she doing at a Le Tigre concert?"

"Old habits die hard," David quipped.

"Did she try to cop a feel?" Lisa asked Harper. "You know, for old time's sake? Jessica always had a thing for Harper," Lisa explained to Wendy.

Harper smiled knowingly.

"Really?" Wendy asked. "I had no idea."

"So, how is Manolo?" David asked Lisa.

"Okay," Lisa said. "He has this weird attitude about the theater. We went to see this off-Broadway play. He told me he felt sorry for the actors. He knew they were following a script, but he was afraid that something bad was in store for them, maybe even involving their being sacrificed to the audience."

"The poor dear!" Wendy said.

"So, what's this business about returning to the Amazon? You can't be serious," Harper said.

"Perfectly serious," Lisa replied.

"But I need you, darling," Harper implored.

"You must stay," Wendy added. "Goodness, what will we do without you? I'm devastated by this news."

David listened solemnly.

"After the thing with Thomas, I need another location to calm myself down and absorb it all," Lisa said. "Don't forget, I still love all of you. But the desire to kill Thomas is still very much with me. I just hope he's hidden himself as far away as possible."

"Forgive me. I'm being selfish. I guess I'm trying to assuage my guilt," Harper said.

"Where is Manolo now?" David asked.

"I don't know," Lisa said.

~

Anxiously, Manolo paced the deserted ramparts of Belvedere Castle, surveying the Great Lawn. He had felt compelled to return to Central Park to commune with spirits from the other world once again before going home. The branches of elm trees swayed in the breeze.

He called out to the stones and trees: "How should I live?"

"You belong to the village," the stones answered.

"Yes, the village," the trees echoed. "It is true that you are at ease in the forest. But you are not *of* the forest."

"Are you sure?" Manolo asked.

"You doubt us?" the stones and trees intoned.

"Of course not. My bad."

The stones told him what had occurred in the village while he was gone. Things had deteriorated. There was dissension among the people. Too many chiefs and no Indians. He must return at once and restore order.

Manolo thanked the stones and trees, and assuming a determined expression, he left the park.

CHAPTER SIXTEEN

David was singing along with a Carmen Miranda CD in his living room. A phone call interrupted him.

"David, old boy, how's it going?" Duncan asked.

"Hi, Dunc. I'm just enjoying some R and R without the missus. Harper and Hester went out to dinner."

"Say, did you hear about Thomas?"

"No." David was intrigued.

"He's gone into exile!" Duncan said excitedly. "Seems he's taken a mental health leave or something from work. And he's left New York."

"Maybe he's following Lisa to the Amazon to try to make amends," David deadpanned.

"You never know. I can picture him there now, in a pith helmet, sherpa—or whatever the correct term is—in tow, hiding behind a bush with a bouquet of orchids. Lisa *does* love flowers."

"Sherpa?"

"What do you think?"

"I think . . . one dart dipped in curare, and that's all she wrote for Thomas! I hear Lisa is handy with a blowgun."

"No doubt . . . Say, what's that music?" Duncan asked.

"Carmen Miranda."

"Hmmm . . . Not bad."

"Well, I can't say I'm sorry to see him go, to be honest."

"Could be the situation hit him harder than we realized," Duncan reflected. "He's human, after all . . . Listen, I'm about to run out the door—I'm meeting Oona."

They said good-bye, and David turned the volume on the stereo up. He stopped in front of the mirror above the mantelpiece to adjust the towel he was wearing as a turban and admire his flaming red lipstick. Then Carmen Miranda's "South American Way" filled the room, and, exhilarated by the song's images of shameless behavior in tropical climes, he joined in, doing an exuberant cha-cha.

~

Outside the village, Lisa and Manolo sat on a rocky promontory that overlooked the Mavaca River valley to the south and the distant peaks of the Sierra Parima to the east. It had been nearly a week since the two of them had returned to the Amazon. With a twinkle in his eye, Manolo offered to double back to New York to launch a raid on Thomas's "village" and take care of him. He made a great show of suddenly getting to his feet with a purposeful look, dusting off his rear end and otherwise preparing for an imminent departure.

"Oh, would you?"

"Should I turn him into a pigeon or have him drawn and quartered?" Manolo asked. "How would you like him? Drawn and quartered or in little pieces?"

"Little pieces, please," Lisa smiled.

He chuckled as he ended his little performance by sitting down again. The conversation turned to Lisa's seemingly precipitous decision to return to the village. He had the impression that her stay with them might be indefinite.

"Any regrets?" Manolo asked with concern.

"No regrets . . ." she sighed.

Manolo thought she looked sad. He put a hand on her shoulder to comfort her. They gazed in silence at the magnificent panorama before them. It was a solemn moment.

Thomas's betrayal had been a brutal blow to her self-esteem. Lisa found it difficult to comprehend that her old life with Thomas had disappeared in an instant. They had been together for nearly five years and married for three.

Though her field research was now complete, Lisa was in no shape to turn out a publishable article. She needed to regroup. Fortunately, the change of scene since she'd returned to the Amazon was having the desired effect. After a few days, the pain had begun to diminish. And there was another reason that Lisa was drawn back to the village: her feelings for Padre Higgins. She had not ventured to the mission since her return. But she planned to do so as soon as she felt up to it.

Esteban was considerate, funny, handsome, wise, and (he had once confided) a talented amateur flamenco dancer. They had developed a strong affection for each other. And . . . and what else? There had been moments when she had sensed some electricity between them. Or was it all in her head? Maybe she'd go elsewhere—Buenos Aires, São Paulo, Quito. She hadn't made up her mind.

Manolo had not pressed her about her intentions, nor had he offered any advice. Instead, he had decided to give her "her space," correctly intuiting that she needed time to find her way.

～

"If you have a romantic nature, the more noble her soul, the more supernal and free from the mire of all vulgar considerations will be the pleasures you find in her arms."

"Stop paraphrasing Stendhal!" Thomas chided.

"I'm quoting, not paraphrasing," Jay grinned. "Look, here's a chance to study your own case."

It was a Saturday afternoon at Nye's on Hennepin Avenue in Minneapolis, where Jay Byrd tended bar. Thomas and Jay had gone to high school together. Thomas had taken a six-month leave of absence from work and moved in with his parents. His father was a classics professor at the University of Minnesota.

"Isn't life wonderful?" Thomas moaned.

"You're drunk."

"Am not."

"Oh, my mistake."

"You know, there's a rumor going around New York that I've moved to Latvia."

"I wonder how that got started?"

"The grapevine," Thomas said dolefully.

"Those grapes will soon be raisins."

"You mean everybody will forget about me?"

"Well, it may be a sign . . ."

"Sign of what?"

"A prompt for you to do the right thing," Jay said.

"Which would be . . . ?"

"Move to Latvia!"

"And return a few years later—older, wiser, chastened, slightly the worse for wear?"

"Something like that. You can sell the Latvian rights to *The Death Machine* while you're there. Say, you remember Marianne Thatcher?" Jay asked.

"Of course."

"Someone hit her in the face with a shovel. Brain hemorrhage."

"What hospital is she in?"

"Cut it out. You're not going to visit her."

"I guess not . . ."

"Besides, that was a year ago."

"How does she look?"

"Askew."

"How sad."

"And you heard about Winters?"

"Yeah, awful."

"He's never getting out."

"No, never."

"So, how about it, pal?" Jay leaned over the bar. "What really happened?"

"Thought you'd never ask . . . Harper liked to talk about what our life together would be like . . . She . . ." Thomas didn't finish his thought and turned his head away.

"Wait a minute, are those tears? Are you crying?"

"No," Thomas protested weakly, his voice cracking.

"You *are* crying! No crying in my bar!" Jay laughed.

"It's not funny," Thomas insisted, with teary eyes.

"Oh, yes it is. Someone get this man a box of Kleenex!"

Thomas laughed through his tears, despite himself.

"I'm getting all choked up myself," Jay added.

"I treated Lisa so shabbily. Why did I do that? And David is a wonderful guy. I completely betrayed his trust. And I screwed things up with Harper."

"You and *I* would make a better match than either you and Lisa *or* you and Harper."

"Maybe so. I failed miserably . . . but, you know, deep in my heart, I still want them both."

"It's a little late for that."

"I know," Thomas said ruefully, and took a sip of beer. "What does Ortega y Gasset have to say on the subject?"

"That poor slob?"

"I've never read him."

"Well, let me tell you," Jay said. He rested his arms on the bar. "He says that 'love affairs' are more or less accidental episodes that happen between men and women. That innumerable factors enter into them which complicate and entangle their development to such an extent that, by and large, in most love affairs there is a little of everything except that which, strictly speaking, deserves to be called love."

"Quoting again," Thomas frowned. "Do you suffer from total recall or something?"

∽

As Lisa rounded a bend in the river, the whitewashed mission came into view in the clearing that had been cut from the rain forest. Cumulus clouds dotted the sky. She was struck by the beauty of the remote jungle scene. All her worries seemed to have vanished. Nearing the shore, she experienced a shiver of nervous anticipation.

At the kayak's approach, Billy squawked, hopping up and down with delight by the water's edge. Upon hearing Billy, Padre Higgins left the house, letting the screen door slam shut, and hurried down to the landing.

Lisa smiled at him from under the brim of her floppy hat.

"I've been waiting all my life for you," he smiled back.

"All our life for you," Billy cooed.

ON MY WAY TO SEE YOU

CHAPTER ONE

Ben Berkowitz sat, naked except for his T-shirt, on the operating table in a small outpatient surgery center. After administering local anesthesia by injection, Dr. Roberts told him they would wait a few minutes for the anesthetic to take effect before beginning the procedure.

"It's nothing personal, but I have to confess I'm feeling a little apprehensive about this. Are there many women urologists?"

"Half the women in my graduating class became urologists. Relax. I've performed thousands of these things and haven't lost a penis yet."

"Shouldn't you be reminding me about the risks of the procedure—that kind of thing? I think I may be having second thoughts."

"Well, as we discussed in the initial consultation, the risks include infection, which could result in the loss of one or both testicles. But that's very rare. We will give you antibiotics, so it shouldn't be an issue. And a small percentage of patients experience reduced sexual desire. That's very unusual too."

"That's right, I forgot about the testicles," he sighed. "I must've blocked it out."

"Also, it's possible the procedure may not take. I'll be back in a few minutes. Hang loose."

When she returned, she prodded Ben's scrotum with the tip of a scalpel. "Did you feel that?"

"No."

"Terrific. We're ready to roll. What kind of music do you prefer?"

"Do you have Zerbinetta's aria, 'Grossmächtige Prinzessen,' from Strauss's *Ariadne auf Naxos*—particularly the 1938 recording with Erna Berger?"

"Oh, God, yes! What intervals! Fastidiously embroidered! Clemens Krauss was at the podium. That'll take your mind off what I'll be doing down there."

"What about you?" Ben shot her an anxious look.

"I won't be listening."

After fitting Ben with Bose earphones, Dr. Roberts snapped on her surgical gloves and nonchalantly went to work, making an incision in the scrotum, through which she could cut and then tie off the tubes.

"You know," Ben said, "when my wife asked me to get a vasectomy, I had to think about it. I went back and forth, before finally making peace with it. Richard Gere's wife asked him to do it, and he said no! He told her that if she and the kids all went down in a plane, he might want to go out and start a new family."

They both laughed.

"It used to be different," Dr. Roberts said. "It's funny, when I first started it was standard practice to have the wife come into the office with the husband for the initial consultation, to make sure everyone was on board with the decision. I actually had one patient whose wife insisted on 'supervising' the procedure. We tried to keep her out, but she poked her head in about halfway through the surgery to make sure I had really cut the tubes!"

"So, how's it going?" Ben asked nervously.

"Fine. How's Zerbinetta doing?"

"Sublime. But now it's too late to start a second family with Erna Berger."

"Remember, you'll have to have at least one million ejaculations, just to give you a ballpark figure, before we'll know for sure that the sterilization was a success. You'll need to bring me samples in a plastic container at least twice a day for us to have tested."

"Okay. How soon can I . . ."

Dr. Roberts looked at him pointedly. "No bike riding, dirt-bike racing, mixed martial arts, soccer, dressage, none of that shit—nothing that will be rough on your balls or bang them up—for a while. They're bruised from the surgery, which is completely normal. I'm going to give you a Percocet prescription. You're going to experience some pain for a few days." She made a grotesque face in mock agony.

"Oh, boy," Ben murmured.

The door opened, and an elderly gentleman peered in. "I wished—"

"Get out, you pig!" Dr. Roberts shouted. The man quickly withdrew.

Ben's eyes bulged. "Wait a minute—wasn't that Clemens Krauss?"

"A nuisance."

"He's still alive?"

"Don't be silly."

There was a knock at the door.

"Diane, get that, will you?" Ben said.

Diane went to the door. "It's Diane," she said.

"Tell her to wait," Ben barked.

"I'm leaving now," the doctor said to Ben. "No baths, though you can shower normally beginning tonight. But no water ballet."

"Why no water ballet?"

"I despise water ballet."

"Thank you, Dr. Roberts, and thanks for the vasectomy!"

"Take care of those sutures."

"Will do, doc."

"Will do what? Were you dreaming?" Diane asked Ben, who was lying in bed.

"No."

"You were dreaming," she said. "Who's Doc?"

"It was Julia Roberts. Should I get a vasectomy?"

"Of course."

"I have to get to work. Should I go to work?"

"If you feel like it."

CHAPTER TWO

Ben looked on those closest to him—father, mother, sister, brother, wife, girlfriend, kids, friends—as bit players, supporting actors of one kind or another or, at least, special guests appearing for an occasional cameo before being consigned to the cosmos, so that he, the star of his own personal after-school special or movie of the week, might shine all the brighter. While it wasn't true that he never thought about anyone but himself, it was fair to say he found it difficult to empathize with others and see beyond his own interests, needs and desires. Ben was a novelist. He liked antiquing, browsing in used bookstores, shopping for vintage prints, trolling art galleries and art fairs, deep-sea fishing, beachcombing, gardening, ultimate Frisbee, mountain biking, hiking, camping, squash, Telemark skiing and snowshoeing. His favorite drink was a gin fizz. His guilty pleasure was taking nude photos of his girlfriends with his medium-format Mamiya and, late at night in the privacy of his study, poring over the album of them that he had compiled over a twenty-five-year period, which he kept locked in a cabinet. Ben's phobias included snakes, spiders, the number thirteen, confined spaces, heights, the sight of blood, hospitals, slime, the color purple, in-laws, loud noises, eels, religious ceremonies, French furniture and

harpsichords. Each evening, after dinner, he enjoyed a shot of
Macallan or Glenmorangie. Once in bed, he read for an hour, typi-
cally something by Ivy Compton-Burnett, Ronald Firbank, P. G.
Wodehouse, Evelyn Waugh, Henry Green, Fielding Dawson, Horace
McCoy, David Goodis, Cornell Woolrich, Edgar Rice Burroughs,
Kawabata, Chikamatsu, Saikaku, Sir Thomas Malory, H. Rider
Haggard, Errol Flynn, Oscar Levant or Harry Mathews. On
Wednesday and Saturday nights, like clockwork, after the kids were
in bed, he and his wife, Tina, locked the bedroom door, took off
their clothes, turned out the lights and had sex. Ben and his girlfriend, Diane, frequently got together for lovemaking sessions in her
apartment, hotels or spas on Monday and Friday afternoons. Ben
was volatile, subject to occasional black moods that dissipated as
quickly as they came on. He would often exhibit a jumble of charm,
intensity, self-possession, fun, charisma, hypersensitivity, alertness
and impetuousness. Finding no need to choose between Tina and
Diane, he felt he was in the fabled circumstance of having his cake
and eating it too. His favorite rock bands were Stereolab, Air and
Animal Collective, but his tastes also ran to the Small Faces, Big Star,
Nico, Echo and the Bunnymen, the Teardrop Explodes, Young
Marble Giants, Gang of Four, Buzzcocks, New Order, Teenage
Fanclub, the Smiths, Guided by Voices, the Bongos, the Lyres, the
Fleshtones, Hüsker Dü, the dB's, Let's Active, Pylon, Southern
Culture on the Skids, Violent Femmes, Broken Social Scene, Sonic
Youth, Yo La Tengo, Dum Dum Girls, Vivian Girls, Grizzly Bear
and Sleater-Kinney. When Ben woke each morning, he assiduously
wrote down his dreams in a dream journal he kept on his nightstand.
After a cup of coffee, he read "Page Six" of the *New York Post,* the
National Enquirer or the *Star*. Tall and rangy, in his late forties, he
was darkly handsome with soulful brown eyes. Since his college days
he had worn his brown hair in a mod haircut reminiscent of Ronnie
Lane's of the Small Faces, circa 1969. Ben's friend Michael Kropotkin

was also a fiction writer. Their bond was formed as MFA students at Brown twenty years earlier, in 1989, and was based on a shared appreciation of each other's work. The two had met on the first day of classes. They enjoyed shopping for housewares and clothes in boutiques, attending rock shows and frequenting strip clubs together and were known among their circle for bickering like an old married couple. Ben's bête noire was Jewish mothers: He could only tolerate them (including his own) in moderation. His favorite childhood toy was a frontier fort with cavalry and Indians. Ben's daytime "uniform" consisted of a T-shirt, jeans with the cuffs turned up and black motorcycle boots with a single buckle. His typical day consisted of taking the kids to school in the morning before settling into a spate of writing in his Williamsburg loft. In the afternoons, depending on the day of the week, he would head to the gym to work out, teach a writing workshop, get together with Diane or have coffee with friends in the neighborhood. His first serious love, April, had been a fellow MFA student. Once, on a summer weekend in Sagaponack in a convertible with another couple, the guys in the front and girls in the back, April, assuming Ben couldn't hear her, breathlessly held forth with a brazen account of all the guys with whom she had been cheating on Ben. Ben heard every word, and the relationship did not make it through the weekend. He was a whiz at Risk, backgammon, Parcheesi, Scrabble, chess, checkers and Chinese checkers. There was an incident during a class field trip to a Broadway show that he had never forgotten: He had almost choked to death on a pretzel. Another boy had dislodged it with a well-timed punch to the solar plexus. His childhood best friend was Tim, who lived in a penthouse apartment on Central Park West with several marmalade cats. Tim's mother, Anita—a glamorous redhead—was a well-known Broadway stage actress and TV personality, who had left a lasting impression. Ben had a fond memory of the Friday night he was invited along with Tim, Anita and Anita's boyfriend, Walter, to attend a Margaret

Rutherford double feature at an Upper West Side art house: *Murder Most Foul* and *Murder at the Gallop*. Anita, dressed in a lavender jumpsuit, had sat in Walter's lap the whole time making out with him. Ben was generally in good health, though he suffered from a mild, if chronic, eye infection, which caused his eyes to burn and itch and required frequent eye drops. He also had occasional pain in his lower back. Ben had traveled extensively in Venezuela, Chile, Argentina, Brazil, Peru, Honduras, Panama, Belize, Germany, Russia, France, Ireland, Scotland and the Hebrides, England and the Channel Islands, Portugal, Greece, including Santorini and Mykonos, Germany, Spain—especially Ibiza, Minorca and Majorca—Austria, Italy, Hungary, Finland, Denmark, Sweden, the Faroe Islands, Iceland, Nova Scotia, Thailand, Vietnam, China, Korea, Japan, Senegal, the Canary Islands and Morocco. He had never been to Turkey. On weekends, he took long solitary walks over the covered bridge and along the Housatonic River in West Cornwall, Connecticut, thinking about his latest writing project. Often, when he was with his family, his thoughts would turn to Diane. Did he reflect on whether he was stringing Diane along? Not really. And Tina was cool with the situation. He just liked to think about Diane and imagine what *she* was thinking. But, quickly, he might shift his thoughts to summer pudding with Chantilly cream, his favorite dessert. His dark secret was that, despite his confident air, he was plagued by self-doubt and feelings of inadequacy. He was inordinately proud of his boys, Henry, eight, and Joe, six, and derived endless enjoyment from their antics and wisecracks. Still, he had mixed feelings about the hard work of parenting and its demands on his time. He thought that, in a perfect world, an English governess or nanny would raise the kids, and he would see them once a day, perhaps after dinner, when they would be trotted out in their finery for a little dog and pony show. His favorite shape was the rhomboid. Ben had grown up in Manhattan and London with his older brother,

Fitz, and younger sister, Heather. Their parents were career academics. A teaching gig in NYU's MFA program allowed him plenty of free time. He taught two workshops each week. He had also taught at the New School for a number of years, before two favorably reviewed novels brought out by a mainstream publisher established him as an offbeat, quirky novelist with a cult following and led to his being offered the NYU job through a friend on the faculty. His work was witty, deadpan and surprising. Its flatness and an absence of figurative language lent it an unstudied, nonchalant veneer. He had carved out an interesting niche writing faux novelizations of the lives of Hollywood stars in which he gave his characters complex psyches that belied their cartoonish existence. Ben's prized possessions were a Victorian carriage clock, a Leica M4, a Trevor Winkfield collage, an art deco flask from the Portobello Road, a collection of Tom Swift novels, a signed first edition of *Now I Lay Me Down to Sleep* by Ludwig Bemelmans, an Omega Seamaster that had been his father's, a polo shirt from Rome and a Stiga table-tennis paddle. After Diane and Ben had been introduced at a party by a mutual friend, they left together and went back to her place. Diane made it abundantly clear early on in their relationship that she had no interest in marriage, kids or giving up other men and women. Three years later, Tina and Ben met in one of Ben's fiction writing workshops, and that was pretty much that. A whirlwind courtship in the library stacks was soon followed by a honeymoon with Tina on the Italian Riviera. Ben's favorite color was lime green. While he was, in fact, a creature of habit who found comfort in routine, in many respects he appeared, to the outside world, an unpredictable, sometimes eccentric character. When Ben first started seeing Tina, did Diane feel as if Ben had been stolen right out from under her, as others in her position might have? Not at all. For her part, she had other lovers of her own to occupy her. Ben and Tina were in love, though Ben was also crazy about Diane. Tina was liberal and allowed, even encouraged,

Ben to continue his relationship with Diane, as long as it didn't interfere with family plans. So Ben continued to see Diane, with Tina's blessing. The marriage went swimmingly. Tina and Diane were friendly but not close. They found each other appealing, but were also wary of one another and kept their distance: They knew the score, and, although there was no manual or etiquette book they could consult for guidance in these matters, they viewed themselves as rivals and rightly sensed that it would be a mistake for them to get to know each other too well. At a late-night loft party they once shared a single kiss after several glasses of wine, but that was the extent of it. Every so often, Ben would wake up at home lightheaded and disoriented, thinking he was with Diane. On one occasion, when they were in bed, he playfully teased Tina about her kiss with Diane and tried to draw her out about how she liked it.

"I know what you're thinking," Tina said.

"What am I thinking?" Ben asked.

"It's not gonna happen."

"What's not gonna happen?"

"What you're thinking."

"Well, it never hurts to ask . . . or think."

CHAPTER THREE

Ben was lying flat on his back in Diane's bed, his eyes closed, trying to catch his breath. Diane was sitting up, drinking a beer, looking out the window. She had pushed Ben onto the bed, quickly stripped him and had her way with him.

Diane lived in a floor-through apartment in Cobble Hill. She was imperturbable, worldly, self-assured, stylish, adventurous and spontaneous. She could, occasionally, become elusive and mercurial. Generally, she and Ben couldn't keep their hands off each other. A graduate of RISD, she was a talented graphic designer with a good eye and a flourishing freelance business.

After a while they dressed, and went into the living room.

"Read this." A poker-faced Diane held out a piece of paper to Ben.

"Read what?"

"This letter. It's about Devin Curtis. It came in today's mail."

"Why would *you* get a letter? *I'm* his friend."

"I don't know. Read it."

He stared at the letter.

Devin Curtis is dead in Paris. His body was discovered on June 20th by the concierge. His door was wide open. His body was sprawled on the carpet. Yesterday he was enjoying life in the city, roaming the Luxembourg Gardens, the Tuileries, the Place des Vosges, the Île Saint-Louis. Today he is dead in his Marais apartment, where he spent most afternoons writing, conjuring up the ghosts of Rimbaud and Verlaine. In the weeks leading up to his death, he had been going to Père Lachaise Cemetery to do stone rubbings with pastels. This morning Paris is less alive without him, certainly more lonely.

The typewritten letter was undated and unsigned. The envelope was postmarked June 28. There was no return address.

"Stone rubbings with pastels? That doesn't sound like the Devin I know," Ben said.

"People change."

"Not like that."

"Maybe you didn't know him as well as you thought."

"Stop it with the past tense!" Ben snapped.

"Do you think it's a hoax?" Diane asked.

"I don't know."

"Maybe he was leading a double life."

"A secret life in which he was a doctor or a lawyer, married with several kids?"

"Something like that."

"I don't *think* so."

≈

Ben and Devin had met through a mutual friend in New York in 1981 at a reading at the Ear Inn on Spring Street, when Devin was editing his journal, *Captain Nero*, and Ben was an undergrad at Columbia. They were both poets then. Devin was living in LA, and the two began corresponding. A charismatic group of LA poets that included Bob Flanagan revolved around Devin. At the time, he was the artistic director of Beyond Baroque, the literary center in Venice. The following year Ben invited Devin to perform in his reading series at Columbia. Soon Devin moved to the East Village. He was an inspiration to Ben; he had impeccable taste. It wasn't until years later that Ben realized Devin's casual, almost offhand recommendations as to which poets to read and which ones to seek out had had a profound influence on the direction both his writing and his life eventually took.

≈

Ben approached Devin's building in the Marais, a four-story, nineteenth-century limestone apartment house with a mansard roof and an inner courtyard. A week had passed since Diane had shown him the mysterious letter. He introduced himself to the concierge, who spoke fluent English. He mentioned the letter he'd received and asked the concierge what he could tell him about Devin. The man seemed puzzled by Ben's concern and assured him that Mr. Curtis was fine.

"Monsieur Curtis is away, and expected back . . ." he said absently.

"May I see the apartment?" Ben asked.

"Yes, but someone is there now."

They walked up four flights to Devin's apartment, where a representative of the building's property management company was poking around.

"What happened?" the property manager asked.

"There was a body, but it was taken away," the concierge responded.

"You didn't say anything about a body," Ben said.

"Didn't I?" the concierge said.

≈

In their family's Williamsburg loft, Henry and Joe, back from morning opera camp at Juilliard and afternoon jiu-jitsu camp at a local dojo, were running amok, cursing like sailors ("fuckhead," "ass wipe," "dickwad," etc.), eating candy and cookies, making prank calls, fighting, tossing water balloons out the window, drinking beer, overturning furniture to make impromptu obstacle courses and clubhouses, and pulling books off the shelves. Tina had given up and retreated to the study with a bottle of wine and a magazine.

That evening, Ben called Tina from his Left Bank hotel.

"These kids are driving me nuts," she complained. Then she laid into him about his gallivanting around Paris while she held the fort with their two wild Indians.

After reflecting for a moment, he said firmly, "Listen. I can't come back yet. Take the kids to Diane's."

"Really? That's revolutionary."

He sensed some of the tension leaving her voice.

"Can I speak to the boys?"

"Boys, Daddy's on the phone from Paris and wants to talk to you."

"Tell him he's a butthead," Henry shouted.

"Yeah, what *he* said," Joe chimed in.

"I'll take that as a no," Ben sighed.

~

Soft Indian music was playing in Diane's apartment. She answered the phone.

"Am I interrupting anything?" Tina asked.

"Oh, no. I was just . . . meditating."

After some awkward small talk, Tina carefully explained that the kids were out of control and she was getting desperate.

"I'd love to help," Diane said. "Really. But I don't know jack about child rearing. I'm not sure I'm the best person for this."

There was a long pause on the other end.

The following afternoon, all was calm in the loft. After taking the boys on a gondola ride to Roosevelt Island and a trip to the Central Park Zoo, Diane kept Henry and Joe entertained with board games and Lego projects (the Taj Mahal, the Pentagon, etc.). Tina marveled at how Diane had them eating out of her hand.

"These kids are a delight!" Diane announced to a grateful, sheepish Tina. "They just need a little discipline, some boundaries. Someone to whip them into shape."

How did Ben know that Diane had such terrific parenting skills? Tina wondered. Diane herself didn't know.

≈

Ben sat at the bar of a Marais bistro with a glass of Brouilly, mulling over the events of the past couple of days, when he saw Devin standing on the sidewalk, and ran outside.

"Devin! They took your body away!" he shouted.

The man turned around. "And you are . . . ?"

"It's Ben."

"Of course. I'm Donald, Devin's twin brother."

"I didn't know Devin had a twin."

"You might say we're . . . estranged."

"Huh . . ."

"Let's go inside and have a drink. I'll explain everything."

Donald was a dead ringer for Devin. Same face, same voice, same everything. Ben was flummoxed. His eyes glazed over.

"Donald?" He stared.

"Yeah, I know, man. It's confusing. There are lots of similarities, but there are plenty of differences too."

"'*Lots* of similarities'?" Ben gasped. "That's the understatement of the century. What about the differences? I can't detect *any*, and I think I know Devin a little better than you do." Ben immediately realized the absurdity of that claim and the utter weirdness of the whole thing. Yet there *was* something slightly off—something he couldn't quite put his finger on.

"If you're not Devin, then what have they done with Devin's body?"

"I'm just as mystified as you are, but I'm certain he's alive."

"Me too."

"Listen, he used to go to Nice a lot. Are you free? Because I think we should look for him there."

"You're on."

They sat and drank and hatched a plan to journey to the Riviera together the next night by train to locate and, if necessary, rescue Devin. After an hour, they came up for air.

"What can we talk about besides Devin?" Ben asked.

"How about me?" Donald replied.

They both laughed.

Ben and Donald looked out the window of their first-class sleeping compartment on the TGV to Nice as it pulled out of the Gare de Lyon. The station was buzzing with activity. It would be a six-hour trip, through the night, to the Côte d'Azur. Ben could barely contain his excitement at embarking on this adventure.

"Tell me about Devin," Ben said.

"What do you want to know? We grew up in a mansion in Pasadena. Our dad played golf with Nixon. Devin was kicked out of boarding school."

"No, I mean his life in Paris."

"Oh. Well, he writes, gives the occasional reading or performance, blogs, works on magazine articles, hits the gay bars every once in a while. That's about it. I live on the Right Bank, in the First. We meet for dinner every few months or so. Devin's favorite bistro is Josephine Chez Dumonet on Rue du Cherche-Midi. We lead very separate lives, and have since we were kids."

"What about stone rubbings?"

"Huh?"

"Never mind. What are the differences between you and Devin?"

"He's secretive. I'm very open. He's become a bit of a recluse. I'm gay too—some would say a flaming queen, even. There's nothing I love more than getting up in drag and going to a wild party. They call me Donna! Devin is, as you know, not like that at all. He's pretty laid-back. In fact, he's a bit dull. All he does is write. Work, work, work. Bor-ing. It bugs him that I'm so fun loving! He thinks people might get the wrong idea about *him*."

A mischievous expression came over Donald's face. "Ben, tell me, have you ever dressed up in drag? You can confide in me—I'm a doctor. You would look so good in a pair of culottes or, better yet, hot pants. Or a micro-mini! I bet you have great legs and wear shorts every chance you get to show them off. We'd need to come up with a drag name for you. Let's see. How about Bunny? Or Betty?"

Ben chuckled. "Hey, let's stick to topic A for a while. Did Devin show any signs of being upset before he disappeared? Did he have any enemies?"

"Let me see . . ."

"Listen, I'm starving," Ben interrupted. "We should grab a bite, but keep talking."

"Okay."

They strolled to the dining car for a late supper, where they continued to explore the circumstances around Devin Curtis's vanishing act. The two tried on various theories for size. Donald vaguely remembered something about a sanitarium near Grenoble and that

Devin had once fantasized about taking a "rest cure." Ben speculated Devin might have gone back to the States because of trouble in his family. The only conclusion that they reached was that they knew less about Devin than they had imagined.

Once back in their compartment, Ben climbed into his berth and reflected. The possibility that Devin might be dead was hard to fathom. He began to feel a deep nostalgia for his youth. Did he still have the chance to tell Devin how much he meant to him? No doubt he was sensing his own mortality as well. Maybe he *wasn't* wrong about claiming to know more about Devin than Donald did—they certainly knew two different sides of Devin, in any event. The more he thought about it, Devin was beginning to seem like a ghostly presence, whereas Donald seemed a reminder of Devin's absence. He imagined Donald and Devin were "one," whatever that might mean. Before long he was asleep.

They were woken by bright Riviera sunlight streaming into their compartment. They sat bleary-eyed, after only a few hours sleep, as the train made stops in St. Tropez, St. Raphael, Cannes and Antibes before finally arriving in Nice. Ben and Donald stumbled out of the station in search of a café. Then they took an early morning stroll along the Promenade des Anglais, past the Hotel Negresco, taking in the view of the pebble beach, the Mediterranean and a cloudless sky. Later that morning they found a turn-of-the-century B and B on a hilltop overlooking the city. The proprietress, a gracious older Frenchwoman, showed them to their rooms.

◇

They sat on the beach and came to a decision. They would go to the authorities and file a missing-persons complaint. The police station was a short walk away. The desk sergeant, a grizzled veteran, interviewed them about Devin, their relationship to him and the facts surrounding his disappearance. Ben recounted the story of the letter

Diane had received in Brooklyn and his visit to Devin's Paris apartment. The police officer made notes, took their contact information and explained to them that he would file a report, which would result in a bulletin going out to police departments throughout the country. He would notify them should there be any developments in the case. However, he cautioned them, it was not entirely clear that anything suspicious had, in fact, happened to Devin. He suggested that it was quite possible that Devin had encountered a case of writer's block and, needing a change of scene, had simply left town without a word.

"I've seen many such cases," he assured them, "particularly among those of an artistic temperament. Everyone's wringing their hands, crying on each other's shoulder, reminiscing about what a great chap Jean-Pierre was, getting ready to call the funeral director to begin proceedings, et cetera. And then suddenly Jean-Pierre walks in like nothing's happened after a couple of weeks of rest in some far-flung locale, wondering what all the fuss is about."

After leaving the station, Ben and Donald wandered Old Nice. They came upon a colorful poster of drag queens pasted on a wall with the legend "Nice in Drag." The fine print indicated that a drag festival, to be headlined by a reunited Deeee-Lite, would soon be coming to Nice. Ben shared with Donald his fond memories of attending Wigstock in Tompkins Square Park years earlier. He could see the wheels turning in Donald's head.

"What are you thinking?"

"We're dolling ourselves up and going . . . to French Wigstock!"

"Can't I just wear my civvies?"

"Absolutely not!"

Donald strolled along the beach as the sun set while Ben sat on a bench on the Promenade so he could call home on his cell phone. Henry and

Joe both answered and informed him that they wanted to go to France for their summer vacation. He quickly got the message that they would not take no for an answer.

"We will *not* take no for an answer," they shouted in unison. "We'll take *o-u-i*!"

"Yeah, I get it," Ben grumbled.

"France, France, France, France!" they cheered. "*Vive la France!*"

"Boys, I'm not staying here. I'm coming home soon. So a family trip to France this summer is not going to work out. But I promise we'll do a vacation in France next summer. How would you like to go to the Dordogne to see the cave paintings? Or the Loire Valley to see the castles? Besides, we've already signed you up for camp at home this summer."

"Daddy, you know what? You're a horse's ass," Joe said.

"Yeah," Henry chimed in. "A really *big* horse's ass!"

"You're both going to have a really *big* time-out when I get home," Ben said curtly. "Now let me speak to Mommy."

Ben brought Tina up to speed. He told her that he planned to leave in a week if he didn't discover anything about Devin.

He called Diane and gave her the gist of what had been happening. She wanted to know what he was going to wear to French Wigstock and ribbed him about Henry and Joe's wanting to join him in France. She suggested that they could prove invaluable in helping him track Devin down, playing Watson to his Holmes.

The following day, Ben and Donald happened into an independent bookstore in Old Nice.

"Do you have any books by Devin Curtis?" Ben asked the girl behind the counter.

"Wait, isn't *he* Devin Curtis?" She nodded toward Donald.

Donald set her straight and explained why they'd come to Nice and the story of Devin's apparent death. After the three introduced themselves, Sylvie, the clerk, expressed an interest in helping. As it turned out, Miss Marple and Nancy Drew were among her favorite literary characters, and she fancied herself something of a girl detective. There was nothing she enjoyed more than a good adventure. She was a student of hard-boiled American crime fiction—Chandler, Hammett, Cain, Macdonald, Latimer, Van Dine, King, Spillane, Thompson, Stout, Gardner, Hughes, Fickling, Alter, Westlake, McBain, Crumley, Parker, Willeford et al. She was eighteen. Ben wasn't sure he wanted her tagging along, but she was insistent. Donald took an immediate shine to her, charmed by her unlikely combination of world-weary sophistication beyond her years and a more fitting naïveté. At his urging, Ben reluctantly agreed to hold an informal "interview" with Sylvie that evening at a bar in the Old Port, to determine her suitability for the new "position" that a few minutes earlier hadn't even existed. It was only when Sylvie took off her rimless glasses, while the three of them were having drinks at the bar, that Ben noticed how beautiful she was and that his initial assessment of her as a mousy intellectual had been far off the mark.

She gushed that the mystery of Devin Curtis, whom she regarded as a daring cult author, was "*très* cool" and that, since it was right up her alley, she simply must help them get to the bottom of it. As a matter of fact, she continued, there was no one better suited to the job. She would draw on all her local knowledge and connections, take a leave of absence from the bookstore, if necessary, and put herself at their disposal. She would make helping them her top priority.

"What do you actually know about Devin?" Donald asked Sylvie.

She launched into an explanation of how Devin had become marooned in Paris by love. Oleg Stolichnaya, his Russian boyfriend, had been unable to obtain a visa to stay in the United States. So, the two were left no choice but to remain in the City of Light, where they'd met. She surmised that being an expatriate comported perfectly with

Devin's own sense of himself, since he generally felt like an outsider. She went on to describe Devin's unhappy boarding-school experience. He was kicked out for smoking dope, but not before meeting the fellow student who would change his life: Kirk Stiles, the inscrutable central character of the so-called Kirk Stiles cycle in his fiction.

Ben and Donald nodded to each other.

Cameron was Sylvie's last name. Her late father was American, and she spoke an offbeat, accented American. "*C'est* cool," "*très* cool," "very much," "not so much" and "cool cat" were among her signature expressions. The quality she most disliked in herself was her fickleness. She gave them a rundown of her romantic history to date. She was the heartbreaker of her set, jaded about the opposite sex and relationships. Writers and writing were what most animated her. She bemoaned the fact that, as she put it, she didn't have a creative bone in her body. But she imagined the next best thing would be to become the muse of someone who *did* have that creative spark. She pictured herself lounging on the deck of a speedboat with a darkly handsome artist or posing in his studio decorated with colorful "synthetic cubist" wallpaper, playing Dora Maar to his Picasso.

Ben was wowed by Sylvie's rambling, emotional "presentation." He decided that she could make herself useful as an aide-de-camp, and considered the "interview" over. The truth was, once she'd removed her glasses, he'd needed no further convincing.

Ben told her she had the job, and Sylvie shrieked with glee. After she'd composed herself, she volunteered to show them around. They all agreed that Devin was likely to have spent time in gay bars. Sylvie drew up a list of the gay bars in town. They arranged to meet later that night at the first bar on the list, Le Code.

Le Code was located on Rue Papon, a dimly lit street. Sylvie's "gang," three boys and three girls, were waiting outside when Ben and Donald arrived. Sylvie pulled up on a Vespa, wearing a fisherman's jersey, Capri pants and Jack Purcells. She introduced everyone. At her suggestion, she and Ben approached the bartender, who knew Devin and had seen him in the bar just a few weeks earlier speaking to Didier, a regular. Sylvie questioned the bartender about Didier, the places he frequented, his acquaintances, etc. Apparently, Didier was a flamboyant, well-known character. The bartender also told them that another establishment, Le Glam, an after-hours club, was a favorite of Devin's during his visits to Nice.

Over the next few days, in between sleuthing, Sylvie introduced Ben and Donald to her hangouts. She and her pals, a collection of punk rockers, literary theorists, drug addicts, conceptual artists, gallerists and postdoctoral oncology fellows, liked to hang out in dive bars in the Old Port and cruise around town on their Vespas. Ben was fascinated by Sylvie's world and felt himself being drawn into it.

"Ben is a writer," Sylvie announced to the group at dinner.

"Be still my heart!" said Véronique, a gang member.

She and Sylvie giggled, gave Ben the once-over, and then exchanged glances.

Sylvie stayed up late that night reading one of Ben's novels, *On My Way to See You,* which she had bought online and downloaded. The book's main character, also named Ben, seemed a lot like Ben.

Meanwhile, at the B and B, Donald complained to Ben about feeling left out. Ben had received all the attention from Sylvie and her friends. It was unfair, he said, since it was he who had championed her in the first place and Ben who had been dismissive.

There was no sign of either Didier or Devin at the various venues they went to, nor were they able to turn up any leads. One afternoon, at Sylvie's suggestion, they went to the beach. Ben was dubious that going to the beach would help them find Devin. She told him to be patient, because this was the beach where Didier liked to hang out with his posse of drag queens. Before long, he appeared. When they approached him, he seemed cagey. He thought Devin may have met with foul play after attending an orgy at the old Roman amphitheater on the outskirts of town. He directed them to a website that featured information about these types of events, in which hustlers charge for viewing of, or participation in, sex with them by groups of clients. Ben thought it sounded very dark. Sylvie was excited by the whole thing. Donald felt it was a promising lead.

The ruins of the deserted amphitheater, which consisted of a hodge-podge of arches, stone steps, fluted columns and blocks of marble scattered about, were located in the old neighborhood of Cimiez on a hillside a few miles from the center of Nice. The sun was setting. The three of them poked around on their own before reuniting at the top of the steps. Did Ben sense Devin's presence? He wasn't sure. He tried to imagine the goings-on that had taken place. Somehow, the mysterious, ritualistic nature of the proceedings outlined on the website that Didier had told them about seemed to suit the impos-ing, ancient setting. Thinking about that put Ben in a solemn frame of mind. Sylvie, on the other hand, was in a dither, titillated by the unexpected collision of sex-for-hire and classical culture.

"I think over there is a likely spot for a blow-bang, or whatever the technical term is," she declared, pointing to the center of the amphitheater. "I can picture it now. I see Devin looking on from the peanut gallery, a shy voyeur, quietly making notes in his journal."

Donald smiled.

They returned to town in their rented Renault with Sylvie behind the wheel. From their vantage point on a remote hilltop road, the first stars were visible in the sky, sparkling above the Mediterranean below.

"Why do I feel like a third wheel?" Donald grumbled from the backseat.

"Not so!" Sylvie reassured him. "We're a team."

When they arrived at the B and B, Sylvie offhandedly told Donald that she and Ben were going out for nightcap. Ben, pleasantly surprised since this was the first he'd heard of it, said nothing, and Donald headed into the house.

"Is this my lucky night?" Ben asked.

"I do believe it is," Sylvie grinned.

"Where are we going?"

"My place."

"So you can have your way with me?"

"As a matter of fact, yes."

Sylvie's mother, an archeologist, was on a dig in Tunisia for the summer, excavating Etruscan ruins. Sylvie's roommate, the daughter of family friends, was out of town, so Sylvie and Ben had the run of the apartment. Tall and willowy, Sylvie had a beautiful body and a pale Modigliani face punctuated by bee-stung lips and framed by chestnut hair pulled back in a ponytail. They fell asleep in each other's arms.

～

French Wigstock, a desultory, rain-soaked affair, was a disappointment.

CHAPTER FOUR

In the Old Port, Sylvie and Ben pulled up on her Vespa outside the dive bar Le Zinc. Sylvie's friends, Benoît, Marie, Robert and Élodie, were already on their third round at an outdoor table. Donald, who was the last to straggle in, was given a round of applause by the group. He took a mock bow before finding a seat.

As a visiting American, Ben was something of a novelty among the clique. Marie and Élodie invited themselves to Brooklyn to crash with Ben and have him show them the sights.

"Why don't I draw up an itinerary for you, to make sure you don't miss anything?" Sylvie said with annoyance.

"Relax, we're not going to jump his bones and steal your man," Élodie replied.

"Speak for yourself!" Marie chimed in.

Sylvie forced a smile. She reached out for Donald's arm and stuck her hand right through it. She screamed. Ben stared at Donald in disbelief. Sylvie was in a state of shock.

"What just happened?" Ben asked.

"There's no need to . . . to be alarmed," Donald stammered. "I won't hurt you. I'm a hologram."

"I thought you were Devin's twin," Ben said.

"That was . . . an untruth," Donald admitted with embarrassment. "I couldn't . . . I'm a high-end hologram—an advanced, experimental model. It's all technics."

"Jesus Christ!" Sylvie gasped. "I need a drink."

"Okay, this is a lot for me to wrap my head around." Ben closed his eyes.

"I know," Donald said. "I feel terrible."

"Why did you . . . why didn't you explain right away?" Ben asked.

"I don't know . . . I didn't want to frighten you," Donald said.

At the other end of the table, the rest of the group was vaguely aware that something had upset Ben and Sylvie, and that Donald seemed to be the cause. Beyond that, they couldn't say.

"Oh, Donald, what have you done this time?" Marie boomed.

"Donald is nothing but trouble! I can't turn my back on him for a second," Élodie added. "He's like a young child."

Robert and Benoît chuckled.

The joking met with a cool reception from Ben, Sylvie and Donald.

$$\sim$$

In bed that night, Sylvie thought sleepily, *Did I really put my hand through Donald, or did I just imagine it?*

"It really happened," Ben said.

"How did you know what I was thinking?"

"I'm psychic!"

"You are not!"

"No. I was thinking the same thing."

Ben and Sylvie mulled over this phenomenal turn of events. Donald was, in fact, "Virtual Devin," identical in appearance to the actual Devin Curtis. How did that affect their plans? Wasn't it still the case that they needed to keep searching for the real Devin? And why, they mused, was Devin now beginning to seem unreal and Donald strangely real? They would need to learn more about Donald before arriving at any decisions.

Later that night Sylvie dreamt that she was the franchisee of a regional chain of transvestite bars.

Ben dropped by. "What are you doing?" he asked.

"Pursuing my dream," she said.

He shot her an appraising look, impressed that she had built a thriving business out of nothing.

∼

In the morning, Ben returned to the B and B. There was no sign of Donald. The rest of the day, neither Ben nor Sylvie heard from him. Over dinner at a bistro near Sylvie's apartment, they worried he might be gone for good, perhaps too ashamed to face them. But after considering the various possibilities, they agreed it was unlikely he'd left town. As a matter of fact, they had a pretty good idea where they would find him later that night, in quiet, solemn reflection.

When Ben and Sylvie entered Le Code around midnight, they immediately caught sight of Donald dancing on the bar in high heels, an angora sweaterdress and pillbox hat, alongside two drag queens.

"I think it's safe to say he seems to be exhibiting a strong sense of remorse," Ben offered.

"No doubt," Sylvie said.

Donald caught sight of them and joined them a short time later.

"Tell me something. Did I really put my hand through you, or was I drunk?" Sylvie asked.

"Yes, you did, but it's no big deal," Donald said. "Listen, I know I screwed up. But this doesn't change anything. If you let me prove myself, I know we can find Devin together."

"What's your story?" Sylvie asked. "We need more to go on, if we're going to take a chance on you."

"I wish I knew. I'm at a loss." Donald shrugged.

Pensively, Ben and Sylvie took his measure.

"So, you're telling us that you don't know how or why you became what you are?" Ben stared at him.

"I swear I don't. I don't know who constructed me or how I work—the mechanisms, I mean."

"So it's like some kind of amnesia?" Sylvie asked.

"Exactly."

Ben reached out to take Donald's hand, but Donald quickly drew back.

"But somewhere there must be someone—some scientists or scientific fruitcakes—who made you and maybe . . . misplaced you?" Ben speculated.

"Ben, I just don't know." Donald put his head in his hands. "In fact, I don't remember much of anything that happened before we met."

"This . . ." Sylvie began.

"Takes the cake," Ben finished her thought.

"Well . . ." Donald sighed.

"I believe him," Ben said at last.

"So do I," Sylvie agreed. "Gee, you poor guy. I'd like to hug you but . . ."

CHAPTER FIVE

Ben and Sylvie dove headlong into their new romance. During the week following their night of magic, they were together morning, noon and night. Some days they joined Sylvie's circle for cocktails, then stayed up until all hours at Sylvie's place, talking, watching Fellini movies and having tantric sex. Other days, they gave a tip of the hat to their search for Devin, checking in briefly with Donald by phone or e-mail to compare notes, before piling into the car for a carefree day trip to St. Tropez or Cannes.

Improbably, though, given the amount of time they were spending together each day, things went wonderfully. Ben and Sylvie felt comfortable around each other. Was it simply an infatuation, a passing carnal attraction, or what—love?

Toward the end of the week, Sylvie began to feel that, given how quickly things were moving, she needed to take a step back. Was she living in a fantasy world, in view of the fact that Ben already had a wife, two kids and a girlfriend back in New York? Was there any future for her and Ben? Was he simply a guy who just wanted to get into her pants and, once he'd tired of her, would let her off by the side of the road? She told him that she was exhausted and begged off going out that night. She slept fitfully, wrestling with her doubts.

At breakfast, Sylvie told Ben that she needed to take a break to protect herself, before she got in any deeper. Ben gently tried to talk her out of it, begging for a chance to prove his good intentions. But reluctantly he conceded that, given his "baggage," her concerns were valid.

∼

Didier was known as the unofficial mayor of Nice among its demimonde. A flamboyant cross-dresser and former nightclub promoter in Paris, he was a popular local character. He was also a onetime paratrooper in the French Foreign Legion, where he had been the notorious "hard man" of his regiment. Once he had done his twenty years, he retired to Paris. At last growing bored with Parisian night life, he moved to Nice full-time, where he had been a member in good standing of the city's small, insular birding community for over ten years. Several mornings each week he could be found stalking rare warblers, finches, woodpeckers, nuthatches and hummingbirds in the forested mountains above the Riviera, Zeiss binoculars in hand. He was expert in their migratory patterns as well as their songs. Birding provided a respite from the hyperactivity of Nice's gay scene. He kept a record of his sightings in an ostrich hide–bound notebook. The local birders formed a cross-section of Nice society: Lacanian analysts, public officials, ex-soldiers like himself, yoga instructors, students, corporate turnaround specialists, cyclists, classically trained musicians and competitive ballroom dancers.

Donald and Didier sat outdoors at a café on Nice's main square, the Place Masséna.

"*Oui*, the gay scene here is not large, and rather tame compared to other cities, *c'est vrai*," Didier remarked.

"I'm not complaining, mind you," Donald said.

"Well, I once visited New York a million years ago—what a scene: Boy Bar, Uncle Charlie's, the Ninth Circle, even the Duchess! And let's not forget the Anvil and the Mineshaft."

"Ooh la la!" Donald chuckled. "It's too early in the morning to get me all excited. I don't know if my heart can take it."

"Say, where are Ben and Sylvie?"

"I think we may have a problem on that front," Donald said pointedly.

"Oh, really? Do tell."

As if on cue, Ben arrived and sat down sullenly. A few minutes later Sylvie joined them.

"The gang's all here!" Sylvie exclaimed.

Ben's expression remained dour.

They took stock of where things stood with their search for Devin. None of Devin's friends in LA had heard from him. Ben had recently reached out to Didier and, with the permission of Sylvie and Donald, had asked him to lend a hand as an ex officio member of the team. At the top of the agenda was determining what unexplored avenues were left to them, then dividing up the labor. Ben raised the possibility of also enlisting Élodie, who had expressed an interest in helping out. Sylvie had doubts about Élodie's motives, suggesting that her true interest lay not in finding Devin but getting closer to Ben. Ben snickered, and Didier nodded knowingly. The matter was tabled.

"Failure is not an option, *mes amis*," Didier concluded grimly. "I don't wish to be overdramatic, but we may be in a race against the clock. Devin's life may be on the line." He pronounced Devin's name "Deh-veen" in his oddly accented English. There was a faraway look in his eyes, and he seemed to be momentarily transported. "Ah, Devin . . ." he muttered. The rest was inaudible.

Ben and Sylvie looked at each other quizzically.

"Excuse me?" Ben said to Didier.

"Oh, Ben, you probably know what I was thinking," Didier confessed sheepishly, and looked down at the sidewalk.

"Okay, then. Now that we've gotten that out of the way," Ben said uncomfortably. He suggested that trying to track down Oleg Stolichnaya,

Devin's boyfriend, was the logical next step. Didier wasn't sure if Oleg had been seen in the area. Ben agreed to work on that angle. He would also phone the concierge in Devin's building in Paris to see if there had been any word about Devin. It was decided that Donald and Sylvie would continue to troll the gay bars for leads. Didier volunteered to follow up with a police detective, Captain Brossard, on the missing persons report. The detective was an old friend of his, though relations between them had cooled somewhat. Still, Didier believed he might be able to pry loose some information that could prove useful.

"Do you and the police captain have a *past*?" Sylvie asked, her interest piqued.

"Oh, boy. I can see where this is going," Ben lamented. "Sylvie, can we keep our eyes on the prize and your mind out of the gutter for . . . at least another few seconds?"

"Do we have to? I suppose so," she giggled.

"*Oui*, to answer your question, the police captain and I do have a past, but not the kind you think," Didier began. "Bernard and I served in the Legion together. We were paratroopers. I saved his life on a mission in the Congo. We were part of a rapid deployment force that had been dropped in at low altitude for a nighttime assault on a rebel compound. The rebels didn't know what hit them. But then a nearby rebel group counterattacked, and a firefight broke out. We lost quite a few men."

"How terrible," Sylvie said. Ben and Donald looked solemn.

"It's still difficult for me to talk about the savagery and butchery of that night. Bernard and our platoon—I was a sergeant, and he was a corporal—made a forced march of ten miles through the jungle that night and early the next morning to an alternate extraction point to be ferried out by chopper. I was not the preening . . . 'metrosexual,' if you will, you see before you, I assure you. *Non*. I was a very different Didier then—a man of iron who kept his emotions firmly in check. Bernard had been wounded, and I carried him on my back the entire way. He has never forgotten it. When we emerged from the jungle that day, no one could believe it. They thought we had perished in the fray because our radio had been knocked out."

"Oh, my," was all Sylvie could manage. Didier's story was rendered all the more remarkable because the teller of that story sat across from them in a Christian Lacroix woman's blouse, chiffon scarf, earrings, short shorts and women's espadrilles.

"Didier, you are a marvel," Ben said in admiration. Didier smiled wanly and looked off into the distance.

Donald ventured a question. "You and Bernard were close?"

"We were as close as it is possible for two men to be. We were like brothers."

"What happened?" Sylvie asked.

"Our falling-out tore apart the local birding community," Didier said. "The Alpine nuthatch had been thought to be extinct for fifty years. But occasionally unconfirmed reports of sightings would filter in from remote areas. So little was known about the species that no one was certain what kind of habitat it preferred once it migrated here from the Swiss Alps for winter. However, I had a hunch . . . I was certain the Alpine nuthatch was not extinct. At last, I had a sighting in the mountains of the interior at the mouth of a cave. I carefully recorded the details in my journal and snapped a few shots with my telephoto lens. There was quite a bit of fanfare around my discovery. But Bernard went to the newspapers, claiming the photos were inconclusive and that it was impossible that I had found an example of a species that had not been seen in nearly half a century. He was always jealous of me. Of course, it could never be the same after that."

After the informal meeting, Ben remained behind to let Didier know about what he and Sylvie had recently learned about Donald. To Ben's amazement, Didier did not bat an eye.

Ben saw Sylvie and an older man in a café on the Place Masséna. He went over, and she introduced him to her companion, Hugues.

"We met at Élodie's party in Cap d'Antibes," she explained. "Hugues is in film production. He came to Cannes for the festival."

They continued to converse, and Ben pulled up a chair. When Hugues excused himself to use the restroom, Ben asked Sylvie if they could have dinner that night.

"Hugues and I have plans," she said coolly.

Flustered by her response, Ben hurriedly made his good-byes, picked up a sandwich to go at the counter and returned to the B and B. In his room, he reflected. Had he just slinked out of the café with his tail between his legs? Was it fair to say he was suddenly wracked with jealousy? He was surprised by the strength of his reaction, unaware that his feelings for Sylvie ran so deep.

If you were to ask Ben about the consequences of his actions on those nearest and dearest to him, you would receive a look of puzzlement. He simply saw no need to deprive himself of something he viewed as one of life's great pleasures. He had an abiding confidence that things had a way of working out. And often enough, they did. This nonchalance that he brought to even the stickiest situations was one of his most winning qualities. The downside of Tina or Diane's learning of his affair wasn't something that gave him much pause. For Ben, it was a vaguely unpleasant thought and quickly forgotten.

How could he win Sylvie back? He would just have to stay loose and hope for the best. The group was scheduled to reconvene in a couple of days to see if they were any closer to locating Devin.

~

Outside Le Zinc, Sylvie greeted Ben effusively, throwing her arms around his neck and planting an enthusiastic kiss on his lips.

"I missed you!" she said.

"Really? What about Hugues?"

"He's history," she sighed. "He was a major-league sex addict, a pig, a creep. All he thought about was pussy."

"I know the type."

Donald and Didier arrived a few minutes later and went to find a table. Ben and Sylvie remained on the sidewalk, eagerly making plans for later that night, happy to put the past few days behind them.

"It's a tearful reunion," she declared, "of two old comrades—"

"Picking up the trail—"

"Of Sir Devin Curtis."

"Why 'Sir' Devin?" he asked.

"No reason. I just liked the ring of it."

"It does have a good ring to it. But you're also a nut."

Back at the B and B, before going out to meet Sylvie, Ben decided to give Diane a ring.

"Is Tina upset with me?"

"Maybe a little. Are you afraid to call her?"

"Should I be? I miss you, Tina and the kids."

"Have you run across any budding Brigitte Bardots over there?"

"In a way . . ."

"We can all be together soon."

"Yes, soon."

"Any progress on the case?"

"Some. The mayor of Nice is assisting us."

"You're kidding."

"He's not the *actual* mayor."

"He's the mayor of the gay scene?"

"You're really something. Though I would say his constituency is a little broader than that."

CHAPTER SIX

A light rain was falling. Inside the amphitheater ruins, the headless, naked body, purported to be that of Oleg Stolichnaya, lay in the fading evening light.

The first police officers on the scene were two patrolmen, Thierry Diaz and his partner, Olivier LeClerc. They were nonchalantly discussing the grisly tableau while they waited for the arrival of other personnel.

"It was an anonymous tip, wasn't it?" LeClerc asked. He had been outside their patrol car when the dispatcher had radioed from headquarters. Diaz had been too distracted to fill him in on all the details as they'd raced to their destination.

"That's right. Apparently, the caller said, 'There's been a murder. Oleg Stolichnaya's body is in the amphitheater,' before hanging up."

"Hard to tell who it is. So find the head."

"Probably rolling down a hill somewhere."

"What the hell goes on here, anyway?"

"S&M, gay porn, snuff films. That kind of thing."

"Really?"

"That's the word on the street."

"Is the captain coming?"

"He'll be here. Had to cut into his poker night, but he's coming."

"There's something eerie about this place."

"You're telling me."

"So what does the captain know?"

"He said the body may be tied to another case he's working on—missing person. Devin Curtis."

"The American writer?"

"You've heard of him?"

"Sure. My girlfriend's read all his books. She's a little kinky herself."

Diaz cracked a smile.

Three squad cars pulled up with lights flashing. Several officers set about cordoning off the area. They were soon joined by two forensic pathologists who arrived in a van. After methodically unloading spotlights, equipment cases and a large field tent to be used as a mobile lab, and stationing an officer at the entrance, the rest of the group went inside the amphitheater to join the patrolmen—and examine the corpse.

At Le Zinc, Sylvie, Ben and Donald discussed the news they'd received from Didier the night before about Oleg Stolichnaya's murder. Didier had learned of it from his detective friend, Captain Brossard. Ben was perplexed and a little frightened, whereas Donald seemed preternaturally calm. It was as if the news had suddenly given him a newfound perspective on life. Sylvie was positively exhilarated at the new turn of events. Ben noticed a sense of excitement in her that, if he was not mistaken, was almost sexual.

What would their next move be? No one was certain, but they were in agreement that they would follow Didier's lead. When Didier arrived, he ordered a drink and, without any fuss, began.

"We've got to stop meeting like this! My assessment of the situation? My old friend, Brossard, has been brought in to investigate. Devin will no doubt become a person of interest, if not a suspect, given his relationship with Oleg. I am, I'm afraid, all too familiar with the workings of the Nice underworld. This is what I think happened: Devin ran afoul of an organized crime sex-trafficking ring while doing research for his latest novel. They didn't want him poking around. When they figured out he was working on a book, Oleg was killed as a message to Devin, and Devin is in hiding—here, Paris or elsewhere. Why not kill Devin? Because no one knew where he was. I wonder if the original letter received in Brooklyn might have been from Devin himself, sent as a coded distress signal. I recommend not getting the police any further involved than they already are or going to them with anything we might uncover, because they'll be suspicious. Even if Devin *was* just researching a book, the police still wouldn't buy it."

Didier turned to Ben. "Brossard knows you are looking for Devin, and he'll want to question you. So be prepared. And, Donald, you, yourself, will have to go into hiding because of the resemblance between the two of you. Anyway, regarding Oleg, I was afraid something like this might happen. However, *mes amis*, there may be another explanation that we have to consider: that the body is not Oleg, and Devin placed the anonymous call to the cops himself to buy Oleg some time, as no one will be looking for a dead man. If Devin suspected that the criminals were onto him, then he would've known that Oleg was also in danger. So, Devin may have conveniently taken advantage of an anonymous body to plant some misinformation, knowing that word would soon spread of 'Oleg's' murder. It may, in fact, be a clever ploy on Devin's part to throw the crime ring off the scent. But how did Devin learn of the body? My guess is that Oleg tipped him off."

"Then," Ben began, "Oleg was—"

"At the amphitheater," Sylvie interrupted. "And he may have witnessed the murder."

"Quite possibly. And he is likely still in the area," Didier added.

"Whose body is it, if it's not Oleg?" Donald asked.

Didier lit a pipe, took a few puffs and looked thoughtfully at the group. "That is something we may never know."

Hand in hand, Ben and Sylvie took a late-night stroll along the Promenade des Anglais overlooking the moonlit Mediterranean. Despite the recent events that had cast a pall over their search for Devin, they both felt strangely giddy.

"You seemed to be turned on by the murder," Ben said.

"Really? You may be right, now that I think about it."

"Sexual turn-ons aside, I feel strongly that we should observe a moment of silence to mark Oleg's passing."

"Would you have any objection to doing so at my place?" Sylvie asked. She paused, then added, "In the nude?"

Ben reflected for a moment. "No. Oleg would have wanted it that way."

Ben and Sylvie had both just drifted off to sleep, after an enjoyable "session" of tantric sex, when the downstairs buzzer rang. Drowsily, Sylvie got to her feet to answer it.

"Hello?" she said.

"It's Donald."

"Donald? What time is it?"

"Is Ben there? I need to see you both."

"Okay." She buzzed him in.

"What's wrong?" Ben asked.

"I'm having a meltdown," Donald announced, joining them in the living room.

"Go on," Sylvie urged. "We're here for you," she added in a motherly tone.

"I don't know how much longer I can go on this way," Donald continued.

"What way?" Ben asked.

"I'm an advanced, experimental model," Donald explained. "I'm programmed to think for myself."

Ben's expression became pensive. "So, is there a problem with what we're doing—looking for Devin?"

"Must we find him?" Donald asked. "I'm just as good as Devin, really, if not better!"

"Donald has feelings!" Sylvie exclaimed. "We've got to look out for his best interests."

"For chrissakes, he's not even real," Ben protested. "He thinks finding Devin will render him superfluous. An instinct for self-preservation has kicked in."

"Oh, Donald," Sylvie said sympathetically. "Is that true?"

He nodded somberly.

"What are we going to do with you?" Sylvie wondered.

"Listen, you're really not programmed for this kind of situation," Ben said. "Maybe you should go back to the factory."

"I wish I could and had some idea where to go," Donald replied.

"Apparently they've built neurosis into Donald's wiring," Sylvie said resignedly.

"Donald, look. Sylvie and I are committed to the search for Devin. Didier said you should lie low anyway. I think the time is right for you to just cool your heels for a while." Ben turned to Sylvie.

"I agree," she said. "Donald, we won't let anything happen to you."

Sylvie's kind words reassured him. The three then made arrangements for Ben and Sylvie to check in with Donald in a couple of days and find him a new place to stay, and with that, Donald made his good-byes.

"Ben."

"Yes, Sylvie."

"Let's pretend that never happened."

"It's almost too much to absorb. Besides, I've got my own problems!"

"There's so much tension in the world. I think this calls for another moment of silence in Oleg's honor."

They tossed off their underwear and hurried into the bedroom.

CHAPTER SEVEN

Of the two boys, Joe, the six-year-old, was generally defiant and adventurous, Henry, eight, more compliant and cautious. But Henry was also prone to sudden, uncontrollable fits of temper when he didn't get his way.

"We're leaving for tennis in a few minutes," Tina warned Joe. "You need to put on sunscreen." She handed him a tube of Coppertone.

"Sunscreen is for dicks," he shot back.

It took Tina a moment to regroup from the riposte. "Listen, buster, you have two choices. You can put on sunscreen, or you can have a time-out. You decide."

"I don't *think* so. Deal with it!" he shouted, casually letting the tube slip through his fingers and drop to the floor while he watched her face for a reaction.

They glared at each other.

"Fine, whatever. Let's go," she said brusquely, after a brief standoff.

"How come I have to wear sunscreen and Joe doesn't?" Henry complained.

"Oh, boy," Tina said.

"Mommy wanted me to, but I just waited until she got frustrated," Joe explained helpfully.

Henry lay in bed in racing-car pajamas reading *The Red Badge of Courage*. The bedroom contained Adirondack-style furniture and antique baseball memorabilia. Joe, who was in the bathtub, had insisted that Tina join him in the bathroom to provide an audience while he held forth on a variety of topics of interest to him.

"You know what, Mommy?"

"What, Joe?"

"Everything Daddy says is kidding, except when he gets mad. Then he starts dropping the F-bomb."

"Ain't that the truth," she chuckled.

After the kids were both asleep, Ben called.

Tina sensed Ben was being evasive when she asked when he was going to wrap things up in France and return home. Finally, she'd had enough of his excuses and interrupted him. "You're not coming back anytime soon, are you?" she snapped.

There was a long pause. "No."

~

Henry and Joe perused the in-flight magazine's list of available movies on their Air France flight to Paris.

"Mommy, is there anything with chipmunks?" Joe asked hopefully.

"Oh, Joe, you're so dumb," Henry lamented.

"I'm afraid not," Tina said sympathetically, after pretending to take a look.

"These movies are all crap," Joe said petulantly, throwing the magazine on the floor. "Why can't we be on a good airline?"

Henry smirked, and Tina rolled her eyes.

"Do you think Daddy will be surprised when we visit him?" Henry asked.

"Oh, yeah . . . Without a doubt." She smiled broadly.

During the flight, Henry and Joe collaborated on a checklist of sights they wanted to visit in Paris, including renting toy sailboats in the Luxembourg Gardens and going to the Picasso Museum. They proudly shared it with their mother, who was suitably impressed.

Once they'd arrived at their Sofitel hotel near the Place Vendôme, Tina called Ben in Nice.

"Can you come up and see us?" she asked.

"I'm in Nice."

"The boys and I are in Paris."

"You're kidding! That was so . . . impetuous."

"Uh-huh."

"Well, I can't wait to see everyone!"

Ben told her he would take the TGV to Paris the following morning.

≈

Tina and Ben's Parisian idyll with their kids went a lot better than anyone could have anticipated. They were surprised at how happy they were to be back in each other's company, and the friction over Ben's lengthy absence quickly dissipated. When he shared with her some details of the search for Devin, he was careful to omit any mention of Sylvie or of Donald's true nature. Tina displayed little interest in it, and Ben was happy to have a break from the goings-on in Nice. Just as he was able to "compartmentalize" his feelings for Diane when he was with Tina, so he was now able to temporarily put Sylvie out of mind and be "in the moment" with Tina. Ben, Tina and the boys rowed a boat in the Bois de Boulogne, visited the Eiffel Tower and the Louvre, and picnicked on the grass in the Place des Vosges.

Over dinner at an old-world bistro in the Sixth Arrondissement, Ben began to tell the boys how much they meant to him and how much he'd missed them. Tina looked on appreciatively.

"Oh, no, oh, no," Joe interrupted. "Don't tell me we're going to have a *moment*."

Ben looked crestfallen, and Tina did her best to suppress a smile. Then Ben asked Henry about a girl in his class at school, Gabby, who had a crush on him.

"She's a whore!" he shot back.

"She's eight years old. How could she be a whore?" Ben asked in disbelief. "And do you even know what a whore is?"

"It's like a prostitute, only you don't have to pay," Henry replied in a measured tone.

Silence.

"Well, I guess we've exhausted that topic," Tina concluded.

The next evening Ben and Tina decided to take advantage of the hotel's day-care center. They were given a claim check by the attendant, a supercilious woman in her twenties, who told them they must present it to pick up their kids.

"What happens if we lose it?" Tina asked.

"We sell your children to the circus," the attendant deadpanned.

"Are you thinking what I'm thinking?" Tina asked Ben.

After a relaxing dinner at a chic brasserie in Saint-Germain-des-Prés, Ben and Tina took a romantic walk along the Seine, past Notre Dame and the Île Saint-Louis. The tone of their conversation was affectionate but also serious.

"What's happened to our marriage? Why have you gone off looking for this guy?"

"I don't know."

"I rest my case. Who *does* know?"

"A therapist?"

The conversation turned to Diane, recently returned from Venezuela.

"Do we both love Diane?" Ben asked.

"You love her, and I admire her. She's much more freewheeling than either of us, and I think we both appreciate that quality."

They agreed they needed more cohesion in their marriage. Tina confessed that she'd come to Paris to prevent things from getting too heavy. While their relationship was on a precarious footing, it had not yet fallen apart, and they concurred that with some work they could right the ship.

"Your children are impossible," they were told angrily by the attendant when they'd returned to the day-care center.

"We know, we know," Ben sighed.

"Something must be done about it," the attendant insisted, before launching into a litany of the boys' misdeeds.

"Got any ideas?" Tina asked.

"Devil's Island," the woman offered.

"Will it cost us anything?" Ben asked.

Despite their blasé response, Ben and Tina were stung by the woman's words. They decided late that night that they could no longer ignore the seriousness of the situation, and they began to reach out for help with the kids. Following an "emergency" long-distance conference call with Tina's mother, Ben's mother, Ben's father and stepmother, and Henry's former therapist, a sporty, bespectacled Freudian psychoanalyst named Dr. George Shulman who was an occasional dinner guest in their home, Ben and Tina resolved they would impose a new world order to take back control: The kids would no longer be running the house. Henry and Joe would be told that back at home, they would be limited to a half hour of TV or video games per day. *Grand Theft Auto, Call of Duty, South Park* and *Family Guy* would be banned from the house. They would have to come to the dinner table when called. Hitting, swearing and breaking things or otherwise disobeying the rules would be grounds for immediate punishment and loss of privileges. Last, they would be told that if they didn't like it, they could find another house to live in.

The next morning Ben called a family meeting. Joe was attentive, excited even, while Henry was apprehensive. They both complained bitterly when the boom was lowered and begged for *Grand Theft Auto*. They promised they wouldn't kill the prostitute after having sex with her and take back their money, if only they could keep the game. Ben and Tina were adamant and held their ground. Henry and Joe didn't know what had gotten into their parents, since they'd never shown the slightest bit of backbone in the past. How and why did they all of a sudden grow a set of balls? they wondered. It was very puzzling.

Once the kids were asleep that night, Tina announced to Ben that she'd had an epiphany. "I've been thinking . . . and have come to the realization I can accept Diane and am comfortable with her and sharing you with her in a way that I haven't been."

"You *can*? You *are*? I'm all ears."

"In fact, I'm going to get in touch with Diane and ask her to join us here as backup. She's the only one who can really control the kids. We'll install her in an adjoining room here at the hotel."

"We will?"

"Yep."

"I'm good with that."

Diane arrived in Paris a couple of days after Tina's invitation. No sooner had she unpacked and joined everyone for an outing to the playground at the Tuileries than Henry and Joe were transformed into models of decorum. It seemed to Ben and Tina as if Diane had cast a spell on them.

∽

Ben sat opposite the eminent French psychoanalyst Dr. Jacques Lowenstein in his elegant Right Bank office. Feeling that he could benefit from professional help, Ben had once again contacted George Shulman, who had referred him to Dr. Lowenstein, an analyst of international reputation who also happened to be the president of the French Psychoanalytic Association.

"Dr. Shulman has told me very little about your living situation but enough to see it's unusual."

"Oh, you're referring to Diane?"

"Yes . . . So, why are you here?"

"I'm not sure."

Dr. Lowenstein nodded understandingly, something that put Ben at his ease and prompted him to continue. He described his current predicament and how confused he was by his reaction to Tina's acceptance of Diane. He was disturbed at not feeling happy at the news. Something was flawed in him, he was certain. What was it? It was almost too painful for him to look into why he wasn't more upbeat in the face of this unexpected "gift" from his wife. He'd never been sure about the relationship between Tina and Diane, and now that the issue had magically resolved itself, it seemed to him that he should be elated. And why, he wondered, was he still interested in finding Devin Curtis at this point? And in romancing Sylvie? He didn't know. But he felt compelled to continue what appeared to be a wild goose chase.

"What's so wrong with not being happy?" Dr. Lowenstein asked. "Why is it important for you to feel happy? If it is, why not finish what you've begun?"

"I know I shouldn't be doing this, but . . ." Ben proceeded to tell the doctor about Donald.

Dr. Lowenstein's impassive expression told him nothing about what he might be thinking.

"You're probably thinking this is just in my head," Ben speculated. "But others have seen him too."

"That's delightful. Whoever manufactured him is a genius."

"We don't know who made him."

Dr. Lowenstein listened attentively. As the session continued, the analyst adroitly drew Ben out about his childhood, his feelings about his parents, his past relationships and his dreams, and, in short order, was able to distill and synthesize for his new patient with remarkable clarity the essential recurring patterns and conflicts that had informed his life.

"You want to understand why you're not happy. But that is the wrong question," Dr. Lowenstein said. "Let me hazard a guess. I think that you want my permission or blessing to continue the adventure—and Tina's. Well, you have my permission."

"I do?"

"Yes, of course."

"What about Tina?"

"Show your love to your wife and how grateful you are. Explain that you must see this adventure through as a moral obligation. But it is important that you promise you will return in a given period of time, and that you live up to the promise. That is, you must make a firm commitment to her, and you must honor it."

"What should I say about Sylvie?"

"You don't have to say anything. She won't be in your life much longer."

"How do you know?"

"I don't."

CHAPTER EIGHT

The pale ruins of the Roman amphitheater were clearly visible in the moonlight. Ben, Sylvie and Didier had launched Operation Spanish Fly because Didier was convinced that those involved with the orgies held at the amphitheater might be able to lead them to Devin. Devin had been a regular, and the last confirmed sighting of him before his disappearance had been at one of the orgies. The group had determined that Ben would go undercover and pose as a client to see what he could learn, while Sylvie and Didier would target Sergei, the leader of the Russian sex-crime ring that was responsible for putting on the orgies.

Around midnight, from her station inside one of the arches, Sylvie could make out disparate groups of orgy-goers gathered about the site in various states of undress. She watched a kneeling male figure perform oral sex on a standing male figure in front of a column. The area was dimly lit by red lanterns. The standing figure wore black-leather pants and a matching leather jacket and motorcycle cap. The kneeling figure was in jeans without a shirt. When the man in leather turned his head, Sylvie saw that it was Ben. His expression suggested ecstasy. *Either Ben is one hell of an actor, or he's really getting into it*, she thought.

Didier was scanning the clients, hustlers and handlers with infrared field glasses from his vantage point along a row of cypress trees on a rise at the back of the ruins. When, at last, Sergei came into view, Didier smiled. He let Sylvie know by walkie-talkie and made arrangements to meet at their rendezvous point outside the amphitheater so they could follow Sergei and confront him.

The festivities were winding down. The hustlers, who were the main attraction, and their handlers had already left. Now the few remaining revelers were filtering out.

Hidden by a row of plane trees across from the entrance, Didier and Sylvie watched Sergei as he walked alone to a side street a couple of blocks from the entrance. Silently, they followed. When he approached his Mercedes and reached for his key, they sprang into action.

"I wouldn't do that if I were you, *mon ami*," Didier barked ominously.

"Why not?" Sergei asked, turning around slowly with his arms outstretched to show he was unarmed. He spoke with a thick Russian accent. Didier, only a few yards away, was pointing a Walther PPK at him.

"Hands on your head," Sylvie said sharply, leveling a 9 mm Beretta.

He quickly obeyed. "Is this really necessary, these weapons?" he protested. "Sergei is lover not fighter."

"We shall see about that," Didier snapped.

"How can I help you?" Sergei asked.

"We need information," Sylvie said.

"Sergei has no secrets. In fact, they say I am guilty of oversharing. What do you want to know?"

Didier led the interrogation. Sergei, who turned out to be extremely talkative, could not have been more cooperative. And, strangely enough, everything he told them had the ring of truth to it. It soon became clear that the body was not Oleg Stolichnaya's after all. Something had gone awry at a recent orgy, and a hustler—also named Oleg—had been killed accidentally by a wealthy client. Sergei had seen the severed head before it had disappeared and was able to verify the identity of the body. He pooh-poohed the notion that Devin might be dead. He was, in fact, looking for Devin himself. To their surprise, Sylvie and Didier learned that Sergei was lovesick, and Devin was the object of his affection! Far from wishing to harm Devin, Sergei wanted nothing more than to spend all this time with him. Alas, his love was unrequited. He confessed that his obsession had, apparently, been driving the famous author crazy, and Devin simply wanted to get away.

At 5 a.m. Sylvie and Didier arrived in his car and Ben pulled up on Sylvie's Vespa at their prearranged meeting spot, an all-night brasserie in the Old Port. Didier and Sylvie shared with Ben what they'd learned from Sergei. The spirits of the group were lifted by this unexpected good news, and Ben was visibly relieved to learn that Devin and Oleg might both still be alive. With some embarrassment, Didier admitted that his more sinister theory about Devin and Oleg's fate had likely been proven wrong by this comic twist: Devin had disappeared in order to flee the outstretched arms of a Russian gangster who had fallen under his spell. But still left unanswered was the question of where Devin and Oleg were now. Over breakfast, Didier also debriefed Ben about anything suspicious he might have witnessed at the orgy. Sylvie recounted in minute detail for Ben how she'd observed him being blown by a hustler so as not to give away his cover, and how she'd loved every second of it. Ben, who seemed puzzled by the scene she described, smiled, sphinxlike.

"Come now, that blow job wasn't so bad, was it?" Didier ribbed him.

Ben paused before responding. "I did it for Devin," he said.

"Yes, for Devin," Didier murmured.

"You took one for the team," Sylvie quipped.

After the check arrived, Ben's expression became contemplative. "You know something? Now that I think about it, that was one great blow job."

Sylvie chuckled, and Didier smiled appreciatively. "We knew you'd come around," Sylvie said.

Then, after rhapsodizing about his participation in the orgy and otherwise milking the situation for a few more minutes, Ben confessed that he was just playing along and that they were mistaken. What Sylvie saw, he said, was someone else wearing the same outfit. "I'd like to say I was blown at the orgy, but it would be taking credit where credit isn't due."

Didier and Sylvie gave him searching looks. Ben remained stone-faced. There was a pregnant silence.

"Okay, if you say so," Sylvie said at last.

"We accept your explanation, but we want you to know that we're very disappointed in you, Ben," Didier said with a smirk.

"That's right," Sylvie chimed in. "We thought we'd learned that you had a hitherto undiscovered dimension."

"Sorry to disappoint," Ben said.

Sylvie and Didier reluctantly let the matter drop and moved on to other topics.

Outside the restaurant, Didier suddenly turned to Ben with a wry smile. "Are you sure?"

"I'm sure," Ben replied.

~

"I have news," Didier announced to Ben and Sylvie somberly the next night at Le Zinc. He explained that he had just gotten word earlier that evening from Captain Brossard. When Ben and Sylvie learned from Didier that the body found in Devin's apartment had been positively identified and was not Devin, they were elated. Only then did the three conclude that Devin was, in all likelihood, still alive.

The body was that of a writer friend of Devin's from the Bay Area who had been staying in his apartment: Kevin Killian. The badly decomposed body had been unrecognizable. A ring with Kevin's initials had been found at the scene, something which, along with the results of DNA testing, ultimately enabled the police to identify the body.

CHAPTER NINE

The party was already in full swing when Ben arrived at the cavernous artist's studio located in a nineteenth-century building in Old Nice. A number of guests among the overflow crowd were gossiping and laughing outside on the cobblestone street, drinks and cigarettes in hand. The host was an artist friend of Didier's who was based in Paris but kept the studio in Nice, where he spent the summers. Large gestural abstract paintings hung on the walls. A star DJ from French Wigstock, who specialized in atmospheric shoegaze and trance, was in charge of the music.

The hip, good-looking partygoers, largely Parisians, included fashion designers, stylists, actors, playwrights, dramaturgs and dominatrixes. Didier, Sylvie, Benoît, Élodie, Marie and Robert were mingling or dancing. Ben had the sensation of feeling very alive. He was startled to find Sylvie talking animatedly to Donald, who seemed to be in his element.

"I'm so glad you're here, but isn't it dangerous?" Ben asked Donald.

"Isn't he great!" Sylvie gushed.

Donald looked bug-eyed. "I was going stir-crazy."

With great relish, Sylvie recounted for Donald the recent events at the amphitheater.

"I'm so jealous," Donald said. "You must have had a great time."

"Well, Ben certainly did!" Sylvie giggled.

"Enough already," Ben rolled his eyes.

"What else have you been up to?" Donald asked.

"Ben and I have been playing house, so to speak. What about you?"

"I've been cooped up in that apartment like a sardine, reading Sade," Donald lamented. "Did you know sardines can read?"

"Good news! We need all the intelligentsia we can get," Ben grinned. "I'm glad you've come up for air. I missed you! We all did."

At the bar, on an upper level of the loft that overlooked the ground floor, Ben and another guest recognized each other from the orgy. The guy cruised Ben, giving him a knowing smile.

"American?" he asked Ben in accented English.

"Yes."

"You look so familiar . . . Do I know you?"

"It's, um . . . not what you think," Ben said awkwardly.

"No? What do I think?" He shot Ben a suggestive look.

"Oh, boy."

"I'm Antoine, by the way."

"Ben."

"Enchanted."

"We Americans would say, '*Enchanté*,'" Ben quipped.

"Why aren't you wearing your divine black-leather outfit, Ben? Are you incognito tonight?"

Ben tried to explain that, actually, he had been in costume that night at the amphitheater, because of certain confidential matters of great urgency, and that what he had on tonight were his regular clothes.

Antoine looked dubious. Carefully, he sized Ben up. "No, no, no, I don't *think* so," he concluded at last, shaking his head.

Sylvie and Didier, who had been eavesdropping, were laughing so hard that tears were rolling down their cheeks. Ben asked them to intercede and explain why he had really been at the orgy, but they politely declined.

"Why don't you just level with him and stop pretending to be straight in public," Didier chided Ben. "That's my advice, for whatever it's worth."

Sylvie kept a straight face.

"Yes, yes, I see, now," Antoine said. "It's just as I thought." He proceeded to tell Ben that he knew just what he was going through and that he could help him with the difficult process of coming out to family, friends and colleagues.

Ben, who had now given up on convincing Antoine of the truth, professed to be grateful. "I have to admit, it's been very difficult to keep who I really am inside," he said confidingly.

"Oh my God, look!" Sylvie clutched Ben's arm.

Ben turned. "Jesus, it's Devin."

From the loft, they looked down as Devin Curtis purposefully crossed the room. Donald, whose back was turned, stood alone facing the dance floor. Devin walked straight into Donald from behind. Donald disappeared in a flash.

"Wow," was all Ben could manage.

Sylvie, who immediately grasped what had just transpired, broke down and began sobbing.

Ben ran downstairs. "Donald? Are you all right? What just happened?"

"It's Devin, Ben. I'm *Devin*. That creep was a hologram. He was a major parasite."

"What did you do?"

"He absorbed all the pieces that they took from me. I *had* to kill him. He was stealing my essence."

"You took him from behind."

Devin cracked a smile. "That would be one way of putting it."

Sylvie appeared at Ben's side, shell-shocked. "Why did this have to happen? I loved Donald."

"He wasn't real," Devin said.

"It all so horrible. I can't stand it. I've got to go." Sylvie broke away.

"Where are you off to?" Ben called.

"Anywhere," she said, without turning back.

"That was awkward," Devin said apologetically. "Who is she? Did I get you in hot water?"

"She'll be okay. Devin, we've got to talk," Ben said. "You have no idea how glad I am to see you."

"I'll call you," Devin said. "Give me your number. I'm wiped out. I need to crash. I promise I'll call."

The next night on the Promenade des Anglais, Didier, Ben and Sylvie went over the astonishing events of the previous night. Sylvie broke down again in tears.

"I don't care if Donald was real or not. He was real to me," she sniffed.

"He said, 'Pieces they took,'" Ben recalled. "Who are 'they'? *What* pieces?"

"Where did Devin go?" Didier asked.

"Maybe Donald came back and reabsorbed him?!" Ben offered. "Who knows. But I have a feeling that we'll know soon enough."

"I missed that whole thing," Didier said. "What did Devin look like?"

"He looked like Devin," Ben said.

"He looked exactly like Donald," Sylvie said. "He murdered Donald. He's horrible."

"Stop it, stop that," Ben said.

Sylvie walked away. Ben began to follow.

"Let her go," Didier said. "She has to get over it. This is really incredible. It's science fiction."

"I don't know if it's science, but it's not fiction. I saw it with my own eyes."

CHAPTER TEN

The message on Ben's answering machine was from Devin.

"Listen, Ben, I'm really sorry about everything. It's a long, complicated story. I understand what you've done, and I appreciate all your efforts. I know you were trying to find me, but I didn't really want to be found. Donald was robbing me of my soul. Please forgive me for not explaining things more fully. You were always a friend."

Sylvie arrived at Ben's room at the B and B in time to catch the tail end of the message. "Who was that?"

"Oh, nobody."

Devin's call was comforting to Ben, though it didn't resolve anything. He saw that there was now no further reason for him to remain in France. He looked at Sylvie longingly.

Ben and Sylvie went to dinner at a Moroccan restaurant in the Old Port.

"I have to go back to America," Ben announced suddenly. "I'll be thinking of you."

He leaned forward and kissed her. She looked at him in wonderment. It was a tender moment.

∼

Élodie immediately saw that Sylvie was not herself when they met for drinks at Le Zinc.

"What is it?" she asked.

"Ben's going back to America."

"Do you love him?"

"Yes . . . no . . . I don't know."

A little while later Didier dropped by and joined them in their booth.

"Ben called me," he said. "I know he's going back home. Are you okay? I'm here. I'm a good listener."

"I'm okay," Sylvie said without conviction.

"You're young, you're beautiful, men will be dropping from the trees for you," Élodie reassured her.

"Of course, it's ridiculous, because I know he's married," Sylvie frowned. "We couldn't have much of a future unless I tied him up and kept him here."

"Well, you did that for a long while," Élodie laughed.

Sylvie smiled weakly, then stared into the distance. Didier and Élodie shared a glance, both now painfully aware of Sylvie's attachment.

∼

Ben walked along the Promenade des Anglais, savoring the picturesque view of the pebble beach and Mediterranean. He was feeling light-headed. A montage of random thoughts flitted through his mind, none particularly noteworthy. He imagined being with the young Bardot in St. Tropez, her telling him, "I just want you to know that I am happy to fulfill your slightly demented sexual fantasies until the cows come home."

CHAPTER ELEVEN

Henry and Joe, decked out in white padded shirts and trousers, donned their fencing helmets and picked up their épées.

"Ready, fence," Joe squeaked.

"*En garde*," Henry boomed.

The two rushed at each other and began to parry and thrust furiously.

"A dozen roses to the widow," Henry shouted.

"Die, Saracen pig," Joe retorted.

"The Saracens used sabers, not épées, you nimrod," Henry responded.

Ben arrived toward the end of the session to pick up the boys, in time to watch each of them in rather sedate bouts with other students. The fencing studio, located in a spacious but dilapidated double-height storefront in the neighborhood, was festooned with awards and medals. Two parrots sat on perches in a corner trading observations about the goings-on. The owner, a sprightly woman with curly blonde hair, had competed for the US Olympic team in the eighties. A change for the better had come over both Henry and Joe since they had, at the suggestion of Diane, taken up fencing and dedicated themselves to the sport.

To his surprise, as they were on their way out, Ben noticed Dr. Shulman engaged in a spirited bout at the far end of the room. It turned out he was a devotee who enjoyed the sport in his spare time.

After Ben took the kids home, he joined Tina on the couch for a glass of wine while Henry and Joe played with the cats. Tina recounted for him how, that morning, Joe had corralled her into providing a play-by-play commentary on his professional wrestling match with Louis, his stuffed gorilla. Joe had been so impressed with the realism of her descriptions, which were peppered with professional wrestling terminology ("pile driver," "dropkick," "body slam," etc.), that he made her promise that this would be a regular occurrence.

"Joe's stage name is the Great Bombo," Tina revealed.

"Who won?"

"It was nip and tuck, but in a last-minute turnaround the Great Bombo prevailed."

"Wow, I can see you're really into it! How do you know so much about it?"

"Who do you think watches it on TV with Joe all day?"

"What's the difference between WWE and WWF?"

"WWE is just like WWF, only not as classy," Tina explained.

"Good to know."

"Say, you've been home for two weeks and haven't told me a single concrete thing about France. What about this Donald character?"

"He was a hologram."

"A hooligan?"

"No, a hologram."

"Wait a minute. A hologram?"

"Forget it."

"By the way, when are you going to get that vasectomy? You keep putting it off."

"So, this is your ultimatum?"

"Not exactly. I will take the kids and leave you if you don't get one."

"Oh, I didn't get the meaning of 'ultimatum.' If I have to . . . I wonder if it will be anything like my dream with Dr. Roberts."

"Huh? By the way, there's some mail for you. It's in the entryway."

Ben found a letter from Sylvie.

. . . I suppose I should tell you Devin and I have stupidly just gotten involved. I don't think it's going to go anywhere. I really miss you. You were so great. Devin is not as much fun as you and compared to you and Donald he is a crashing bore. I miss Donald. Write to me. I'm staying at my mother's. Didier sends his love . . .

CHAPTER TWELVE

Diane and Mavis pulled off their bikini tops and took turns licking and sucking each other's nipples. Mavis's erect nipples were one inch long. Gently, Diane took one between her teeth while flicking her tongue back and forth.

"Jesus! So . . . good," Mavis whispered. She reached down and caressed Diane's crotch, working her fingers under the fabric and into her moist vagina.

Before long, Diane pushed Mavis onto the bed, pulled off Mavis's bikini bottom, got on her knees and began tonguing Mavis's pussy and clit, over and over. She held her by the ankles and pulled Mavis's legs back over her head and licked furiously. In moments, Mavis became sopping wet, soaking the sheets with wave after wave of thick, flowing pussy juice.

"Yes, oh yes. Oh, oh, shit, oh fuck!"

Mavis's whole body shuddered as she came. She would never experience an orgasm like that again. Diane was a magician.

Once Mavis caught her breath, the two switched positions, and Mavis eagerly went to work on Diane, diving into her pussy with abandon. Diane held Mavis's head in her hands, pushing her mouth deeper into her cunt. Mavis's tongue was long and hard. In seconds,

Diane was coming, squealing with delight as her cunt squirted uncontrollably, dousing Mavis's face, neck and hair.

"Yikes!" Mavis squeaked, and they both broke into a fit of giggles.

Brent coughed. He had been watching all this time from behind the bathroom door.

"Hey, guys, that was wonderful. My penis is throbbing."

"Agh!" Diane exclaimed. "Brent, you weren't supposed to see that."

"Too late. Who's going to come soap my balls in the shower? Diane?"

"No thanks. Not even your monster cock could satisfy me like this girl just did," Diane laughed, circling an arm around Mavis.

"I need to take a shower and wash off all your sweet cum," Mavis said softly to Diane. They kissed, sucking each other's tongues, then Mavis went into the bathroom, where Brent stood naked, his eleven-inch cock at half-mast.

Diane's phone rang. It was Tina.

"What's going on?"

"Oh, honey, this place is too good to be true. And remember that department store thing I told you about? The thing with the woman from Bergdorf's?"

"Vaguely . . ."

"Well, she's down here with her husband, and I think they're going to come through for me with some catalog-design work. More money for everybody!"

"When will you be back? I need you."

"Early next week. Listen, Tina, you're doing great. The kids are gonna turn a corner. C'mon, brighten up!"

"Yeah . . . I don't know . . ."

"Listen, I gotta go. There's some people here."

"People? Are you fucking them?"

"Don't be silly."

CHAPTER THIRTEEN

Princess Attila entered the salon. "Where's Priscilla? I can't find her anywhere. Goddammit! I want Priscilla."

"How about a straitjacket, dear? I have one just your size, made to measure," Princess Attila's mother, Marina, suggested indifferently from a chaise longue.

"What's a straitjacket?"

"You'll find out one day."

"Mother! There's Priscilla! Under the couch!" Attila got down on one knee, reached under the couch and grabbed the doll by the leg, happily holding it up for her mother to see.

Marina looked up from her magazine and cast a bored look at Priscilla. "I'm so glad you two have been reunited. I was afraid she might have lost interest in you, the way you've been treating her lately."

"What's wrong with the way I've been treating her?" Attila frowned.

"Oh, you know, flinging her around, spilling juice on her, threatening her, jabbing her with scissors, generally beating her up."

"I'm punishing her. Sometimes she needs punishment."

∼

Attila's father, Roger, was on the beach below the house with his research assistant, Miss Burgoyne, who was pale, wore bright red lipstick and was dressed in a tartan skirt, kneesocks, jumper and horn-rimmed glasses. Roger proceeded down the beach with his mason jars and notebooks in search of rare mollusk specimens. Miss Burgoyne, who was conveniently wearing a bikini under her outfit, spread a blanket and lay down to sunbathe. After a while, Roger returned and lay down next to her. He traced circles on her stomach with a finger, and she did not object.

∾

The guests began to arrive around 5 p.m. for cocktails on the wrap-around porch of Roger and Marina's palatial beach house, with views of the dunes and ocean. Roger and Miss Burgoyne were there to greet them along with Attila and Marina. Roger insisted that every-one wear a funny hat from his travels, and he handed out the head-gear to the amusement of the group: fez, pith helmet, kepi, beanie, sombrero, straw boater, ten-gallon hat, tiara (for Attila) and top hat (for Roger). Only Marina demurred and declined to wear a hat.

"You look ridiculous, Daddy!" Attila said.

"We're *all* ridiculous, darling, with or without our hats," Roger laughed. He assessed the arrivals—all long-standing friends: Jim and Sophie Brownstein, he a successful Bay Area businessman in the shower curtain game, garrulous, funny, a gifted storyteller, she a bit dim; Randall and Marguerite Dubois, both fellow scientists, friends from graduate school, currently stationed outside Cleveland, sharp, alert, preppy, peppy; and Gerard Atkinson and April March, a "live-in" couple, both families described as "San Luis Obispo roy-alty going back to the early part of the twentieth century," loaded with cash and property, often, if not always, drunk, good-looking, adventurous, entertaining, speaking with Locust Valley lockjaw, which they'd picked up at Eastern Seaboard private schools.

Attila freely interrupted the grown-ups' conversations as she wandered about with Priscilla in tow.

"Mustn't be rude, poppet," Marina scolded.

"What an adorable child," Sophie Brownstein smiled.

"*Sort* of," Marina shrugged. "We call her Attila the Hon."

Still wearing their funny hats, each carrying their chosen cocktail, the group strolled along a wooden walkway through the dunes down to the beach, where they removed their shoes and, led by Roger and Miss Burgoyne, explored the tidal pools.

Attila remained behind with Priscilla, making a partially successful sandcastle or "sand land," as she called it. "Well, Persilly," she addressed her doll, "What do we think of Miss Alverna Burgoyne?"

"She's putrid," Priscilla replied. "Your father's totally cuntstruck. It's going to break your mother's heart."

"Stuff and nonsense!" Attila shot back. "Mother couldn't give less of a flying fuck *what* Daddy does with his fingers. She's the Rock of Madrid!"

"Gibraltar," Priscilla corrected her mistress.

"Whatever. Hey, what's this?" Attila picked up a small red-and-black-speckled snail. "I better take it to Daddy."

She hurried, snail in hand, back to the gaggle of adults. On close inspection, Roger determined that Attila had likely found a new species of mollusk, similar in type to recent discoveries off the southern Australian islands.

In the house, Attila flung herself around her bedroom, scraping her elbow on a stanchion. The maid, a slim Latina whom Attila called

Blobbo for reasons no one could discern, but who was actually named María, bandaged the wound in the bathroom.

By the time everyone sat down for dinner, Attila had changed into a pink tutu and tiara and performed for the guests: an impromptu dance to spring, accompanied by Blobbo on the harp.

"Thank you, my dear, that was wonderful," April enthused. The guests murmured in agreement.

Then Blobbo gave a scintillating rendition of Debussy's "La cathédrale engloutie" from his first book of *Preludes*, adapted for harp. It brought down the house.

The sun was sinking below the dunes. Blobbo served dinner to Attila in front of the TV in the family room. Afterward, Attila wandered outside to the gazebo and admired the sunset. All at once, it hit her: *Jesus Christ! I left Priscilla on the beach after I found the snail! She's probably dehydrated! Possibly dead!* She rushed to the ocean's edge and found Priscilla, a bit bedraggled but quite alive, sitting in the sand, playing twenty questions with herself.

"What's the point, if you already know the answers?" Attila asked the oblivious doll.

"I don't know *all* the answers," came the reply.

Back at the gazebo, Attila and Priscilla made themselves comfortable in the fading light.

"Persilly, I've become completely taken with Vladimir Propp's *Morphology of the Folktale*."

"Oh, really? I've heard of it, but I'm embarrassed to say I haven't read it."

"He breaks down Russian folktales into their constituent parts, which he calls morphemes and narratemes."

"How does it work?"

"Well, the motifs and characters are interchangeable from folktale to folktale. For example, the villain may be a dragon, a devil, a bandit, a witch or a stepmother. The villain typically attempts a disguise. A dragon can turn into a handsome youth. Or a witch can pretend to be a sweet old lady. Later the villain abducts somebody. A dragon kidnaps the king's daughter. Or an older brother abducts the bride of a younger brother."

"Fascinating!"

"The hero's means of transportation may be a steed, a magic carpet, a bird or the back of a giant."

"Oh, you know what that reminds me of? Poussin's *Blind Orion Searching for the Rising Sun.*"

"Fabulous painting. It's at the Met in New York."

The conversation continued in this peripatetic fashion for some time until Attila, too exhausted to continue, doll in hand, went inside and threw herself on her bed.

The sun sparkled on the Pacific. An impressive breakfast had been laid out on platters and chafing dishes on the buffet in the dining room: eggs Benedict, fresh raspberries, pineapple, melon, grapefruit, croissants, scones, toast, jam, yogurt, bacon, smoked salmon, kippers, oysters, coffee, tea, orange juice, champagne and Bloody Marys. In need of a little "hair of the dog," Gerard and April were the first to arrive for breakfast, impeccably turned out, visibly no worse for wear. They quickly began downing Bloody Marys one after the other until they lost count. The Brownsteins were the next to arrive, followed in short order by the Duboises. Roger and Marina had elected to sleep in, and Miss Burgoyne had gone for a walk on the beach.

Suddenly, there was an enormous crash. Everyone shuddered and turned in horror to find that Gerard, who had been leaning back in a Louis XV chair, had lost his balance and tumbled backward. The chair had splintered into pieces. April screamed. Blobbo rushed in from the kitchen and calmly took Gerard's pulse. He was out cold but otherwise fine, she reassured the group. Following Blobbo's orders, Jim and Randall carried Gerard onto the chaise longue in the salon while she went to prepare a cold compress. April, Sophie and Marguerite continued with breakfast as if nothing had happened.

Attila and Priscilla were in Attila's bedroom engaged in a furious argument.

"Of all the Russian formalists, Viktor Shklovsky was the most brilliant. His ideas about *ostranie*, or defamiliarization, and the laying bare of the device have been very influential," Attila asserted.

"I disagree. Shklovsky was charismatic, a gadfly, true. But I think Roman Jakobson was the most theoretically rigorous of the group," Priscilla insisted. "The notions of *fabula* and *sujet* all begin with him."

"How can you say that? That is so wrong. No, no, no!" Attila shouted, turning red with frustration.

There was a knock on the door.

"Shit, who could that be?" Attila asked meekly.

She peered through the keyhole.

It was Tina.

"Hey, honey, look who's back from St. Bart's, and she got the new client!" Tina called to Ben through the door of his study.

"Gee, that's great, but I'm in the middle of this paragraph," Ben said.

"Sorry, honey. Take a break and come join us," Tina said.

"Who is it?" Priscilla asked.

"Nobody. Probably just the wind," Attila replied.

~

Diane and Tina sat on the couch having a glass of wine. Henry and Joe were at the house of friends for a sleepover, so the loft was unusually quiet.

"Where did you stay in St. Bart's?" Tina asked.

"The Guanahani."

"Oh, fancy! So, you had your own cottage with a private pool?"

"Of course."

"I'm impressed."

Then Diane recounted the dramatic landing when she'd first arrived: The puddle jumper from St. Martin had suddenly dropped down between two mountains onto an old airstrip the size of a postage stamp! She described how she rented a Mini Moke to get around the island and explore the beaches.

"I'll bet you were a holy terror on the road," Tina laughed.

Ben joined them on the couch. He was steaming inside. The flow of his novel had been interrupted just when he had found a groove.

"My tie was on the doorknob," Ben scolded Tina. "You know that means no interruptions."

"Doesn't a tie on the doorknob generally mean you have a girl in the room, and your roommate shouldn't come in?" Diane asked.

"Yeah, if you're living in a college dorm," he glowered. "Here it means I'm writing, and I'm not to be disturbed."

"Sorry." Diane studied her lap.

"Actually, I'm happy for you, Diane. Will you still be able to work from home?" Ben asked.

"Yeah, for the most part," Diane said.

Ben nodded, then excused himself and returned to the study.

CHAPTER FOURTEEN

Over a period of a week, Ben's initial minor reservations about going to Yaddo had developed into full-fledged misgivings. Unhappy with his work on the novel, he had begun to have serious doubts about his writing generally. He questioned what had possessed him to sign on for the retreat in the first place. Tina and Diane encouraged and even pushed him to follow through with the residency. Only half-kidding, Ben accused Tina of wanting to get rid of him so she and Diane could have each other.

Tina tried to get Ben to look on the bright side: The change would do him good, and he would be getting a free pass from parenting duty while she was stuck with the kids. Even though his departure was still several days off, she helped him pack his duffle bag and Dopp kit and, to lighten the mood, suggested he take along a special outfit to write in—fisherman's jersey, board shorts and camp moccasins—and another outfit for cocktails to make a splash: seersucker sports jacket, polo shirt, Bermuda shorts and white bucks. He was still on the fence, but she could see that he was weakening. As an afterthought, she suggested he bring the tattered tartan golf bag of antique golf clubs that stood in the corner of the study. Suddenly his expression brightened: She'd won him over.

~

In an effort to whip the kids into shape, Dr. Shulman referred Ben and Tina to Dr. Zakir, a behavioral psychologist. A change of approach from individual therapy would be well worth a try, he thought. In their initial consultation with Dr. Zakir, in his tasteful, midcentury modern office in Brooklyn Heights, they gave some choice examples of the boys' temper tantrums, fights, cursing and general acting out at home, and they were impressed with his descriptions of the techniques with which he had had success in tackling similar issues in the past.

A few days later, Tina brought Henry and Joe in for their kickoff session with Dr. Zakir. The boys made a particular effort to give a good impression and were exceedingly polite and reasonable.

"Where did you go to school, Dr. Zakir?" Joe asked.

"I got my degree at Harvard."

"That's terrific," Henry said.

"Doctor, we've heard about Islam," Joe said. "What's your opinion? Can you show us your rug?"

"I'm not sure that that would be appropriate," Dr. Zakir smiled.

The boys stared at him expressionlessly.

"I'm only kidding, kids. I would be delighted to, but another time. Right now we need to get down to business."

He consulted with each of the boys individually to discuss their thoughts on the other members of their family. When questioned privately, each confided that he would like to get along better with his brother. Next he worked with them both together: The three of them played Clue, in an effort to foster a spirit of cooperation and teamwork. Dr. Zakir was enthusiastic, kind and sympathetic. The boys took an immediate shine to him, sensing that he genuinely liked them and would be an advocate for them with their parents.

When Tina picked up Henry and Joe after the session, they were in an upbeat, talkative mood and, unprompted, gave her a blow-by-blow account of the session in the car ride home, including how well behaved they'd been and how well they'd gotten along together.

"Are you boys just blowing smoke?" Tina asked circumspectly.

"What does that mean?" Joe asked.

"Never mind," Tina replied. "I'm just glad to hear that it went well."

"Mommy, when is our next appointment with Dr. Zakir?" Henry inquired.

"Are you looking forward to seeing him again?" Tina asked, trying not to sound too eager.

"Yes, we are," Henry said matter-of-factly.

"Fine," Tina said. "I'm sure he will be pleased. I'll call and set it up."

The boys beamed.

That night, after the kids were in bed, Tina brought Ben up to speed on the boys' session. He thought it was a resounding success.

"Honestly, I'm not so sure," Tina said. "I have my doubts."

"How so?"

"I kinda think the boys were just putting on a show for Dr. Zakir and telling him what he wanted to hear. As soon as we got home, they were up to their old tricks, going at it like mixed-martial-arts cage fighters."

"Hmmm . . . Well, let's see how it goes. I wouldn't take such a jaundiced view. It's a process—it's not going to happen overnight. I really think they *do* want to change."

Tina's dubious expression told him that in her mind the jury was still out.

During their sessions over the next several weeks, Dr. Zakir, Henry and Joe went fishing together, read *Huckleberry Finn* to one another, joined a barbershop quartet and began predevelopment work on a design for an energy-efficient, single-family dwelling.

~

The night before Ben was to leave for Yaddo, he and Tina went out to dinner with Michael Kropotkin, a writer friend of Ben's since their days in Brown's MFA program, and his wife, Lara, to a hip, bustling "hunting lodge" in Williamsburg. It wasn't lost on anyone that Ben consumed three martinis in quick succession soon after they arrived.

"What are you celebrating, Ben?" Lara smiled.

"Ben, we've asked the bartender to cut you off!" Michael cracked.

"Really?" Tina asked hopefully.

"No . . . but we're thinking about it," Michael reflected. Lara nodded in agreement.

"Michael, as usual I knew I could count on you for some unsolicited snide commentary," Ben shot back.

"He doesn't want to go to Yaddo," Tina interjected.

"That explains it," Michael said. "Do you want to see my father? I can get you a consultation with him, maybe even a special friends-and-family discount."

"I was wondering when *that* shoe was going to drop," Ben snapped.

"Now, now. No need to be snippy," Michael replied.

"Maybe I should get Ben a session with Dr. Zakir?" Tina chimed in. "I hear he's a whiz at Clue. He may even show Ben his rug."

"Dr. Zakir!" Lara exclaimed. "We know all about Dr. Zakir."

"You do?" Tina said.

"Yep," Lara responded. "He's big on team building. He had us hiking the Appalachian Trail, orienteering and technical rock climbing with Josh and Max before all was said and done."

"Wow, that's right up Tina's alley," Ben deadpanned.

Tina rolled her eyes. "Did it work?"

"Not really," Michael said. "Camping out on the Appalachian Trail, everyone had assigned tasks and chores, like gathering firewood and carrying fresh water. Each night we told ghost stories. Lara thought mine were very 'Michael' in their details as well as very imaginative, by the way. And then before bed, just for good measure, Josh and Max would wind each other up and land a few good punches inside the tent before crawling into their sleeping bags."

Ben, who had continued to drink throughout the meal, was now more than a little woozy. Of the group, only Michael, the designated driver, had abstained. After dinner, the couples walked in a light summer rain shower to Michael's car, which was parked a few blocks away on a quiet side street.

Exhilarated by the rain, Tina and Lara began to sing. "Ooh, walking hand in hand with the one I love . . ."

Michael helped Ben into the car.

"I think I'm going to be sick," Ben moaned.

"Oh, Ben. *Really?*" Tina said.

Ben doubled over and threw up on Michael's shoes.

CHAPTER FIFTEEN

*R*oger *stroked Alverna's thigh. They lay in their underwear on the bed in their suite at the Waldorf Astoria in Key West, overlooking the swimming pools and ocean.*

"Alone at last."

"Isn't it wonderful?"

"You bet."

"Make love to me."

"Must I?"

"You must." She dangled her bra high above her head.

Alverna Burgoyne's reverie continued in this fashion as she strolled past the tidal pools in her jumper, skirt and kneesocks.

Meanwhile, Attila and Priscilla continued their spirited debate on Russian formalism, this time focusing on the merits of Shklovsky's study of Sterne's *Tristram Shandy*.

They heard a knock.

"Tell them to go away," Attila barked.

Priscilla went to the door. "Who is it?"

"It's Jennifer Eastman. Is Ben there?"

"Ben, it's for you."

"Tell her I'm busy," Ben said.

"You tell her," Priscilla replied.

"Hey, Ben, why don't you come out and play?" Jennifer asked through the door of Ben's studio.

"I'm working," Ben explained impatiently.

Jennifer cleared her throat. "I'm wait-ing," she called in a high-pitched, singsong voice. She could hear the clacking of keys. Squatting, she prepared to wait for as long as necessary.

Jennifer Eastman was a clean-cut blonde with a healthy sexual appetite. A photographer, she was a graduate of Yale's MFA program, where she'd been a student and protégé of Gregory Crewdson. She had already had her first one-person show at White Cube in London and was currently with the Zwirner Gallery. She specialized in large-format color photos consisting of elaborate outdoor pre-Raphaelite-style nude self-portraits and tableaux that were meticulously arranged, lit and shot. She was thirty-two and had grown up in a large, prosperous family in Shaker Heights.

"C'mon out, Ben. I have this terrific location for a shoot that I want you to see. I need to get there for the golden hour."

"Are you part of Eastman Kodak?" he asked, from behind the locked door.

"Distantly," she responded.

Somehow, that seemed to do the trick, and he unlocked the door. Jennifer stood before him in a red bikini.

"Praise the Lord and pass the ammunition. I'm bored with the people here. They take themselves too seriously. You don't really fit in at Yaddo. You're a wild card. I like that."

"I see." Ben looked at her blankly.

They dropped by her cabin to pick up her camera equipment and then hiked in the late-afternoon sunlight to a remote clearing by a pond in the woods on the sprawling Yaddo property. Jennifer made a big show of ignoring Ben and intently began to set up for the shoot. Absently, he pulled leaves and berries from a bush.

While his back was turned, she slipped out of her bikini.

"What's so great about that bush, Ben? Come and look at mine."

He turned and stared.

"We're not really here for a shoot, are we?" he asked.

"Not really."

She went to him, helped him peel off his clothes and pulled him down onto the damp grass.

Ben was at Yaddo for a two-week residency to work on his novel. He had never been to an artists' and writers' retreat before. There were fourteen other residents.

Yaddo's main structure was a nineteenth-century stone castle. A massive pergola covered in grapevines formed the centerpiece of the formal gardens. For the residents, their daily routine began with a communal breakfast in the dining room before they dispersed to work in individual studios. Lunch was taken alone, followed by more work. Cocktails were served in the library at five before a communal dinner in the large dining hall. The evening usually ended in the library with semi-impromptu group activities: a performance, a recital, a reading, board games. An informal "silent-ballot" election ("best dressed," "most sexy," etc.) had become a nightly ritual and a favorite among the residents.

Although Jennifer Eastman had taken a shine to him, Ben was viewed as a wet blanket at Yaddo. He came across as neurotic, even unpleasant, rejecting all overtures of friendship. He declined to participate in any group activity. Jennifer was the only one able to make any inroads with him. He confessed to her that he had arrived at Yaddo depressed, and that the daily routine and goings-on only made things worse. Possibly at the root of his malaise was his ambivalent attitude about his novel—his uncertainty and insecurity about whether it was turning out as he'd planned. He was secretly pleased when, after dinner in the library one night, he was voted the least popular person at Yaddo. There was even talk about beating him up.

Others had their problems too. Jed Wurtzel and Stuart Wertheim were poets. Both were forty-five and taught poetry workshops at small Midwestern colleges. Having gone to graduate school together, they had known each other for years and could fairly be described as jealous rivals. In fact, Jed would tell any Yaddo resident who would listen unflattering gossip about Stuart. For his part, Stuart was only too happy to make Jed look bad whenever the opportunity arose. Each had, to the dismay of the other, received several grants and awards, with the result that their work was taken seriously in an ever-widening circle of those who, like them, were especially undiscerning.

One night in the library after dinner, a contest was held to see who could write the worst poem. Everyone except Jed had a lot of fun. He thought the whole thing was in poor taste and refused to join in. Stuart, however, surreptitiously submitted an actual poem by Jed under Jed's name as a practical joke, and it won. The assembled group concurred that Jed's poem was a real stinker. Jed was livid with anger. Someone else had submitted under his own name a poem by Forrest Gander, also as a practical joke, and it came in a close second.

"Congrats, Jed," Stuart said sarcastically.

"Stuart, you're a real asshole!" Jed shouted, before storming out of the room.

Everyone turned and stared.

"What just happened?" someone asked.

"That went well," Jennifer said. "I thought he was going to take a swing at you."

Stuart smirked.

Ben, in the meantime, was holed up in his studio, agonizing over his book.

≈

Emily Yates was an extroverted pixie hipster. Known for her racy, autobiographical bad-girl fiction, she also wrote an online sex column for *Salon* and regularly published idiosyncratic, opinionated reviews and articles for *Time Out* and the *Observer*. Originally from Grosse Pointe, she had graduated from Berkeley ten years earlier.

Jennifer and Emily immediately hit it off at Yaddo. They admired each other's work and were delighted to get to know each other and become friends.

A week after the Jed-Stuart incident, the residents were gathered in the library after dinner. Ben quickly polished off several martinis.

Emily approached him. "I wish you'd read a bit of the new book to us."

"A bit? Are you trying to undermine me?" Ben snapped.

"No, we all want to hear it. It's the truth," Emily said guardedly.

"Here's the truth," Ben responded. He slapped her face.

Emily screamed. "Ben, what the fuck?!"

Everyone froze. Jennifer was horrified.

"Are you drunk?" Emily asked. "What is your problem? You need to get your head fixed."

Somewhere in his drunken fog, Ben realized that he'd possibly misunderstood Emily's intentions and had overreacted. He turned on his heels and hurried out of the room.

Furious, Emily approached Jennifer. "Don't you have any control over him? Go talk to him!"

"What's that supposed to mean? What does this have to do with me?"

"Jennifer, I think you know."

"Hmmm . . ."

They glared at each other.

"All right, people, let's all chill out," Stuart admonished the group.

"Everybody just calm down." Sensing that he had everyone's attention, he became reflective. "How odd, that *I*, of all people, should be the voice of reason, but there you have it."

The residents nodded in agreement.

A short time later, a small group, led by Stuart, went to Ben's room to check up on him. They correctly inferred that Ben was experiencing a meltdown of some kind and could use some moral support. And for the sake of everyone's peace of mind, they wanted to make sure that the scene in the library didn't take on a life of its own.

Ben heard voices outside and assumed the worst: that the residents had come to confront him. He remained silent as he listened to them speculate on his mental state. He fished in his overnight bag for his Mauser, then remembered that it was at home in the safe.

~

Diane and Tina sat at a table at Peter Luger having dinner with Alex and Luca, clients of Diane's who were executives in the New York office of an Italian fashion design house. Diane had been hired to design their US catalog. In need of another woman to round out the group, Diane had asked Tina to join her, and Tina had reluctantly agreed. Since Ben was away, Diane reasoned, it would be good for Tina to call a babysitter and enjoy a night out.

Luca, who cut a dashing figure, seemed to take a keen interest in Tina. He was generous with compliments and expressed curiosity about her: where she was from originally, where she grew up, where she went to college, etc. Was he flirting with her? Tina wondered. He told her about his summers spent on Sardinia, and how much he would enjoy showing her the Costa Smeralda. Charmed by the unexpected show of attention, Tina became unusually animated. When Luca suggested that she give him her phone number so that they could make plans, Tina was at a loss as to how to respond. There was an uncomfortable silence.

Diane, who had been monitoring the situation, quickly sprang into action. "Excuse me. Tina, would you mind joining me in the ladies' room?"

"So, what do you think of Luca?" Diane asked, once she and Tina were alone in the bathroom.

"Well, he seems nice," she said noncommittally.

Diane smiled knowingly. "I love you, but I can't be a moral arbiter here. You should do what you really want to do, but keep in mind that it could become messy. I don't want anything bad to happen to you."

"I know, I know . . ."

Once they returned to the table, Tina was visibly more reserved, and the dinner proceeded without incident. Seeing that he had perhaps been too forward, Luca, who himself had a wife and three children, as well as a mistress named Coco, at home in Milan, was on his best behavior.

"I knew you would do the right thing," Diane said to Tina in the cab on the way home. "It was important that you reached your own decision."

"Thank you for your support," Tina said, hugging Diane.

≈

After breakfast, Ben confronted Jennifer outside the dining room. "I need to speak to you," he said curtly.

As soon as they were in her room, he let loose and blamed her for his being stymied with his novel.

"You're being irrational."

There was a long, awkward moment.

At last Ben responded. "You're right. This is not like me. It's totally out of character, believe it or not."

"I know, Ben."

"You do?"

"Yeah."

Suddenly Ben got choked up and broke down and cried. She held him and tenderly embraced him, something which touched him deeply.

When he recovered his composure, they made out and screwed for about forty-five minutes.

"Ben, when are we leaving this dump?" Attila asked.

"There are two more days before the residency ends," Ben replied.

"Jesus, this is *the* most boring place!"

"I second that emotion," Priscilla said.

Ben turned off his computer. "Sit tight, girls, there's something I've gotta do."

Ben knocked softly on a door. Emily Yates opened. She backed away when she saw who it was.

"You're not going to slap me again, are you?"

"I came to apologize. *I'm* the one who deserves to be slapped."

"That's very kind of you. Apology accepted." She threw her arms around him and gave him a long soul kiss, catching Ben completely by surprise.

"Wow, I didn't see *that* coming."

Emily shrugged.

"I would love to chat, but I've got to pack. I'm leaving soon."

"I understand," she said. "I'm sorry we didn't get to know each other better."

"Me too," he said over his shoulder as he turned to go.

Ben left Yaddo a day early without saying good-bye to Jennifer. He slipped a brief note under her door:

Jennifer,

Perhaps this has been a turnaround for me. Anyway, it was wonderful meeting you.

Ben

On the way home, Attila and Priscilla sat in the backseat.

"Jesus, that was some wringer you put yourself through," Attila said.

"Yeah, that's not going to happen again," Ben replied.

"I was scared for you," Priscilla said.

"You're awfully quiet, Ben."

"I'm thinking of someone."

"Who?" Attila asked.

"A woman—Sylvie."

"Is she nice?" Priscilla asked.

"She's young and beautiful, and she does dumb things."

Attila and Priscilla exchanged bewildered looks.

CHAPTER SIXTEEN

While Ben was still at Yaddo, Tina and Diane arranged babysitting for Henry and Joe, so they could again go out for the evening.

The babysitter, a cute teenager from the neighborhood named Maggie, was an aspiring actress. Joe had her sit on the couch with him and watch his favorite movie, *Happy Gilmore*. The two of them giggled together. Later, for a game of chess with Henry, she adopted a more sober, thoughtful mien. Each of the boys was smitten.

Over dinner at a Japanese restaurant in Diane's Cobble Hill neighborhood, Tina and Diane discussed Ben's character. They agreed that Ben, who wanted everything, had become emotionally shaky. Ben was a good father up to a point. The kids loved him. He did lots of stuff with them: skiing, snorkeling, spelunking, collecting fossils, etc. But his particular shortcoming as a parent was his inconsistency when it came to imposing discipline.

"What are his finer points?" Diane asked.

"Self-absorbed?" Tina said.

"Check."

"Self-indulgent?"

"Check."

"Soulful brown eyes?"

"Definitely."

"Extremely vain?"

"Always has his puss in the mirror."

They both laughed.

"What can we do to help Ben improve?" Diane wondered.

"Is that a rhetorical question?"

"Yes!"

"Listen, Di, I know it's an odd situation, but I want to tell you how much I appreciate you. What you do with Ben is okay, as long as you don't take him from us. You're part of the family."

Diane squeezed Tina's hand.

"You know, you never did tell me how you and Ben met," Tina said.

"Didn't *he* tell you? We had adjoining concession stands at Coney Island."

"Oh, yeah. He *did* tell me. On your first date you won the Nathan's hot dog–eating contest, and Ben was runner-up."

"Nah, you know we met at a party."

"Yeah, I know."

∾

When Ben returned from Yaddo, a letter from Didier was waiting for him at home. Its contents sent him reeling. Just as he'd finished it, Tina walked in on him staring out the window.

"What is it?" she asked.

"The French girl that I . . . who helped us in the search for Devin—she's dead."

"I'm so sorry."

He handed her the letter.

My Dear Ben,

I don't know what to say, other than how very sad I am, *mon ami*, to have to tell you this awful news. I am still recovering from the shock of it, as are Élodie and Marie.

So, I will just come out with it. Sylvie died suddenly last week in an accident on her Vespa. She was hit by a truck in downtown Nice on her way to Le Zinc. She died instantly, as did her companion. What a tragedy. Her laugh was infectious. She brought the enthusiasm and inexperience of youth, together with, at times, a wisdom beyond her years, to all she did, as well as great beauty and style. Was she a bit all over the place? Perhaps. I must admit that, in matters of the heart, she gave me a lot of good advice that I never took and a lot of bad advice that I followed!

I know how difficult leaving her was for you. I shall never forget her, and I know that you won't either.

I hope that you are well. We are all of us thinking of you, and send you our love.

Bisous
Didier

Tina put the letter down on an end table and quietly left the room. She wondered who the French girl was and what she meant to Ben. She left him alone with his thoughts, not wishing to intrude.

The whole episode with Sylvie seemed even more like a dream to Ben. He couldn't understand that she was gone. He thought of their first meeting in the bookstore, the first time they made love, all their adventures searching for Devin Curtis and their eventual breakup. He wanted to tell Tina everything, how he felt when he was with Sylvie, how he felt now. He knew he would have to put it out of his mind—but not yet. Tina would be kind, but she would be hurt. Maybe if he spoke to Diane . . . but he wasn't sure if she could help.

∾

Over the next two weeks, Ben moped about the loft, haggard and unshaven. He spent the afternoons sleeping. He didn't work on the novel and had next to no appetite. He showed little interest in the kids. Tina would bring him chicken soup on a tray at dinnertime but otherwise left him undisturbed. Understanding it was going to be difficult for him to get over the shock, she was willing to allow him all the time he needed and would make no other attempt to smooth things out.

"You know, we don't have to talk about it," Tina told him. "Just let me know if I can help in any way."

One morning, Henry and Joe approached Ben, who was lying in bed.

"Daddy, can you can take us to the aquarium?" Henry asked.

"Dad's not feeling well," Tina interjected.

"Can't you see he's depressed, Henry?" Joe said.

"You mean he's retreated into his shell?" Henry responded.

Tina raised an eyebrow in surprise. "More or less."

When Tina told Diane about Ben's affair with Sylvie over the phone, Diane's reaction to the news was matter-of-fact. "Well, it was to be expected," she said. She let Tina know that she was there for her until Ben came out of his funk. They spoke by phone a couple of times a day. Tina was grateful for her support. Oddly, Ben's sinking into a mild depression drew Tina and Diane even closer together.

One day, without warning, Tina found Ben in his study humming, showered and dressed, intently working on his book. She smiled and said nothing, delighted that his "dark night of the soul" had finally passed and that he was once again himself. For his part, Ben recognized how compassionate Tina had been and how lucky he was to have her and Diane.

To Tina, Ben now seemed noticeably more attentive than he'd ever been, and she wondered what had gotten into him. Diane experienced the same thing when she and Ben met for coffee a couple of days later.

"Have you noticed something different about Ben?" Tina asked Diane on the phone.

"Yeah. Strange, isn't it?"

"It's going to take some getting used to."

CHAPTER SEVENTEEN

The downstairs buzzer rang in Ben and Tina's loft.

"Ben, it's Devin Curtis," Tina called.

Ben was caught totally off guard. The one time he'd seen Devin in France was like a hallucination.

Devin appeared at the door dressed like a big kid in a T-shirt, jeans and Converse sneakers. He was just as laid-back as he'd always been. After Tina made them some tea, she went out to pick up Henry and Joe from school. Ben and Devin sat in the study.

"I'm sorry about Sylvie." Devin's affect was flat.

"Yeah, I'm still numb about it."

"I should tell you that Sylvie and I had a fling. I wouldn't want you to hear about it from somebody else. She was still sweet on you. She pursued me, but I was just something that happened on the rebound. I think she thought I was pretty boring and that I turned out to be not at all what she expected."

"I appreciate your telling me. It's fine."

Ben brought up Donald's demise at the party in Nice, something which turned out to be a taboo subject with Devin. "I just can't talk about it."

"Okay."

"Tell me what you're working on now," Devin said.

Ben described the characters in his novel, including Attila and Priscilla.

"I've been thinking that Attila and Priscilla are real," Ben said casually. "These characters sort of visit me. I don't know what to make of it."

"I understand. I once got so involved with a character I thought I *was* that character."

Devin spoke briefly about his new project, a novella.

"Teenagers in LA in the seventies meet at the Frolic Room and form a punk band together. They are molded by a charismatic Svengali, who turns out to be a vampire." Devin grinned.

Ben looked perplexed.

"It's kind of a YA thing."

"Oh, wow! I wish Kevin Killian were alive to enjoy it!"

"I loved Kevin. *Shy* and *Arctic Summer* are two of my favorite novels. His death was so awful. I have no idea how that happened. Kevin had a key to my apartment. His body was unrecognizable, so I can see why people might have thought it was me."

"Is your publisher bringing out your new book?" Ben asked.

"No. You could say I've been let go. They're dropping all their so-called innovative writers."

"Huh . . . I would've thought you were a feather in their cap."

"Well . . . seems they have other ideas about the direction they want to go," Devin said resignedly.

"I can put you in touch with my editor. He's a fan of your work. Who knows?"

"Fantastic. I'd be really grateful."

"Happy to do it. Say, you know what I saw a couple of months ago? Your favorite film, Bresson's *Lancelot du Lac.*"

"Oh, yeah . . . I love how he defies traditional notions of quality—what's 'good' and what's 'bad'. I think of him as a great stylist above all."

When Tina returned home with Henry and Joe, she reminded Ben that he had to take them to fencing, so he invited Devin to tag along. On the street, Ben realized he'd forgotten his wallet and keys.

"Devin, can you keep an eye on Henry and Joe for a minute while I run back to my place?"

"Sure."

"Thanks. They're a bit of a handful. See if you can keep them entertained," Ben called over his shoulder. "Boys, I'll be right back."

Ben assumed that Devin hated kids, and worried that when he got back he would find that Henry and Joe had left Devin for dead, but Devin soon had the boys doing jumping jacks on the sidewalk and seemed to be enjoying himself. As far as Ben could tell, Devin actually liked kids after all. He marveled at how Devin continued to remain a mystery.

～

Tina masturbated in bed. Disparate images flew through her head before she had an orgasm. She closed her eyes, fell asleep and had a dream.

"Shall we order?" Devin said.

"Do they have that cassoulet?" Tina asked.

"You bet."

"I love this place. There's this one wine I've heard about."

"Let's see if they have it."

After dinner, Devin and Tina relaxed over glasses of Armagnac, savoring the old-world charm of the Michelin-starred restaurant.

"Boy, the food was just sensational," Tina sighed.

"I'll say," Devin replied. "You know, life with you has been wonderful. You've been a great wife, a great mother. I'm so glad we came here for our anniversary. You've always wanted to."

"Shall we go watch the movie?"

"Yeah, they're projecting it onto a cloud."

They left the restaurant in the Place des Vosges. The movie began. It was a highlight reel of their life together: visits to a bullfight, Roman ruins, a parade of lights, a sex club, a natural history museum, the Blue Angels, cave paintings.

ACKNOWLEDGMENTS

The following in chapters two and four of *Are We Done Here?* were drawn from actual incidents described by Napoleon A. Chagnon in his study *Yanomamö*: the discussion of poor bartering skills, the description of the treatment of outsiders, the ministering to the sick tribesman, the discussion of the audience with the pope, the warrior lineup and discussion of the reason for it, and the deplaning in Caracas.

Both fight songs in chapter six of *Are We Done Here?*, "Bulldog" and "Bingo, That's the Lingo," are by Cole Porter.

The two interview questions and responses in chapter eight of *Are We Done Here?* are based on my recollection of part of an interview with Kathy Acker that appeared in the magazine *BOMB* in the 1980s.

ABOUT THE AUTHOR

Photo © 2010 John Sarsgard

Michael Friedman is the author of two full-length books of poetry, including *Species* (2000), and four chapbooks. His work has appeared in many journals and anthologies, including *Great American Prose Poems*. His first novel, *Martian Dawn*, was published in 2006 by Turtle Point Press. Previously, he was the chair of The Poetry Project at St. Mark's Church and an adjunct faculty member of Naropa University's MFA writing program. He is the cofounder of the literary journal *Shiny*. He lives in Denver, Colorado, where he practices law.